Changing Yesterday

Sean McMullen is one of Australia's leading SF and fantasy authors, with seventeen books and seventy stories published, for which he has won over a dozen awards. His most recent novels are *The Time Engine* (2008), *The Iron Warlock* (2010) and *Before the Storm* (2007). In the late 1990s he established himself in the American market, and his work has been translated into Polish, French, Japanese and other languages. The settings for Sean's work range from the Roman Empire, through Medieval Europe, to cities of the distant future. His work is a mixture of romance, invention and adventure, while populated by dynamic, strange and often hilarious characters. When not writing he is a computer manager, and when not at a keyboard he is a karate instructor.

.

Also by Sean McMullen

The Centurion's Empire
Souls in the Great Machine
The Miocene Arrow
Eyes of the Calculor
The Ancient Hero (The Quentaris Chronicles)
Voyage of the Shadowmoon
Glass Dragons
Voidfarer
Before the Storm
The Time Engine

CHANGING YESTERDAY

Sean McMullen

FORD ST

First published by Ford Street Publishing, an imprint of
Hybrid Publishers, PO Box 52, Ormond VIC 3204

Melbourne Victoria Australia

© Sean McMullen 2011

2 4 6 8 10 9 7 5 3 1

This publication is copyright. Apart from any use as permitted under the Copyright Act 1968, no part may be reproduced by any process without prior written permission from the publisher. Requests and inquiries concerning reproduction should be addressed to Ford Street Publishing Pty Ltd, 2 Ford Street, Clifton Hill VIC 3068.

Ford Street web site:
http://www.fordstreetpublishing.com/

First published 2011

National Library of Australia Cataloguing-in-Publication data:

McMullen, Sean, 1948- .

Changing yesterday/ Sean McMullen.

ISBN 9781921665370 (pbk.).

For young adults.

Time travel – fiction

A823.3

Cover design © Grant Gittus Graphics
In-house editor: Saralinda Turner

Printing and quality control in China by Tingleman Pty Ltd

CONTENTS

Prologue	1
1: Sleepwalker	14
2: Traveller	50
3: Photograph	77
4: Bystander	116
5: Engineer	153
6: Musician	188
7: Castaway	221
8: Warrior	258
9: Hunter	289
10: Hero	328
Epilogue	369

PROLOGUE

A prince was coming to Albury. He would not be there long; in fact, he would just be passing through, but he was heir to the British throne. One day he would become the most powerful king in the entire world. Nobody so important had ever visited Albury, so everyone wanted the town to look its best.

In the shunting yards at Albury Railway Station the rubbish had been collected, the weeds between the tracks were gone, the buildings were newly painted, and even the steam engines gleamed like new. The yardmaster watched with satisfaction as a shunting engine moved three trucks to beside the line where the royal train would pass. They were being placed to hide some things that could not be easily moved or neatened: piles of track ballast and a stack of rusting rails. The wagons were new, and while not actually beautiful themselves, they would prevent his royal highness seeing anything that was actually ugly.

Three miles away, two people on a bushfire watch tower were paying very close attention to the wagons. One of them was watching through a telescope, and while this should have been innocent enough, the telescope had crosshairs, and was part of a gun. The assembly of black tubes, pipes, cables, panels, studs and mountings did not look like a gun, however. It was the fourteenth of May 1901, and plasma lance assault rifles would not be invented for another century.

'Er, ya not gonna do anythin' weird with that thing, are ya, Miss Liore?'

The speaker was four foot eleven inches tall, and had the sort of slightly scruffy, commonplace appearance that blended easily into crowds. This was a big advantage when he was blending into a crowd with a pocket watch that belonged to somebody else. His name was Barry Porter, but he was better known as Barry the Bag because he always carried a battered leather bag of stolen goods with him.

'Barry, surroundings, check,' said Liore.

'I checked the bleedin' ground already, didn't I?' muttered Barry.

'Check again.'

Liore was twelve inches taller than Barry, and had cold, sharp blue eyes that would make the average guard dog back away very hurriedly and look for someone else to bark at. She was dressed as a youth, and in clothes that were as shabby and unremarkable as those that Barry was wearing. Barry was fairly sure that he had been born in 1886. Liore would not be born for another ninety-five years.

On the platform of the distant railway station Daniel Lang had a camera set up on a tripod, and was making a big show of finding the perfect angle to photograph the royal train when it passed through on the following day. He was dressed in his school uniform to give the general impression of being harmless. On a nearby bench his sister Emily was reading a book, and doing her best to look as if she had nothing to do with Daniel. Her knitting bag was beside her on the wooden bench, which she had to herself. People avoided Emily, because her look and manner were rather like that of a particularly strict school headmistress, or perhaps the governor of a women's prison.

The stationmaster regarded Daniel with approval. He would take a fine photograph of the royal train passing through his station. The shunting yards beyond the platform were looking tidier than they had since the station had been established, so the photograph would be fit to hang on the wall of his office. *Must get the boy's address and ask him to send me a print,* he thought.

Fox was about Daniel's age, but was dressed in a long, shabby coat, had a scruffy beard glued to his face, and wore a hat pulled down to his eyebrows. He had been pacing slowly about the platform, as if he had arrived hours before his train was due and was now at a loose end. His hands were in his pockets, and in his left hand was a device that should not have existed for several more decades. It vibrated silently. He lifted it to his ear, pretending to scratch his beard.

'Three reporting, serial K37WCB0542, trans,' he said to the device.

'BC, status ready,' said Liore's voice in the small black box. 'Fox S3, report status. Trans.'

'On platform, crew, FoxS3, DanS2, EmilyS4. Status, ready. Trans.'

'Plan Scramble, initiate. Verify. Trans.'

'Lockdown, trans,' said Fox after one last scan of the platform.

'Lockdown, trans, out,' said Liore.

Putting the shiny black device back in his pocket as he walked, Fox now strode briskly for the seat where Emily was sitting. As he passed her he snatched up her bag then broke into a run and made for the platform gate. Emily screamed several times, then shouted 'Stop, thief!' as she ran after Fox.

Everyone on the platform now dashed after Fox and Emily. This included Daniel, who was carrying his camera and tripod. Just seconds later the platform was completely deserted.

Far away on the watchtower, Barry confirmed that

nobody was nearby. Liore touched her thumb to a pad on the side of her weapon, and a small red light came on. Barry watched with interest as she made an adjustment to it.

'So the red light means ya can shoot now?' asked Barry.

'On target,' said Liore, looking through the telescopic sights again.

'Can ya see the Lionheart cove wot ya gonna give the big push?'

'Targeting wagon.'

'Oh. But are ya sure ya not gonna kill some innocent bystander?'

'On target.'

There was a series of soft clicks and cheeps as she made more adjustments to her gun. In the distance, the steam engine was backing away from the three wagons.

'Look, I know a thing or two about guns,' continued Barry. 'I got a mate, Luker the Lurker, an' he knows guns so he told me stuff. He reckons ya can't hit nothin' with a rifle more than half a mile off, an' that wagon's about ten miles off.'

'Three miles, seven hundred and twenty-six yards.'

'How'd ya know that?' asked Barry, sounding doubtful.

'Gun.'

'The gun? That's horseshit. Guns can't talk.'

'Has display.'

'Wot ya mean?'

'Displays range.'

'Yeah, well, even if yer gun could talk, it can't hit nothin' that far off.'

'Target clear. Lockdown.'

There was a shrill squeak from Liore's weapon as she squeezed the firing stud. A bright flash burst out from the direction of the shunting yards, then a red and orange cloud boiled up into the sky, raining glowing fragments that trailed sparks.

'Frig me doggles!' exclaimed Barry. 'It blew up!'

'On target,' replied Liore.

'But it blew up wi'out no noise, an' that's –'

After travelling for seventeen seconds at seven hundred and seventy miles per hour, the thunderclap blast from the wagon's annihilation burst over the tower. It was followed by a series of echoes.

'Bleedin' hell!' exclaimed Barry.

'Assess damage,' said Liore, handing Barry a brass telescope.

Barry trained the instrument on the distant shunting yards, where the dust and smoke were now dispersing.

'Er, there's a bleedin' great hole where the middle wagon was, and the other two wagons aren't there neither – oh wait up, yeah they are, but they're a lot further away now an' they don't look much like wagons any more.'

'Good.'

'So wot now?'

'Lionheart evidence, destroy,' said Liore, pointing her weapon elsewhere. 'Target clear. Lockdown.'

There was another squeak from the weapon, then another, and a third. Barry put his hands over his ears and braced himself for more explosions, but none came.

'Thought ya never miss,' he said.

'On target.'

'But ya missed then.'

'Rooming house, oil lamps, on target.'

Barry looked out across the roofs of Albury with the telescope. Smoke was starting to pour from a distant building.

'Friggin' frig! Why'd ya do that?'

'In building, evidence planted, by Lionhearts. Provoke Century War, with Germany.'

Muriel Baker was in central Albury, flirting with some of the local boys. This was something that she did particularly well, for she was very pretty, wore her flame-red hair brushed out, and was dressed more stylishly than the local girls. She was also putting on a French accent and telling everyone that she was Michelle, an artist from Paris.

The sound of the wagon blowing up had the effect

of freezing everyone in the street for a moment. Muriel shrieked, and threw her arms around a boy known as Slim. A second or two later the cloud of smoke and dust became visible, showing that the explosion had come from the direction of the station. Some of the boys now dashed off to investigate, but Muriel held on to Slim very tightly.

'No, no, please stay and protect me, I am very frightened!' she pleaded.

Sensing that this was a chance to embrace a beautiful girl and be a hero without doing anything at all, Slim made the sensible decision and stayed with Muriel. Three other boys also stayed, hoping that they too might get a chance to protect her. Staring over Slim's shoulder, Muriel watched the upstairs windows of a nearby rooming house. Suddenly there were three flashes in quick succession, accompanied by the tinkle of breaking glass. Muriel waited some moments for the flames to get properly established before speaking.

'Monsieur Slim, that building!' she cried. 'It is on fire!'

Slim and the other boys dashed across to the rooming house and raised the alarm. Before long everyone inside had been safely evacuated, and the boys were being hailed as heroes. Slim would have preferred to have been in Muriel's arms as well, but she was nowhere to be seen.

❇

Liore and Barry descended the steps of the tower, then walked across to where their horse was tethered. Liore mounted and pulled Barry up behind her, then they set off for the town.

'In Albury, shocked bystanders, we are,' said Liore. 'That's an easy.'

When they reached the railway station they learned that frantic efforts were already under way to fill in the crater and repair the tracks, so that the prince's train could pass through on schedule the next day. However, that was not what most people were talking about.

'Lucky it blew up today,' a man in a railway company uniform was saying.

'Jeez mate, ya call that lucky?' exclaimed a youth, gesturing at the distant hole and wreckage. 'Yarder says there were seven railway guards in the next wagon and four in the one behind.'

'Are they all right?' asked a woman with an English accent.

'All right?' exclaimed the youth. 'Yarder says they was smeared over the insides of the wagons like raspberry tarts.'

'Oh my word!' exclaimed the woman.

'It could have been much worse,' said the conductor. 'That wagon was right beside the line where the crown prince was due to pass tomorrow. If it had blown up while his carriage was passing, well, what do you think?'

'Australia would be having its first royal funeral,' the youth concluded.

'Too right.'

Barry took Liore by the sleeve and led her away from the group. It was a cool, clear day in late autumn, but his face was beaded with sweat.

'Bleedin' hell, did ya know them coves was in the wagons?' he whispered.

'No.'

'So that was an accident?'

'Is war.'

While Barry was quite accomplished as a petty thief, he tried to avoid violence because he was very small and would always lose any fight. Eleven deaths, accidental or otherwise, were enough to leave him very unsettled.

'So them coves in the wagon, ya reckon they was Lionhearts?'

'On target. Dynamite, were guarding.'

'So no more fighting?'

'Perhaps.'

Barry shivered. Standing beside Liore was like being in the same cage as something very large that ate meat. One had to stand quite still and hope not to be noticed.

Slowly the members of Liore's unlikely squad gathered on the street outside the railway station while police and railway officials hurried about. Fox had discarded his coat, hat and beard, and was now carrying a sketch pad and box of pencils. He was pretending to be Muriel's brother, who did not speak English. Daniel and Emily were bickering about who had left their tickets back to Melbourne in the bag that Fox had stolen and discarded. Muriel took Daniel by the arm and sneered at Emily.

'Silly cow, my Daniel would not do something as stupid as losing the tickets,' she said. 'He arranged for Fox to take your silly tickets out of the bag before he threw it away.'

'Squad, to me,' said Liore. 'Debrief.'

'Plan Scramble worked perfectly,' said Emily, glaring contemptuously at Muriel as she spoke. 'We got everyone off the platform and chasing Fox before the explosion. No innocent bystanders were hurt.'

'Plan Windows worked even better,' said Muriel, putting a hand on her hip and casting another sneer at Emily. 'I attracted a crowd of boys by being so charming that they even stayed with me after the explosion. When the rooming house began to burn I sent them over to raise the alarm. Nobody was hurt.'

'You probably attracted them by taking your clothes off!' snapped Emily.

'If *you* had taken your clothes off they would have run away!' retorted Muriel.

'I've spoken to the stationmaster,' said Daniel before the exchange became any worse. 'A train from Melbourne is being held at the edge of the shunting yards, and it will be turned around and sent back. It will have us home by this evening.'

'So that's the end of them Lionhearts, then?' asked Barry.

'On target,' said Liore.

On the surface, the little squad was functioning perfectly. Only five days earlier they had prevented the bombing of Australia's first parliament, and now they had stopped the shadowy Lionheart conspirators again. The two cadets from the future and their four recruits from 1901 had changed history twice, so the world had been saved from the Century War. As far as Daniel was concerned it was time to live happily ever after with Muriel, while Emily had no plans other than persuading her brother to break up with her worst enemy. However, everyone else was thinking through far more devious agendas as they set off for the train. In its moment of triumph the squad was already falling apart, but superficially it was as strong as ever.

Barry's plans were particularly ambitious.

Well, I reckon it's over, he thought as he walked. *No more Lionhearts, so no more fightin'. If there's no more fightin'*

I reckon that Liore won't need that fancy gun wot she brung from the future. Reckon the king would like that gun. Reckon he'd change me name from Barry the Bag to Sir Barry Porter if I give it to him.

Chapter 1
SLEEPWALKER

The last day of May 1901 was like the end of any other school week for Daniel Lang. He was in his second last year at an expensive private school, and life was going very well for him. For the first time in his life he had acquired a sweetheart in the form of Muriel Baker, a beautiful classmate of his sister's. For Daniel, this was even better than getting a medal. Muriel knew that Daniel was a hero, and for Daniel her opinion was the only one that mattered.

As usual, he took the local steam train home from school to North Brighton. It was a very pleasant autumn day, the sort that seemed wasted on school. Daniel had plans to get back on the train once he had finished his homework. He would meet Muriel at her mother's shop in Balaclava, and they would go to a local café, there to sit holding hands and talking for an hour or so. Daniel was fifteen years old, six foot one inch tall, and startlingly thin, but that did not seem to matter to Muriel.

Daniel's friend Barry was working at North Brighton Station when he got off the train. Barry was also technically a schoolboy, but in practice he spent most of his time helping his father at the station, receiving stolen goods, and picking pockets. It was a rather unlikely friendship. Daniel was from a moderately rich family and generally came first in everything that he did at school. Still, their friendship had somehow endured for five years.

'That Muriel baggage were 'ere this arvo,' said Barry as he collected Daniel's ticket.

'Muriel, here?' exclaimed Daniel. 'You mean she's waiting for me at home?'

'Nah, she come an' she went. Caught the same train on its way back to Flinders Street. It were just after ten this mornin'.'

'You mean she missed school today?' exclaimed Daniel. 'Did she look sick?'

'Danny boy, I miss school nearly every bleedin' day, yet I'm not sick.'

'What did she say?'

'Muriel Baker talk to Barry the Bag? Give it a rest, Danny boy.'

'Perhaps she left a note at home.'

'Yeah, I reckon.'

Daniel turned to go, but something was on Barry's mind. Dumping the tickets he had just collected into the fire bucket, he hurried after Daniel.

'Oi, Danny boy, I need to ask somethin',' he said as he caught up with Daniel. 'It's about our mates from the future, Liore and Fox.'

'I have not seen much of either of them for a fortnight.'

'I just need advice about 'em, sorta. They're from the future, an' they come back a hundred years to stop parlyment gettin' bombed, 'cause that would start a war. That's right, isn't it?'

'Yes.'

'An' we helped stop parlyment gettin' bombed, but nobody knows.'

'Yes.'

'So why'd Liore explode that bleedin' railway wagon in Albury? Jeez, I nearly laid the brown egg when that wagon blew up.'

'The bags of dynamite that were inside the wagon were what exploded,' said Daniel. 'If she had not destroyed it, then when the Duke of Cornwall and York came past in his special train, those Lionhearts would have blown up the wagon, killing him. Evidence would be found in the rooming house that she set on fire. It would have put the blame for the duke's death on German secret agents. The Century War between Britain and Germany would have started. The Lionhearts want to start the war to unify the British Empire, but it would be a catastrophe for both sides. Now both the wagon and evidence are gone.'

'But wot if them poor coves guardin' the wagon

were innocent railway workers? I mean bleedin' hell, *I* work for the railways.'

'Nobody who loaded that wagon was an innocent bystander, Barry. They were all Lionhearts, dedicated to provoking the Century War between Britain and Germany. They would not have given up until war was declared.'

'But they were doin' it to save the Empire, right?'

'Yes, but they were misguided. Misguided men are just as dangerous as those who are evil.'

'So why don't she kill the leader? Like, so the others won't know what to do?'

'Barry, she can't know everything.'

'Well if she knows about 'em she must know who gives the orders.'

'Barry, you're a member of the British Empire and the king gives the orders, but I bet you don't know the king's name.'

'Yeah I do! It's . . . er, King Arthur.'

'Rubbish, it's Edward.'

'Oh. Yeah, well, anyway, how'd she know about the wagon?'

'She told me that new memories slipped into her head after we stopped the bombing of parliament, memories of the Century War being started by the assassination of the crown prince by German agents in Albury.'

'Yeah? I reckon she's dippy. I reckon she's not good

at nothin' but killin', so she makes up excuses to kill.'

'Well I trust her,' said Daniel huffily.

'But I bet she'll get some new inspirational to kill more coves she reckons is Lionhearts.'

'She told me she now has memories of another war that starts in four months, but –'

'See? See? Told ya!'

'Perhaps there is no hope of avoiding a century of war,' said Daniel defensively. 'Perhaps time heals itself whenever someone from the future tries to change the past.'

Metaphysics was not one of Barry's strong points. He had understood little of what Daniel had said, and believed even less. He opened his mouth to ask another question, scratched his head, and failed to think of anything sensible to ask. Having decided that Daniel had confirmed his worst fears about Liore, he finally folded his arms and shrugged.

'Okay, so maybe yer may be right. Now what? What about us?'

'We no longer have to help.'

'She made us help blow up that bleedin' wagon.'

'Liore and Fox could have done it without us. They are stronger, faster and better than us in every way. Fox even saved me from drowning.'

'Then why'd they make us help?'

'Barry . . . it's like Joan of Arc and Robin Hood walked into our lives for a few weeks, then left to have other adventures. We just taught them a bit about how things are done in Australia, in 1901. Now they are better at fitting in, they can do things for themselves, and they are so much better than we are that they will probably never need our help again.'

'So we don't owe them nothin'?'

'We have nothing that they need, Barry.'

'Yer daft sister Emily reckons we orta still do stuff for 'em.'

'Emily thinks they're exciting. Just think about it. Fox is the perfect boy: strong, handsome, clever, well-mannered and absolutely loyal. She probably even wants to, er . . .'

'Rip his drawers off?'

'Barry!'

'Yeah, anyway, so Fox and Liore don't need us no more?'

'No. We should just get on with our lives.'

'So we don't owe 'em nothin'?'

'For the second time – no, wait, I do owe Fox my life, and so does Emily.'

'But wot about me?'

Daniel stopped, put his schoolbag down, stood before Barry with his hands on his hips and looked him in the eyes.

'You owe them *nothing*, Barry. Is that the answer you want?'

'Er, yeah, I reckon,' said Barry, scratching his head again.

'Then go back and mind the railway station. I have homework to do.'

Having finally shaken Barry off, Daniel hurried on home. Only a few weeks earlier he would have stayed at the station and kept talking to Barry until he uncovered whatever was on his friend's mind. Barry was clearly concerned about something, but for Daniel there was nothing as important as seeing Muriel. Since she had first kissed him, four weeks earlier, Daniel's life had been transformed. Although he was still a schoolboy of fifteen, being Muriel's sweetheart had changed him into a young man. All his classmates knew about her, and most of them had never even touched a girl, except at dancing lessons. Muriel gave Daniel status.

For Daniel, Muriel was not just a symbol of growing up, however, she was a declaration of independence as well. With Muriel in his life he could no longer be dominated by his sister Emily. While Emily was like a policeman, always ready to pounce and point out what he was doing wrong, Muriel could get her way by just flashing a winsome smile or by batting her eyelashes. Emily could not do either to save herself. Dangerous thoughts slipped into Daniel's mind when he was with Muriel. Rather than becoming a solicitor or judge, he could see himself playing the piano in dingy coffee houses while strangely-dressed people talked about art, anarchism and absinthe.

The maid, Martha, was sweeping the porch when he reached the gate.

'Yer friend Muriel came past this mornin',' she called as Daniel came up the garden path.

'Yes, I know,' said Daniel. 'What was the matter? Was she sick?'

'She looked well, but sort of worried about somethin'. She gave me a note for passin' on, but said it's not urgent or nothin'. I left it on yer bed.'

Daniel found the note on his pillow. The border of the envelope was fringed with briar rose tangles drawn in green, red and brown ink, and Daniel's name was written in flowing script at the centre. The flap was sealed in three places with red sealing wax, and Muriel's seal, a majuscule M, was impressed in all three patches of wax. Not wanting to disturb Muriel's artwork, Daniel took his pocketknife out and slit the flap neatly, then unfolded the letter. Even when he saw that the lines were widely spaced, and that each word dripped a tear drawn in light blue ink, Daniel did not suspect that the news was going to be very bad indeed.

> Dear Daniel,
>
> There is no way that I can break this to you kindly, so I shall just tell the cruel truth. Fox and I are in love and have left for Paris to develop

our artistic careers together. I am truly, truly sorry, but while I hold you in the highest esteem, Fox and I are sweethearts bound together by our passion for art. Daniel, please try to forget me. We are not of a kind, and never could be. By leaving you now, I am saving you more intense pain in the future.

My deepest regrets,

Muriel.

Three hours later Emily went upstairs to see why Daniel had not come to dinner. She found him sitting on the edge of the bed, his tears dripping onto the letter that was by then nearly illegible. He had reread Muriel's letter over five hundred times, hoping that the words would change, but the message stubbornly remained the same.

'Daniel?' said Emily from the door, realising at once that something was terribly wrong.

'The boy who saved my life has taken my sweetheart,' responded Daniel without looking up.

Some miles away, in St Kilda, Barry was on the way to an appointment with one of his business associates. Although Barry was a hardened petty criminal, he was not entirely without moral scruples. Thus he always gave himself a reason whenever he did something wrong. This meant that it was all right to steal things that were already stolen, steal from rich people because they had lots more, steal from people who deserved to be stolen from, or steal what did not matter. Stealing Liore's plasma lance assault rifle was a little more difficult to justify, but Barry was very resourceful.

That Liore, she don't really need somethin' wot can sink ships, he thought as he walked. *She can kill them Lionheart coves with a bleedin' pistol. The best thing for the good of the British Empire were if the king had that death ray rifle thing.*

Luker the Lurker was always the person of choice when disposing of stolen goods, but Barry was not entirely sure how to introduce the subject of a super-weapon from the future. He decided that the idea was so fantastic that someone like Luker could not possibly understand it. Barry was also fairly sure that one demonstration of its power would guarantee a sale to any of Melbourne's criminals, but he had developed ideas of improving his status in society as well as just making money. The king could make him important as well as rich, and Barry wanted to be both. Thus he needed to contact someone who knew the king, someone wise and clever enough to understand his story about warriors from the future with an absolutely fantastic weapon. As Barry reached the Acland Street coffee house where Luker was to be found at that time of day, he decided to use shock tactics.

'Oi, I got a job where there's profit for ya,' Barry began as he stopped at Luker's table.

'What've you stolen now?' asked Luker without turning.

'I got a thing wot I gotta give the king.'

'Give?' asked Luker, now turning to face him. 'To the king? You mean Jim King at the South Melbourne market?'

'Nah, the real king. The one wot runs the Empire.'

'Come off it, little bagman. *You* have something for the *king*?'

'Well, in exchange for rekkypence for me expenses. Say two hundred quid, no questions asked, no names named.'

'Who says I know the king?'

'Well, do ya?'

Luker was bright enough to realise that Barry might have something very valuable. He decided to humour him.

'I reckon I know someone who knows him.'

'Yeah? Wot's his name?'

'King Edward.'

'I mean yer contact.'

'Not tellin'! What you got?'

'It's a gun.'

'The king's got plenty of guns, Barry boy, he runs the bleedin' army. Why should he pay two hundred quid for yours?'

'It's special. It's sorta secret.'

Luker the Lurker frowned.

'Listen, little bagman, you're wasting my time and it'll cost you.'

'Lurker man, have a listen. I can prove it.'

'I bet you stole some new gun from a drunk soldier while he was sleeping it off. I bet there's a reward for gettin' it back.'

'Luker, mate, trust the bagman. Remember that railway wagon full of dynamite that I sent your way last month? We sold that lot for eighty quid.'

'Yeah, and five days later another wagon full of dynamite blew up in Albury, shovin' eleven coves off to meet their maker. I reckon it belonged to the same push what we stole the other load from. I reckon that second wagon was rigged to explode, and I reckon we're damn lucky we got away with our lives when we stole that first load. You keep whatever it is you stole. While you're at it, get away from me before whatever you got blows up.'

'I haven't got it here,' said Barry.

'Then don't bring it here.'

'It's a gun, not dynamite.'

'You sure it's just a gun?'

'Yeah, an' it's small, but real powerful. It can sink a ship, yet it fits in me bag.'

For some reason this particular wild claim made sense to Luker the Lurker. After all, two men with a

Gatling gun had the firepower of an entire brigade of soldiers with rifles. If Barry had stolen some secret weapon that could fit in his bag yet sink a ship, it might fetch two thousand pounds, and probably more.

'All right then, little bagman, I'm hearing. Where's the gun?'

'Not sayin'. Anyway, I gotta bag it first.'

'I'll want to see it work before you get a farthing.'

While it was not entirely true that Emily Lang was a bully, she did tend to get her own way by humiliating other people into doing what she ordered. Her brother Daniel had been her favourite target for most of her life, because he was younger than her, male, and a natural born victim. Whatever Daniel accomplished, it was never good enough for Emily. Whether it was his examination results at school, table manners at home, choice of clothes, piano playing at family song nights, or even the Christmas presents he gave her, Emily always found a reason to make Daniel squirm.

Daniel tried to fight back with his choice of friends. While Barry the Bag was fairly close to the bottom of Emily's list of preferred people to be seen with, he was another person who Emily could dominate, so she tolerated him. Muriel Baker had been a classmate of Emily's, and was at the very top of her list of most hated people in all the world. When Daniel and Muriel had begun courting four weeks earlier, it had been Emily's worst nightmare. Daniel had begun breaking free of Emily under his sweetheart's influence. Now Muriel was gone, but everything had not returned to normal.

At first Emily was overjoyed to learn that Muriel and her brother had broken up, but when Daniel did not respond to her displays of sarcasm, wit, rhetoric and abuse, she realised that he had not been returned to her in his original condition. All of Friday evening Emily tried to persuade Daniel to eat something, to change out of his school clothes, to do his weekend homework, and even to admit that she had been right about Muriel Baker. Daniel did not move and hardly spoke. He spent the entire night on the edge of his bed with Muriel's letter in his hands. By the morning the Lang family was growing alarmed.

Emily had read about people losing the will to live and just fading away. Now it was happening to her brother, and for the first time in her life Emily felt a twinge of genuine concern for him. Shouting at Daniel, reasoning with him, and saying some very cruel but witty things about Muriel had raised not so much as a grunt of acknowledgment from him. Their parents could do no better. By Saturday morning Emily was so frightened that she was forced to admit defeat and call upon her last resort. Chaperoned by Martha, she went in search of Barry the Bag.

Barry was sweeping the station platform when Emily and Martha found him.

'Something terrible has happened to Daniel!' called Martha as they hurried toward him.

'You must come and speak to him,' cried Emily. 'He needs his friends.'

'Jeez, if ya think he needs *me* he must be bad!' said Barry, holding his broom between himself and Emily. 'Wot's the problem?'

'That floozy Muriel Baker has jilted my brother for Fox!' exclaimed Emily. 'They have run off to Paris to be artists!'

'Friggin' hell – er, sorry, miss.'

'Daniel has taken it very badly. I fear he has even lost the will to live. You *must* come and talk to him.'

'Yeah, yeah, I'll come over. Tell ya wot, though, that Liore would be good for Danny boy as well. They're mates. I'll just pedal over an' give the word.'

'Yes, yes, Liore would be perfect!' exclaimed Emily, jumping up and down on the spot. 'Liore's an officer, and they know what to do in emergencies.'

As was nearly always the case, Barry had his own agenda. He knew where Liore lived because he had followed her home from the railway station one evening. Since then he had even cycled past the end of her street, but he had been too frightened to ride past the actual house. Perhaps she would be looking out of the front window, and would see him. How could he explain riding past the house where she lived, except to spy on her? He already knew what girls from the future did to spies. Now, at last, he had an excuse to call on her at home.

Barry turned into Liore's street, and located her house. It had a picket fence and two gates. An elderly, bad-tempered black Labrador patrolled the front yard. It took an instant dislike to Barry and directed a barrage of asthmatic woofs at him.

'Just my luck,' he muttered. 'Almost got me hands on the most powerful weapon in the world, yet I'm stopped by a bleedin' dog.'

The situation was not encouraging. In order to even knock at the front door, he had to get past the dog.

'Barry Porter?' said a voice behind him.

Barry literally jumped with fright, then turned. Liore had come up behind him in absolute silence, like a cat stalking a mouse. She was dressed as a rather more respectable boy today, like Daniel when he was not in school uniform. She was now attending lectures at the University of Melbourne after passing some special test. Apparently they did not wear uniforms there.

'I, er, come to see ya,' he babbled.

'Why?'

'I was gonna go in an' tell ya something, but the dog don't like me so I couldn't go knock on the door.'

'Wellington, stand down,' she said, reaching over the gate and scratching the dog behind the ears. 'Wellington's bark, alerts landlady.'

While Liore was able to speak normally, she had recently been using the combat language, battlespeak, nearly all the time. It was as if she were on a battlefield, continually on alert.

'Well the bleedin' dog's been barkin', but she never come out.'

'Saturday morning, is shopping. Well?'

'Well wot?'

'Yourself, here. Why?'

Yeah, why am I 'ere? screamed in Barry's mind. *This is Liore, an' she's from the future, an' girls are tougher than friggin' prizefighters in the future, an' they kill spies, but first they do horrible things to their tenderest anatomicals, an' – an' why am I 'ere?*

'Oh! Er, yeah, it's Danny boy,' Barry suddenly remembered. 'Ya gotta go see Danny, he's real bad.'

'Accident?' asked Liore, her eyes widening. 'Details, trans?'

'Nah, it's that daft baggage, Muriel Baker. She's given Danny boy the big heave an' run off to Paris with Fox.'

'Fox? Paris?' said Liore sharply. 'When?'

'Well I only found out this mornin' when Emily come lookin' for me. She said –'

'Room, must check. Barry Porter, fall in!'

Liore led Barry to the side gate. The dog growled at Barry.

'Bike! Guard!' said Liore, pointing to Barry's bike.

The dog had apparently learned to obey orders when they came from Liore, so it seated itself beside the delivery bike that Barry had borrowed from North Brighton Station.

Liore took Barry down a path beside the house. She lived in a former servant's room built at the back of the house. The door opened onto the backyard, so that she could come and go as she pleased along the side path without disturbing the landlady. The girl from the future unlocked the door and they went inside.

It was the neatest room that Barry had ever seen. There was a bed, a cupboard, a chest of drawers, a cast-iron stove, a table and a chair. The only personal item visible in the room was a trunk beside the table. Its lid was secured with a padlock. Liore dropped to one knee beside it and took out a key.

'Penalty, death, for desertion,' said Liore coldly. 'Equipment, must check.'

Just then someone knocked at the door. It was the landlady, back from her shopping.

'Oi, Master Liore, a lad called Fox left a parcel for ya yesterday.'

'Mrs O'Brien, my thanks,' said Liore, standing up.

'I got it in the kitchen, come along.'

Liore looked down at Barry for a moment, as if making up her mind about something.

'Barry Porter, stay here, returning soon,' she said. She closed her eyes and added softly, 'By your leave, speaking courtly,' before walking out.

Liore was barely out of the door when Barry opened his bag, took out his pickwires and got to work on the padlock on her trunk. It was a new lock, and a challenge to open. Just as it yielded to his pickwires, Barry heard Liore thanking the landlady. He lifted the lid, caught a glimpse of the deadly plasma weapon, and then frantically set about locking the trunk again. The padlock was just as stubborn about being locked as it was about being picked open. By the time he had it locked again Barry only had a moment to turn around and sit on the trunk before Liore stepped through the door. The pickwires were concealed in his hand. She now looked a lot less alarmed. She also noticed that Barry's bag was open.

'Your bag is open,' she said suspiciously.

'Er, I were just takin' stock.'

'If you have taken any of my stock, I shall kill you.'

'Barry's bag got lots of things that people want,' said Barry defensively. 'That's why I gotta check it.

Stuff gets nicked if I leave it for even a minute.'

'Get a padlock, like mine. Five shillings at Wentworth's, unless you want to take your chances and steal one.'

Barry put his hand into the bag and placed the pickwires inside as he pretended to check the contents.

'Artistic postcards, rubber medicals, baccy tins, handbooks of an improvin' nature, yeah, it's all 'ere.'

'And pickwires?'

'Yeah, they're okay –' For a moment Barry nearly lost his bladder control, but he forced himself to stay calm. 'Oi, how'd ya know about them?' he asked off-handedly.

'I am a battle commander. I know everything.'

'Yeah, well ya didn't know about Fox and Muriel.'

'Fox left a parcel,' said Liore, ignoring the comment.

The brown paper parcel contained a uniform, a pair of boots, a small, sleek black box, a pen with no nib, several coins and some other oddments that Barry did not recognise. It was everything that Fox had brought from the future, and he had done the honourable thing by leaving them with Liore before fleeing to Paris with Muriel.

'I must secure all this,' said Liore. 'Barry, out.'

Barry stepped outside and looked down the side path. The dog was still guarding his bike, but after one glance at Barry it decided that the bike needed to be defended from whoever he was. With another barrage of woofs it began an arthritic charge along the path beside the house.

'There's a savage dog –' began Barry, banging on Liore's door.

Liore flung the door open just as the dog arrived.

'Wellington, friend!' she said firmly to the dog, holding Barry off the ground by his coat collar with one hand and pointing at him with the other.

'Er, g'day, Wellington,' said Barry.

The dog was clearly still suspicious, but accepted that if Liore trusted Barry, then Barry was not to be bitten. She put Barry down and went back inside. Barry waited for some agonisingly long seconds, but Liore found nothing amiss with her trunk as she added what Fox had given her to the contents. She was smiling enigmatically as she stepped outside.

'Fall in,' she said as she walked for the bike.

'So we're goin' to see Danny boy now?'

'Espionage first, Daniel second.'

Barry sat in the bike's delivery basket as they left the house and set off down Union Street. He was unusually quiet as they made the trip to Carlisle Street, where Muriel's mother had an artists' supply shop. Like a true professional, Barry was recalling every detail that he could remember of Liore's room. Now that he knew where the PR-17 weapon was hidden, it was only a matter of stealing it without getting killed, then handing it over to a buyer.

By Saturday afternoon Daniel had still not eaten anything. He remained in his school uniform, sitting on the edge of his bed. Downstairs Emily and her parents held a family conference over lunch, and then went upstairs to confront Daniel.

Mrs Lang had decided that self-discipline was what Daniel needed, so she shouted at him to pull himself together. Daniel ignored her. It was Emily's turn next, and her theory was that Muriel Baker was not worth crying over, and that he should come out to tea parties with her and meet some more socially suitable girls. Daniel did not so much as blink. Mr Lang asked just who this Muriel Baker was, and if she was from a good family. Emily explained that she was Daniel's secret sweetheart, Emily's worst enemy at school, and the daughter of an artist.

'An artist!' exclaimed Mrs Lang, scandalised. 'That will never do.'

Mr Lang decided that the nonsense had gone far enough, and that some even louder old-fashioned shouting would clear the air.

'Daniel Lang, if you will not stop this nonsense at once you can get out of this house!' he thundered, like a vicar preaching about hellfire and damnation.

Daniel stood slowly, straightened, and walked out of the room.

'Daniel, come back here at once!' shouted Mrs Lang.

As Daniel walked down the stairs, Emily suddenly realised that he might be doing the very thing that she did when all else had failed: causing extreme and excruciating embarrassment. There was something about the way he was walking, something grim and purposeful.

'Daniel, come back this instant!' shouted Mr Lang, setting off after him. 'I'm the head of this house; you will do what I say! I paid for everything you think is yours, I own every stitch of clothing on your body.'

Daniel had reached the front door. He stopped, and then proceeded to strip off his school uniform. Mrs Lang, who was on the stairs, screamed and collapsed onto her husband. Both of them tumbled down the remaining length of the staircase. Emily had been following. Stepping over her parents, she ran to the back of the house to fetch the maid and groom.

Leaving Martha to attend her parents, Emily dashed out of the front door with John. Daniel was sitting in the gutter in front of their house, as naked as the day he was born. It was Saturday morning so people were out and about. At least a dozen neighbours had gathered to stare. Emily and the groom stopped to stare as well. Mr and Mrs Lang now limped through the front door, both leaning on Martha. At the sight of Daniel, Martha screamed and fainted, bringing the Langs down with her.

Emily forced herself into action.

'John, attend me!' she called to the groom.

Emily and John walked down the garden path and out into the street. Emily stared down the neighbours, her hands on her hips.

'My brother is suffering from a fever, and has been sleepwalking,' she improvised. 'Do nothing to wake him. It is very harmful to wake sleepwalkers.'

John took Daniel under the arms and Emily took his legs. Together they carried Daniel back into the house and into the bathroom. There he was placed in a tub, and Emily carried in hot water while John hurried off to fetch a doctor.

Not only had Daniel broken Mr Lang's resolve, he had shattered it and jumped up and down on the pieces. Mrs Lang was made of sterner stuff, and she managed to rally. As long as there was someone to blame, she could cope. Her husband was definitely worthy of blame.

'You own every stitch of Danny's clothing, do you?' she shouted as the family gathered in the bathroom around Daniel. 'You will go straight to your study and write out a deed that grants Daniel legal ownership of all his clothing, everything in his room, and fifty pounds.'

'But my dear –'

'One hundred pounds!'

'I was only –'

'Two hundred pounds!'

'Yes, yes, yes, I'm going now,' whimpered Mr Lang as he hurried out.

'And as for you, Emily, for a girl of sixteen that was a most admirable display of quick thinking, out on the street, with the neighbours and with Daniel. You certainly did not get that sort of backbone from your father's side of the family.'

Daniel had been bathed, dried, put into his nightshirt and taken back up to his bedroom by the time Liore and Barry arrived. Because the Langs believed Liore to be a boy from an aristocratic family, and because they also believed that aristocrats were a superior type of species, Mr and Mrs Lang were sure that Liore could help. Their feelings for Barry were quite the opposite, but he was a friend of Daniel's and he was with Liore, so he was allowed in as well. Emily showed them upstairs to Daniel's bedroom.

'By your leave, speaking courtly,' said Liore as she entered.

'Sorry, what do you mean?' asked Emily.

'Yeah, ya don't have to ask me to do nothin',' added Barry.

'The apology is a formal declaration that common classes must use when speaking to the nobility in courtly language.'

'But those nobles are a hundred years in the future,' said Emily. 'Why use it when speaking to us?'

'It is a little convention that reminds me of who I am. Your time, your world, your society, none of them are mine. My world was horrible, but it was familiar. I feel that I am losing my identity, so I try to follow old rules and standards. They remind me of who I am.'

'You shouldn't feel that way,' began Emily.

'Enough, I am not the one in need of help,' said Liore impatiently. 'Daniel, I am told that Muriel jilted you.'

'I'se warned ya 'bout that Muriel baggage,' added Barry, who had never liked Muriel and had trouble coping with girls in general. 'Don't trust 'er, says I, she'll make ya betray the Empire for a smile.'

Daniel said nothing. Emily sat beside him and put an arm around his shoulders. She was not used to being sympathetic to anyone, however, and so was unsure of what to say. She looked imploringly to Liore. She was a Battle Commander from 2011, and would know what to do.

'I have conducted some espionage,' Liore said to Daniel. 'I visited Muriel's mother. After that I broke into the journal cache of Fox's radiocomm.'

Liore held up a smooth, black thing about the size of a cigar case. Like her weapon, it would not be built for another century.

'Thought that thing were a telegraph wi'out wires,' said Barry.

For a moment Liore searched for common words.

'It is also a notebook, calendar, diary, encyclopaedia, motion picture camera, phonograph and ... other things. Fox deleted his diary before he returned this unit, but I am an officer. I have access to the Lazarus buffer, so I can restore his deletions.'

'Lazarus buffer?' asked Emily.

'It restores deleted records to life.'

Liore touched a number of coloured studs with letters and numbers on them, then held the unit up.

'*Twelve May, attended art lesson, Muriel Baker, invitation,*' came Fox's voice from the radiocomm. '*Subject, nude sketching, one hour. Made progress.*'

Liore pressed a stud and the voice stopped. For a moment there was no sound at all in the bedroom, apart from the grinding of Emily's teeth.

'Continue playback?' Liore asked.

Emily and Barry nodded together. Daniel did not move. Liore pressed the stud again.

'*Thirteen May, attended art lesson, Muriel, conducting,*' continued Fox. '*Subject, nude sketching. Duration, one hour. Then talked. Two hours. Muriel said, soul mates, we are. I asked, of Daniel. She said, his soul, is wasteland. Fourteen*

May, attended art lesson, Muriel, conducting. Subject, nude sketching, one hour. Then talked, five hours. Did also —'

'Enough!' exclaimed Daniel.

Liore keyed the radiocomm silent.

'Aw, Danny boy,' protested Barry. 'He was up to the good bit.'

'The devious trollop,' said Emily. 'Only five days earlier she was saying she loved Daniel.'

'I also visited Mrs Baker,' said Liore. 'I said I was a friend of Fox's, and needed his address in Paris because I was going there. She gave me the address. She also gave me these.'

Liore held up a sketch. It was a very faithful rendering of Muriel lying back on a lounge chair and wearing nothing but a rose behind her left ear. Daniel's jaw dropped open. Emily gasped, blushed, put a hand to her forehead and considered fainting, then decided against it.

'The wanton baggage!' she said through clenched teeth.

'Give ya two bob for it!' exclaimed Barry eagerly.

'Dated, twelfth May,' said Liore.

'The faithless . . .' Emily trawled her memory for some suitably abusive word, but being from a sheltered background could manage only, 'Hussy!'

'Fox has a good way with shading and texture,' said Daniel in a hollow, helpless voice, staring at the sketch.

'I do believe she looks a little plump,' said Emily contemptuously.

'Daniel, was there a problem of the heart between Muriel and yourself, before the, ah, art lesson?' asked Liore.

Daniel hung his head and clasped his hands together very tightly.

'Two days after we – we saved parliament from being bombed, Muriel asked . . .' Daniel's voice cracked.

'Try to speak in a detached manner,' said Emily. 'Speak without feeling, as if you were Barry.'

'Now just a minute!' began Barry.

'Silence!' commanded Emily.

Daniel took several deep breaths.

'Muriel asked if I would like to learn about being an artist. We had been boating that day, and I was walking her home. I said that I had done some sketching at school but would like to learn more. She has a room over her mother's shop, so we went there and she gave me a sketch pad and a charcoal pencil. Then she went behind a screen to change. I thought she was getting into a costume, but she came out wearing nothing at all.'

'Blimey!' exclaimed Barry.

'I – I snatched up a coverlet from her bed and held it between us. I told her that we should not tempt ourselves to do shameful things, even in the name of art.'

'Bravo!' cried Emily.

'Then wot?' asked Barry, sounding disappointed.

'She snatched the coverlet from me, threw it on the floor and told me to get out. On the following Tuesday I called at the shop after school but it was closed.'

'No doubt for private art lessons!' said Emily.

'I left a note under the door apologising for being a little abrupt, and inviting Muriel to the circus matinee the following Saturday. On the Friday a letter arrived saying that she would be delighted to go to the circus with me. I saw her lots of times after that, mostly on the railway platform at Balaclava. I would get off on the way home from school, and we would spend the time together holding hands until the next train, then I would go home. I thought our misunderstanding had been resolved.'

'I warned you about those artists!' said Emily sharply.

'Just vanishing and leaving a note is the coward's way,' said Liore.

'Typical artists,' added Emily.

'Ya got any more sketches?' asked Barry.

Liore had another ten sketches. The dates on them spanned a two week period, the last being the 27th of May. Fox did appear to have been doing some genuine artwork along with whatever else had transpired between him and Muriel. One of the sketches was only the size of a postcard. Muriel was posing in a feathered hat, with a fencing sabre held jauntily over her shoulder. Daniel stared at it for a long time.

'Emily, could I have some hot chocolate and shortbreads?' he asked with a very slight grin.

'Oh, Daniel, wonderful!' she exclaimed. 'I thought you were going to do something stupid like die of a broken heart.'

As soon as he heard Emily's shoes clattering down the stairs, Daniel held out his hand to Liore.

'Could I have the little sketch?' he asked.

'Why torture yourself?' asked Liore.

'Yeah, I'll take the lot off ya hands for a guinea,' said Barry.

'All I have of Muriel are the two strips of her petticoat that she used to bandage you and me after the fight to save parliament. The picture is more substantial.'

'I ask again, why torture yourself?' said Liore.

'One pound ten, that's me final offer,' added Barry.

'To remind myself that I once had a sweetheart all to myself.'

'Take them all,' said Liore, handing the sketches to Daniel.

The sketches were safely under Daniel's mattress by the time Emily returned. Daniel drank the hot chocolate listlessly, then dutifully finished all six shortbreads that she had brought on a plate.

'You should get on your telegraph thing and tell Fox he is a scoundrel, a cad, a bounder and a deserter,' Emily told Liore as Daniel munched.

'Fox left his radiocomm here,' said Liore, holding both units up for Emily to see.

'How's a raddycom work without wires?' asked Barry.

'It's a Marconi wireless,' said Daniel.

'What would you know about things that have not even been invented?' snapped Emily, forgetting to be sympathetic to her brother by sheer reflex.

'We learned about Marconi wirelesses in school,' said Daniel. 'By using them, two people can speak to each other at great distances.'

'Radiocomms can also locate each other,' said Liore, holding the units up again. 'On the battlefield it is useful.'

'That weapon thing's more of a worry,' said Barry, gently steering the conversation to his own agenda. 'Wot if someone 'alf inches it?'

'Half inches, no target,' said Liore.

'Pinches,' explained Barry.

'Steals,' said Daniel.

'That's wot I said. Anyway, I reckon ya could start a war with that thing. Probably win it, too.'

'A security pad locks the weapon,' said Liore. 'No clearance, no shot.'

'Wot ya mean?'

'Liore's weapon will not activate unless she touches the pad,' said Emily, who had once been cleared to use the weapon. 'It can recognise people who are allowed to use it from the touch of a finger.'

'What if ya finger's blown off?' asked Barry.

'Barry!' shrieked Emily. 'What a thing to say.'

'Any part from my body activates it,' said Liore. 'Even blood or hair will do. It scans for my DNA.'

'DNA?' asked Barry.

'Future discovery,' replied Liore.

'I think the future should be left alone,' said Emily firmly.

That terminated the discussion, but Barry had comprehended just enough to make himself dangerous. He already knew that the weapon recognised who was allowed to use it, but now he knew how that was done.

A piece of Liore, thought Barry. He could demonstrate the weapon to Luker the Lurker. Luker would then introduce him to someone who knew the king. *Gettin' a piece of Liore's the problem, though.*

Liore left, saying that she had other matters to attend to, and Emily went downstairs with her to see her to the front door. Now that they were alone together, Daniel picked up a pencil and opened his address book.

'Barry, where were you when Mrs Baker gave Muriel's address in Paris to Liore?' he asked.

'Outside, mindin' the bike.'

'So you don't know it?'

'Nah, but I seen it.'

'Where?'

'On the envelope wot the nude piccies were in, down on one corner.'

'Liore took the envelope with her . . . but I wonder . . .'

Daniel took out the sketches and examined them carefully, then rubbed at a corner of one sketch with the side of the pencil's lead. The address appeared as white letters on a black background.

'Blimey!' exclaimed Barry. 'That's one trick I gotta remember. Oi, but yer not gonna write to her or nothin', are ya?'

'Write, oh no,' said Daniel. 'Writing to Muriel is the last thing on my mind.'

Any bit of her body, Barry thought as he rode the delivery bike back to North Brighton Station. *Needn't be attached, neither. Wot's a bit of body? Fingernails? Snot? Hair? Hair!*

Barry remembered the comb on Liore's chest of drawers, but it had been as clean as new. The floor of her room had been swept, and even the wastebasket had been empty.

I bet the tidy baggage cleans her place every friggin' mornin'. Oi, now there's an inspirational. Where's the rubbish go? The dustbin? Yeah!

The sixth of June was the next moonlit night on which there was a garbage collection. The moon rose at 9 pm, and was nearly full. Barry was ready with the station bike as the first moonlight glowed from the eastern horizon. Minutes later he was in Keys Street, where Liore lived.

Rubbish bins stood outside each house for the collection the following morning. Barry rode up and stopped outside number eight. To his relief, the dog had decided that the night was too cold to be on patrol, and was nowhere to be seen. Taking a potato sack from his bag, he removed the bin's lid, decanted the entire contents into the sack, then rode away with the sack balanced in the delivery basket.

He made straight for North Brighton Station, where he emptied the sack onto the mail room floor. Mostly it was kitchen scraps and other household rubbish, but something else stood out. There were seven little packets of newspaper, all neatly wrapped and tied with string. Barry unwrapped one. It contained dust, crumbs and a few strands of hair. The boys at university wore their hair fashionably long, and Liore had grown her hair out to look like one of them. The strands were the right length for Liore's hair, and when twisted together they were also the right colour.

Blow me down, so the murderin' baggage does clean her place every day, thought Barry as he unwrapped the next packet.

Soon he had enough for a thin braid of Liore's hair, along with the pile of reeking garbage. He burned what he could in the station's fireplace, then carried the rest a short distance along the railway tracks and dumped it into the grass. The mail room continued to smell of kitchen refuse, so he left the door open while he fanned the air with some newspaper. Finally he locked the door, made up a mattress of mail bags, pulled a blanket from under the counter and settled down for the night. His father had rooms above a nearby shop, but made Barry sleep at the station to deter thieves.

By the moonlight streaming through the window, Barry carefully wound the strands of Liore's hair into a braid as he lay there, then fashioned this into a ring that fitted over his right thumb.

'Reckon you're a bit of Liore,' he told the ring of hair. 'Reckon you're gonna make me Sir Barry Porter, richest knight in the empire.'

Chapter 2

TRAVELLER

Because Barry was so very frightened of Liore, he decided to let some time pass after stealing Mrs O'Brien's garbage. Each day he lived in fear of Liore arriving at the station and threatening to kill him, but she did no more than buy a ticket for Flinders Street. Slowly Barry's courage returned, but it was still two weeks before he approached her house again. This time he was far better prepared. He bribed the watchdog with a cream bun, picked the lock on Liore's door, and let himself in. By now he had been studying her movements at the railway station very closely, and knew when she took the train to go to university lectures. As he entered the room his heart was pounding so loudly that he thought the landlady might hear. The place was still meticulously clean and orderly.

That's how the bagman likes it, he thought as he looked about, locking the room's layout into his mind. *Neat is easy to remember.*

A quick search of the drawers and cupboard revealed nothing that would be out of place in mid-

1901. Next Barry set to work on the trunk. This time he was more familiar with the brass padlock, so he had it open sooner. The weapon was still within, along with two uniforms, a tiny medical kit, the small, smooth black thing that was Fox's radiocomm, some papers written in a code that he did not understand, and two pairs of boots. There was nothing that looked as if Liore would need to use it every day.

Putting on a pair of gloves that he kept in his bag, he noted the exact position of the weapon, then lifted it from the trunk. It was not as heavy as he had expected. He saw that it was switched off, because the little red light was not glowing. Barry removed a glove and touched his thumb to the security pad, as he had seen Liore do. The recessed red light did not come on. Barry put the ring of Liore's hair around his thumb and touched the pad with it. This time the red light glowed into life.

'Man o' mine, Barry Bagman!' he exclaimed, then remembered where he was. Nobody came to investigate his cry of triumph, however, not even the dog.

Barry now pushed the door open, raised the weapon and looked through the gunsights. The magnified image of the top of a distant gum tree presented itself as a suitable target. He gently pressed the firing stud. There was a sharp, shrill squeak. The tree's crown gave a little flash, then flames burst out amid the leaves.

'Barry boy, have you got a deal for that king or wot?' he whispered with satisfaction.

Again Barry pressed the ring of hair against the pad, and the light winked out in its little recess. He put the weapon in his bag, locked the trunk, checked that everything was precisely as he had found it, then stepped out, locking the door behind him. He had reached the front yard when the dog looked up, failed to recall who Barry was or that he had just given him a cream bun, and charged him with a barrage of barks. As Barry vaulted the front gate he heard the dog's jaws click shut, but it was on space that he no longer occupied. He set off along the street, but the neighbours were looking at the burning tree so nobody paid him any attention.

After all the trouble he had taken to steal Liore's weapon, Barry had been expecting at least a little awe and respect from Luker the Lurker when he put his bag down on the café table and opened it. Luker looked into the bag, frowned, then turned to Barry.

'That's no gun,' he said.

'Yeah it is,' said Barry, throwing caution to the wind and lifting the weapon out.

Luker peered at it. A few other patrons glanced at it as well, decided that it looked like part of some steam engine, and went back to their own business.

'Two barrels got glass in 'em, there's no trigger and there's no stock,' said Luker. 'Did you pay some cove real money for this?'

'Luker, man o' mine, this is a very special gun,' said Barry, putting the weapon back into his bag. 'Come outside. I'll show ya.'

'Shove off, I'm havin' a coffee.'

'But I gotta demonstrate it to ya.'

'Do it here.'

'I can't. All these people will see.'

'You mean all these people will see it do nothing.'

Barry was almost frantic. Every moment spent arguing with Luker the Lurker was a moment less before Liore returned to her room. Barry knew that he could stage a spectacular demonstration of the weapon's power within the café, but then rumours would quickly spread that Barry the Bag had a fantastically powerful weapon. Liore made it her business to keep track of unusual rumours.

After considerably more pleading, and finally offering Luker half a crown if the weapon did not work, Barry and Luker emerged into Acland Street. They entered a lane, and Barry took the weapon from his bag.

'This better be good,' said Luker.

'Trust the bagman,' said Barry, slipping the ring of Liore's hair onto his thumb and touching the security pad. 'See that streetlamp?' he said, pointing at a cast iron gaslight lamp in Acland Street.

'What about it?'

Barry pressed the firing stud as he waved the barrel in the general direction of the gaslight. There was a flash high on the cast iron stem of the pole, then the top four feet toppled and fell to the gutter with a loud crash, spraying broken glass all about. The white hot edge of the severed metal ignited the gas that now gushed free, sending a long tongue of yellow flame into the air. Women screamed, men shouted, horses reared and bolted, and every dog in the street either fled or began barking. Nobody thought to glance down the lane.

'Bleedin' hell!' exclaimed Luker. 'Even a new Lee-Enfield couldn't do that. Give it here, you little pisser.'

Barry backed away, the barrels pointed at Luker. Remembering what had just happened to the gaslight, Luker stopped and raised his hands.

'Now just you listen,' Barry warned. 'This thing can blow up a train, an' it did.'

'Blow up a train? You mean that wagon in Albury last month?'

'Yeah, yeah. There was secret spies. They used this.'

Luker considered the situation carefully. Again, what Barry was saying had an oddly genuine feel to it, and the proof was pouring flames into the air out in Acland Street.

'Righto little bagman, what's your terms?'

'You just tell someone wot knows the king about this implemental. Tell that king that it's 'is in return for rekkypense of expenses incurred by a loyal subject. That's two hundred quid.'

'You didn't spend two hundred quid stealing this!'

'The king's not gonna know that, Luker, matey. Oi, make that two-fifty, then it's fifty for you.'

Barry was the only person not crowding about to view the broken, burning gaslight as he got back onto the station bike. Half an hour of frantic pedalling had him back at Liore's place in Keys Street, and this time the dog was nowhere to be seen. He entered very quietly by the side gate and wheeled the bike up the path. In the backyard he saw Wellington chewing on a large bone. Being a little deaf, the dog did not turn around as Barry set to work picking the lock on Liore's door. Once safely inside the room, Barry picked the padlock on the trunk, then replaced the weapon. He was outside again and had just locked Liore's door when Wellington stood up, looked about for somewhere to bury his bone, and spotted him.

Barry tried to ride down the side path while Wellington ran beside him, barking furiously and snapping at his legs. Barry raised his legs to the handlebars, then noticed that he was rapidly approaching the front gate. The bicycle collided with the gate and Barry fell on Wellington. The dog yelped, then ran back up the side path with his tail between his legs. Having reached the backyard, the dog turned around to bark at Barry, who had the side gate open and was wheeling the bike into the street. By the time Mrs O'Brien came out to see what the dog was barking at, Barry was around the corner and pedalling down Union Street, swearing to himself that next time he would bring two cream buns and a bone to keep the dog occupied.

It was not often that Daniel's father called a family meeting. Outwardly he was the head of a very conventional household, but in fact his wife's family had most of the money and all of the authority in his business. Most of the time she was happy enough to let him run things, but when he failed in something important she took over at once. Because he had failed so spectacularly in the matter of Daniel and his obsession with Muriel, Mrs Lang had sent numerous telegrams to her relatives in England. They decided what was best for Daniel, and Mr Lang was told what to announce.

'My boy, we are seriously worried about you,' said Mr Lang, standing with his back to the living room fire as his wife, Daniel and Emily sat in a semicircle around him. 'It has been six weeks since that, that *girl* saw fit to abandon you, yet still you are moping. I am informed that you are failing all your tests and essays at school after being top of your class. This is simply not good enough.'

'I'm sorry, Father,' said Daniel, staring past him into the fire.

'Well, it's too late for regrets now. There is a school in England named Harlingford. It specialises in tutoring the sons of gentlefolk in preparation for university.'

'You plan to send me there next year, Father.'

'Well, plans change. Because of all your moping, your mother and I have decided that you need a regime of hard work and discipline at once. You are booked to sail for Britain on the steamship *Andromeda* in six days. Harlingford should have you prepared for Oxford University as early as this time next year.'

'Thank you, Father,' said Daniel listlessly, feigning that he did not care what he was being told. All the while his heart was pounding with excitement.

'You will have a first-class cabin all to yourself,' said his mother. 'This will be a wonderful and exciting adventure. It will change your life forever.'

'Thank you, Mother,' said Daniel. *But the real adventure will be in Paris.*

'And don't even think about going to France and visiting Paris,' said Emily, as if she were reading his mind.

❇

It took a month before Luker the Lurker finally managed to contact someone in authority who could safely be told about Barry's secret. The key word was *safely*. Luker could easily contact a large number of people in authority, but all of them were more likely to have him flung into jail than come along for a discreet meeting with Barry the Bag about a stolen weapon of quite fantastic power.

Finally he was introduced to a former soldier who was down on his luck and making ends meet by selling rifles stolen from local rifle clubs. This man introduced him to an officer with the local militias who was buying the rifles at a reduced rate, and from here Luker slowly made his way into the establishment until he met with someone who had letters after his name. Luker left his office with a man who was introduced only as Sir Bernard.

'I am told that you want to meet someone who has the ear of the king,' said Bernard as they walked along Collins Street.

'That's right, I got a matter of high importance,' said Luker, who was very much in awe of the knight. 'I'm in delicate circumstances, you know? I'm a shady cove, I'll grant you that, but I'm still a patriot and I love king and crown. I'll not sell them out for anything.'

The man smiled and nodded. This reassured Luker.

'A patriotic criminal,' he said. 'In wartime, we call you heroes when you go against the enemy. Tell me, why did you not volunteer to fight the Boers in Africa?'

'Got a tropical disease. Can't go anywhere hot or it flares up.'

'Oh? How unfortunate. What disease is that?'

'Malaria,' guessed Luker.

'You poor man. Well then, how do you wish to support king and country from here?'

'I've been hearing talk from the local coves. Talk about a load of dynamite being stolen from a railway wagon in Melbourne on the day parliament opened, then a few days later another railway wagon full of dynamite blows up in Albury. I asks myself, is this something to do with enemies of the king?'

Bernard leaned slightly closer to Luker as they walked, and paid him very close attention.

'Go on,' he prompted softly.

'Well now, a while back this ratty little push boy comes up to me with a story about stealing a secret weapon. I thought it was just talk, but I happen to know that he was mixed up with the coves who stole that load of dynamite.'

'The load that did not blow up?'

'That one, yes.'

'And?'

'Well, that's all. He wants to meet someone from the king before he'll hand the weapon over. He wants two thousand quid for it.'

'What does this weapon do?'

'It sort of cuts through stuff like a red-hot knife. I saw it slice an iron pole in half.'

'Obviously some sort of trick, but tell me, how do you know that your associate was involved with the theft of the dynamite?'

'Oh, I got a few contacts who need things moved along for a consideration, no names named.'

'So *you* took part in the theft?'

'Not as such. I was just contacted about moving a load for profit. Like I said, no names, no questions. Now what about this weapon, then?'

'I believe I may be able to put you in contact with someone who would give you a hearing.'

After enduring a month of waiting, Barry was growing so frantic that he was not far from giving up on Luker the Lurker and writing to the king directly. After all, there was only one king of England, so if he wrote *The King* and *England* on an envelope it was sure to arrive. Finally Luker announced that a meeting had been arranged. Barry was provided with an address, a time and a password, and told not to be late.

The address turned out to be a club for very rich gentlemen in the centre of Melbourne. Although thoroughly intimidated by the building and the uniformed doorman, Barry boldly walked up, stopped and stood his ground.

'I'm Barry Porter, an' I were told I should come 'ere an' say *lion*.'

'Barry Porter, lion,' replied the doorman smoothly. 'You are expected, Master Porter. Do enter. An official will escort you to the correct room.'

Once inside, Barry looked about the club in awe. He had not been aware that such opulence existed. There were huge paintings on the walls, and even the wallpaper was decorated with gilt leaf. A chandelier a yard across hung from the ceiling, and the carpet was so thick that his shoes actually sank into it. The reception area featured suits of armour, crystal cabinets full of silver trophies, and the biggest armchairs that he had ever seen. Barry had just settled down in one of the armchairs and was kicking his legs in the air when a man in a suit arrived and held up a little white card.

'Master Barry Porter?' he called.

'Reckon that's me,' said Barry, clutching his bag and standing up.

'Come this way.'

Barry followed the man up a staircase of polished wood that was such a deep shade of red that he thought at first it had been painted. He was shown into a room furnished with yet more huge armchairs, and here he found Luker the Lurker waiting. With him was a broad-shouldered, middle-aged man in an embroidered waistcoat who he introduced as Sir Bernard, and a woman whose name was Lady Conrad. She was dressed in clothes that were close to the height of fashion. Barry was good at picking fashionably dressed people; they were the best to steal from. A fishnet veil hung from her hat, obscuring her features, but she looked to be about forty. A waiter brought in coffee on a tray with four cups on saucers. Barry suspected that the silver spoons were real silver, but he had the sense not to pocket one.

'Er, so ya know the king?' Barry asked Bernard once the waiter had left.

'Lady Conrad knows the king,' replied Bernard. 'I am her personal assistant.'

'Yer a knight, yet ya gotta work?' exclaimed Barry.

'Even the king works for the good of the empire, so why not the rest of us?' said Bernard.

'I am told that you have important information,' said Lady Conrad. 'I am very anxious to hear what you have to say.'

'Could we 'ave Luker out of 'ere first?' asked Barry, correctly suspecting that Luker was trying to take over the sale of the weapon.

'Now just a minute,' began Luker.

'Leave,' said Lady Conrad.

The authority in Lady Conrad's voice as she spoke that single word told Barry that nobody who knew what was good for him argued with her. Luker left.

Lady Conrad turned back to Barry. 'Continue.'

'Yeah, well, this is gonna sound like a load of horsey, but I met a couple of coves back in April wot come from a time wot hasn't happened yet and brung a weapon like ya wouldn't believe,' Barry began.

There was a long and uneasy pause during which Barry panicked, lost his nerve, and forgot what he was going to say next.

'So these two people came from the future?' prompted Lady Conrad.

'Er, yeah.'

'And they brought a weapon from the future?'

'Yeah.'

'Rather like Sir Bernard taking a Maxim machine gun back from today to the Napoleonic Wars.'

'Er, wot?'

'A machine gun, Barry,' said Bernard. 'A Maxim gun can fire two hundred times more bullets in a minute than a soldier with an old-fashioned musket. One man with a Maxim would be as effective as two hundred soldiers during the Napoleonic Wars. His bullets would also travel over a mile, so he could fire at the enemy for almost half an hour before they marched close enough to shoot at him. He could defeat a whole army if he had enough bullets. Is that what your weapon from the future can do?'

'Um, yeah, except that it can cut through iron from three miles off.'

'You mean it can shoot bullets through iron from three miles away?'

'Er, yeah. That is, no. I mean it sort of melts stuff.'

'With hot bullets?'

'I'm not sure. It just sorta melts through stuff. Yeah.'

'This sounds like a lie to me, Barry,' said Lady Conrad in a very unsettling tone of voice.

'No, no, I can prove it. I got it.'

'Where?'

'I got it hidden. Like, if yer Bernard cove had a weapon like that, he'd hide it, too.'

Lady Conrad and Bernard conferred quietly for a moment.

'On another matter, Barry, there was a wagon load of dynamite stolen from the Jolimont railway yards in May. Mr Luker said you were involved. A very fat man named Lurker the Worker was involved too, and a railway clerk named Wreder.'

Now Barry had a dilemma. If he denied all knowledge of this theft, he would lose credit for stopping the bombing of parliament. Luker the Lurker, Lurker the Worker and Wreder the Writer would get the credit, the rewards, and the medals.

'Er, yeah, we was helpin' the two coves from the future,' said Barry, deciding that trying to tell them that Liore was a girl warrior was stretching belief just a little too much. 'These two coves were Liore and Fox. They come back in time to stop parlyment bein' bombed by coves called Lionhearts. Them Lionhearts are British, like us, except that they're tryin' to start us fightin' the Germans so the empire will stay together.'

Lady Conrad and Bernard exchanged glances again.

'So two soldiers from the future came back through time to stop the bombing of the first Australian parliament by British agents who were going to blame it on Germany?' said Lady Conrad with a condescending smile.

'Yeah, ya got it.'

'Where is their time machine?'

'It was a sort of time cannon. It shoots people back through time but stays where it is, in the future.'

'So no time machine?'

'No.'

'What about the time travellers?'

'Well, after they saved parlyment, Fox ran off to Paris with an artist floozy to learn to paint.'

Lady Conrad rubbed her temples. Bernard patted her on the shoulder.

'Go on,' she said without looking up.

'Liore's at the university, learnin' to be a doctor.'

'So a warrior from the future is learning to be a doctor at the University of Melbourne?'

'Yeah.'

'Just how did you people save parliament?'

'Well, Liore an' Fox knew what would happen, 'cause they was from the future. They didn't know where the bombs were, though, but I found out, so I stole them with a little help from Wreder the Writer, Lurker the Worker, and you already know about Luker the Lurker.'

'And where is the dynamite?'

'We sold it.'

'Again, no evidence.'

'No.'

'And I suppose you will claim to have destroyed the wagon in Albury, too.'

'Yeah – er, not quite. That was Liore, with the future weapon gun thing.'

'I heard that it was one of the guards, smoking.'

'Nah, it was Liore with her weapon. Then she burned a hostel where some evydence about Germans killin' the prince had been planted.'

'I heard it was flaming wreckage from the explosion that started the fire.'

'Look, lady, I know this all sounds like a load of cocky cacky, but I can prove it with the weapon.'

'When?' asked Lady Conrad, looking as if she

now needed something a lot stronger than a cup of coffee.

'Three days,' said Barry desperately. 'Three days. You bring two fifty quid an' I bring the weapon.'

'Luker said it was two thousand pounds.'

'Did he? Jeez, that Luker, ya just can't trust nobody. I said two hundred an' fifty quid. No more, 'cause I'm doin' it for the king.'

Finally Lady Conrad smiled. Had Barry not been sitting down, he would have collapsed with relief. At last, someone who knew the king believed him.

'Barry, here are my terms,' said Lady Conrad. 'You bring your weapon and all your fellow conspirators to North Brighton Station in three days, and I shall be there with Bernard and your money. If the other men confirm what you say, and if the weapon works, you get what you asked for, a medal, and a meeting with the king. If not, Bernard will kick you from one end of the station platform to the other, then back again.'

'It's true, I swear!' babbled Barry.

'What time?'

'Three in the afternoon.'

'I shall be there, and I shall expect convincing proof.'

Railway Pier was where people left for overseas, and

for many it was their last view of Melbourne. Daniel was about to leave, but he did not care whether he ever saw the place again. Even six weeks after he had been rejected by Muriel, his pain was still intense.

He was driven to the pier in the family carriage, accompanied by his father, mother and sister. The ship carried a thousand passengers, and several times as many had come to see them off. Thus the pier was more crowded than a football match, and everyone was either waving, shouting or crying. The groom whistled for a porter as they arrived, and Daniel's luggage was carried away to the ship.

'Now remember, you are going to a very exclusive English school,' said Mr Lang as the family escorted him onto the pier through the press of the crowd. 'Study hard and forget all that silly girl business.'

The advice was sensible, but memories of the only love of Daniel's life were still clear and agonising in his mind. In his luggage were also two strips of Muriel's petticoat and some nude sketches that he used to renew his memories of her.

'She was a worthless baggage anyway,' said Emily. 'She was an artist, what do you expect? Artists run away with other artists. That's what they do.'

Daniel made no attempt to argue or fight back. Very soon his family would be on the pier, waving as the *Andromeda* pulled away, with him aboard. He could then dream of holding hands with Muriel without anyone bursting in and telling him to pull himself together. His only regret was that Barry and Liore had not come to see him off. On the other hand, Daniel had not been particularly good company for anyone in the weeks just past, so it was only to be expected.

The Lang family finally reached the gangway of the *Andromeda*, which was easily the largest ship docked at the pier. To Daniel's relief, his sister was so thoroughly awestruck by the ship's sheer size that she stopped ordering him about.

'It's so big, how can it possibly move?' she exclaimed as she gazed upwards.

'Nonsense, the bigger the ship the faster it travels,' scoffed Mr Lang. 'Everyone knows that.'

Acutely embarrassed, Emily was immediately silent. The Langs climbed the gangway, found a steward, and were shown to Daniel's cabin. His mother snatched the key from the bed and dangled it before Daniel.

'This is the key to your cabin, now put it in your pocket and don't lose it. Always lock the door whenever you leave, you never know what sorts of riff-raff will be on the ship.'

'Mother, he's a first-class passenger, the riff-raff are not allowed in this area,' said Emily.

'Well one of them might climb up here on a rope or something. You know how good sailors are with ropes.'

'This is a gentleman's cabin, so always act like a gentleman,' said his father. 'Be sure to play some deck games, but only the right sorts of games. Deck cricket to establish yourself with the other young men, and quoits so that you can mingle with young ladies from good families.'

'Do not volunteer for the amateur theatrical shows, only vulgar people do that,' said his mother. 'Remember, if there is a fancy dress ball, I have packed a mask and a cardboard dagger, so you can wear your Harlingford academic gown and go as a spy. That will look very dashing.'

Daniel's cabin was on the port side, and Mr Lang pointed out that he would have a view of Brighton Beach as the ship sailed south down Port Phillip Bay. Emily looked out through his porthole.

'So big,' she cried, still trying to comprehend the size of the ship. 'The people down on the pier are like little dolls.'

'Ten thousand tons gross weight,' said Mr Lang, who had read a pamphlet about the ship. 'All driven by triple expansion steam engines and twin screw propellers. Her service speed is between eighteen and twenty knots, so Dan will be in England in only six weeks.'

Daniel's luggage began to arrive at the cabin, and he did not even bother to protest as his mother and sister began unpacking his trunks and putting his clothes away. The strips of Muriel's petticoat and the sketches of her were safely hidden in the lining of the suitcase, thanks to some advice on the art of smuggling from Barry the Bag. His father now took him out to the promenade deck, where he gave him a small camera and told him to photograph significant things on the voyage, such as the Suez Canal and the Rock of Gibraltar.

'You must remember to get photographs of people, too. Make friends with some young man and have him snap you in the company of important people. Photos like that can have a great bearing on how others view you in later life.'

To Daniel's relief the ship's horn sounded a warning for visitors to leave. He saw his family to the gangway.

'Don't forget to send letters from Ceylon and Egypt,' said Emily.

'Always lock your cabin,' said his mother.

'Remember that place on the promenade deck I showed you,' said his father. 'We will be looking for you there.'

Once they were out of sight Daniel turned – to be confronted by Liore. As always, she was dressed as a boy. Daniel blinked, unsure if his imagination had spilled over into the real world.

'Me, it is,' she said.

'I – I thought you might not come along,'

stammered Daniel. 'Barry said you are at the university a lot.'

'My friend, you are. Am late, I apologise.'

'That's quite all right. Just to see you at all is better than a whole morning of Emily.'

Liore looked down at the deck for a moment. *She is unused to compliments,* thought Daniel. *Before Muriel, I was, too. Strange how a few soft words can shake up invincible people, just as surely as weaklings like me.*

'Your sister, means well,' said Liore.

'But she can't stop nagging.'

'Her downfall, it is.'

'She tries to hold people too tightly, then wonders why they slip through her fingers.'

'True.'

'Liore, you're using battlespeak again.'

'By your leave, speaking courtly.'

'And you don't have to apologise for speaking normally.'

'Daniel, try to understand me. My world is over a hundred years in the future. I am finding it harder and harder to . . . to maintain discipline over myself. I have to play games with myself, like pretending that people like you and Emily are the nobility, and that I must apologise formally before I speak what I know as courtly to you. Little rituals like that are all that I have to remind me of who I am.'

'Oh. Sorry.'

'Think nothing of it. Now Daniel, the Century War may start while you are studying in Britain. If Britain is invaded, you can never return to Australia.'

'With luck I may die in the invasion,' said Daniel.

'I have given you my warning. Lockdown?'

'Lockdown,' said Daniel.

'Goodbye, Daniel Lang. Try to stay out of the House of Death.'

Because Liore was dressed as a boy, they had to part as boys. They shook hands, and Daniel heard something pop among his metacarpals as he tried to squeeze back against her grip. Suddenly he felt that he should leave Liore on a more positive note.

'Liore, will I ever see you again?' he asked as they drew apart. 'I mean, I rather like having you around.'

Even as he spoke the words Daniel felt as if he were betraying Muriel, yet he wanted to at least try to be nice to Liore. Apart from Muriel, she was the only girl he had ever liked.

Liore smiled, but shook her head.

'Unlikely,' she said, then turned away and hurried down the gangway as the ship's horn gave its final warning.

She is like a wild fox that has learned to trust me, thought Daniel as he gazed after her. *She is so dangerous, and even though I enjoy her company, it is a relief to have her gone.*

Daniel remembered to go to the place on the promenade deck that his father had pointed out.

The Langs were gathered at a particular bollard on the opposite side of the pier, all waving red handkerchiefs. Daniel even noticed that his mother and sister were dabbing at their eyes from time to time. He could not see Liore.

Suddenly Daniel realised that the ship was already moving. He waved. Barry had, of course, not put in an appearance. *Probably trying to talk his way out of some police station,* thought Daniel. The wind blew a plume of sooty smoke from one of the tugs between the ship and the pier. By the time it had cleared, Daniel was no longer able to distinguish anyone. He stayed on the promenade deck to get a photograph of Brighton Beach as the ship steamed past some minutes later, but to his surprise he found that the bayside suburbs looked rather like bushland when seen from a ship, and that nothing was familiar. Daniel decided that if he could not identify Brighton Beach with his own eyes, his family would not be able to do any better with a photograph posted home. He snapped off a picture, then returned to his cabin.

Daniel felt decidedly cheered, not because he was at the beginning of a great adventure, but because he had six weeks of peace and solitude ahead of him. Six weeks to dream about his lost love, and six weeks of not being shouted at and told to pull himself together. Six weeks of not being a schoolboy, and not going to classes at all. After that, he still had the two hundred pounds from his father. That would be more than enough to get him from London to Paris.

Once in Paris, I shall challenge Fox to a duel, Daniel decided. *He shall kill me, and Muriel shall know that I died of my love for her.*

Just over two hours later the ship passed through the Heads at the south of Port Phillip Bay. Daniel had been hoping to see the fortifications at Point Nepean, but the cannons installed there were in low, squat blockhouses, and did not look at all impressive. On the other side of the Heads, his favourite holiday town, Queenscliff, was only visible as a few buildings on the horizon. Daniel concluded that views from the ship were always going to be pretty uninteresting, and that he was in for a very boring voyage.

Once the *Andromeda* was clear of the Heads and steaming into Bass Strait, things became anything but boring. Although the sky was clear, a rolling swell had been generated by a distant storm. The swell was strong enough to make even the ten thousand ton *Andromeda* wallow and pitch as it made its way west to Adelaide, its last port of call in Australia.

At first Daniel thought that he was handling the motion of the ship very well, and that a vessel in rough water was no worse than a fairground ride. He soon realised that a fairground ride seldom lasted more than a few minutes, and that one could get off. It was not at all like a rowboat's rocking, because one had a feeling of falling for several seconds, then one was suddenly heaved upwards very sharply. This sensation was entirely new to Daniel, and it was very unpleasant. He tried staring at the coastline. He tried to tell himself that he enjoyed the motion. He tried thinking of Muriel kissing him. He imagined himself duelling with Fox. Nothing worked. At last he made the worst mistake of all.

'It's going to be like this all the way to England,' he whispered to himself.

That thought was too much for Daniel. Gripped by nausea, he leaned over a rail and threw up his going-away breakfast before he realised that a lower deck, and not the ocean, was directly below. A cry of outrage floated up to him, and he collided with a steward as he hurriedly turned away. The steward guided him to a bathroom.

Chapter 3

PHOTOGRAPH

Barry knew that Liore would be gone for a long time because she was seeing Daniel off. According to Daniel, Emily had invited Liore to lunch after the ship had left, so she was likely to be away until at least mid-afternoon. It was a perfect time to steal the weapon, sell it to the king's envoy, then hide the money and act innocent. He arrived in Liore's street just after 2 pm, because he now knew that the landlady had a sleep after lunch. He tossed Wellington a cream bun before the dog had a chance to bark, opened the gate and wheeled his bicycle up the side path to Liore's room. The lock on the door seemed to take forever to pick, but Mrs O'Brien apparently remained asleep and Wellington had forgotten about Barry by the time he had finished the cream bun. When the lock finally yielded to Barry, he took the bicycle inside and pulled the door shut.

The padlock on the trunk still took a depressingly long time to pick, but finally Barry had the trunk open. He lifted the weapon out, placed it in his bag, then looked at the trunk's other contents. He decided that if he stole everything, it would look like a random burglary. If only the weapon were missing, the finger of suspicion would be pointed at someone who knew the weapon's value. Of the six people who knew that, two were in Paris, one was on a ship to London, and two more were seeing that person off. That left Barry.

Nah, gotta make this look like a randomly, he thought as he emptied the trunk's contents into his bag.

He examined the radiocomm with suspicion. There was only one in the trunk, which meant Liore had the other. Thus she could locate this one if it were switched on. Recalling that her devices always had a little light to show that they were working, he checked it for glowing lights. Finding none, he put the radiocomm into his bag. Barry checked the drawers and cupboard again. In one of the drawers was a toy steam engine connected to something that looked electrical, some things with wires wound in coils, a few tools, a clasp knife, and a Bergmann automatic pistol.

Reckon a burglar boy would take you two, he decided, then put the knife and gun into his bag.

As a final touch, Barry put an identical padlock on Liore's trunk and locked it with a key. His reasoning was that she would try to open it with her own key, assume the lock was broken when it failed to open, then call a locksmith. All that would take time, and would allow the trail leading to him to go cold.

The dog was waiting outside when Barry emerged from the room.

'Nice, er, Nelson,' said Barry, reaching out to pat the dog.

Wellington growled and snapped at his hand.

'Nice Lancelot?' ventured Barry.

Wellington barked. Barry tossed his second cream bun to the dog. Wellington gulped it down as Barry tried to use his picklock to relock the door, but the dog started barking again before the door was secure.

'Oh friggin' hell, shut up, Galahad!' shouted Barry desperately.

Mrs O'Brien's face appeared at the kitchen window, her mouth open with surprise. Barry instantly concluded that all was lost and decided to flee. Keeping the station bicycle between Wellington and himself, he hurried down the side path. He had just opened the gate when he heard, 'Stop, thief!' behind him. Barry dashed through the gate and pulled it shut. Mrs O'Brien appeared, holding a shotgun. She fired it into the air, and again shouted at him to stop. Fortunately the gun had only a single barrel. He leapt onto the bicycle and began pedalling frantically as she reloaded.

Mrs O'Brien fired low, meaning to hit the back wheel of the bike where it was in contact with the road. Instead she hit the road about a yard behind the bike, showering Barry's legs with dust and stones but doing no damage. This put the fear of death into the fleeing youth, who pedalled harder. By the time she had reloaded, Barry was around the corner. She opened the gate and told Wellington to go after him, but the elderly dog lumbered off in the wrong direction.

Barry's legs were burning with exertion as he reached North Brighton Station. He put the bike away, opened the door to the mail room, then froze. Luker the Lurker lay dead, a single bullet hole between his eyebrows.

'Liore!' exclaimed Barry, convinced that she was nearby. 'Don't shoot, they made me do it.'

When Liore did not appear, Barry riffled through Luker's pockets and found two pounds, then twisted the heel of one of his snakeskin boots. It popped off, and within the hollow was a gold coin. The other heel had a similar bonanza, and there was another five pounds hidden in his belt. Barry stole the belt, then paused to think.

Liore was definitely nearby and trying to kill him. How to get away, and where to go? Barry had Luker's money, and more money hidden in his bag. The fastest thing on earth was a train. Nothing could catch a train, especially over distance. The Adelaide

Express would be leaving in an hour. Daniel's ship would sail from Adelaide the very next day. Barry realised that if he could get onto the Adelaide Express, nobody could catch him before he could board the ship and go to England. There he could hand the weapon to the king in person.

'Don't shoot!' whimpered a voice from behind the counter.

'Lurker the Worker!' exclaimed Barry softly, as a pair of hands then a chubby face appeared. 'What are you doing down there?'

'Luker said to come here for a bit of easy profit. I just lay down back here for a little snooze, 'cause I came early, you know how it is, got all me weight to carry and so much work.'

'What the frig happened to Luker?'

'I heard his voice, and there was two coves with him. They asks where's the other two traitors, an' he says they orta be here by now. That weren't good enough for them, 'cause I heard a bang and a thump. That was Luker gettin' shot.'

'That's a bleedin' obviously.'

Somewhere in the distance there were raised voices. Barry put a finger to his lips.

'That's me old man!' gasped Barry. 'I gotta warn him.'

Going out onto the platform with Lurker, Barry looked about. There were a dozen or so people waiting for the next train, and another three waiting at the ticket window. One of them held up his pocket watch.

'I say, I've been waiting here for five minutes and forty seconds,' was as far as the man got before there was a loud bang from the signal box.

Barry turned in time to see a figure stagger backwards, burst through a window and plunge fifteen feet to the platform. A moment later two men and a woman dashed out of the door to the signal box and clattered down the stairs. Barry recognised Sir Bernard as the man with the gun. He fired two warning shots into the platform.

'All of you, back!' he shouted, then the woman clutched his arm and pointed.

'There, the boy and the fat man!' she exclaimed, her voice unmistakably that of Lady Conrad. 'Lurker and Porter.'

Bernard fired at Lurker, and the bullet removed his cap and a few strands of hair. There was a click as the pistol's hammer came down on a spent shell.

'Come on, hurry!' said the other man.

Lady Conrad and Bernard glared at Barry and Lurker for a moment more, then they jumped down onto the railway tracks, hurried to the street and made off in a carriage that yet another man was tending.

Barry ran up to the body on the platform. There

was a bullet hole at the centre of his forehead.

'Dad, oh frig, Dad!' exclaimed Barry, trying to comprehend that his father was dead.

'Barry, mate, them's rough coves,' said Lurker behind him.

'They killed Dad! Just like that.'

'Reckon they'll be back for us?'

'That's an obviously. Worker man, we gotta get west on Australia's fastest wheels before that cove reloads and comes back.'

'Yeah, I'm all for that.'

'I say, shouldn't someone call the police?' asked the man from the ticket window, who was still holding his pocket watch.

'Yeah, ya better do it now before they friggin' escape!' said Barry. 'They murdered me dad.'

The man hurried off. Barry considered going through his father's pockets, but everyone on the platform was watching. Besides, the body was his father's, after all, and even Barry had standards.

'Can't believe he's friggin' dead!' squeaked Lurker. 'I was havin' a beer with him only lunchtime.'

'An' he's me dad an' all. I mean, he wasn't much of a dad, but he was all I got.'

'They shot him, just like that.'

'We gotta leave,' said Barry. 'Go to London, tell the king important stuff.'

'Yeah?'

'Ya comin'?'

'Me? See the king?'

'Yeah! Ya gotta back up me story 'bout all the dynamite that was gonna be used to blow up parlyment.'

'Yeah, but d'ya reckon we might 'ave to give back the money we sold it for?'

'Worker my man, I reckon the king will give us both an extra hundred quid an' a medal.'

'Yeah?'

'Besides, we gotta tell him 'bout those coves wot killed Dad so they can be strung up for murder.'

'Yeah, and before they murder us.'

'So we gotta go.'

'Where?'

Barry already had a plan in his mind as he led Lurker from the station platform. The Adelaide Express was leaving within the hour, and Daniel had said his ship was calling at Adelaide. Adelaide was a safe, distant place to wait for a ship. Daniel had told him his first-class ticket had cost his father seventy-five pounds. He had asked if he could go second class and keep the extra fifty pounds, but his father had refused. Fifty from seventy-five was twenty-five pounds. That was probably enough to go to England second class, and Barry now had about that. If steerage tickets were correspondingly less, Lurker and he could sail together.

Wreder the Writer was a clerk in the railways, and had a talent for forging documents and tickets in return for money or favours. Barry had enlisted Wreder to help with the theft of the dynamite intended for the bombing of parliament, and he had been given a share of the dynamite's sale. He worked at Spencer Street Station, and this was where the train left for Adelaide. Barry was sure that he would jump at the chance to be involved in another such scheme.

'We gotta get to Adelaide, but still have enough pay paper left to get tikkies on the ship,' said Barry. 'Ya reckon Wreder the Writer could do us a deal?'

'Reckon we could give him a couple o' quid as a consideration, an' say there was more in it for him if we swings a deal with the king,' replied Lurker.

'He'd never believe a couple of lads like us had anything the king would want.'

'He would if we said it was about the explosion in Albury.'

'Yeah, yeah. Reckon that's proof. Come on, we gotta go to my place for some stuff – oh jeez no, them coves are probably waitin' there! We gotta get to Spencer Street Station, and I got the mail bike 'ere.'

'I can't ride.'

'Friggin' hell, Worker man, then just sit on the bleedin' seat an' I'll pedal.'

❇

Half a mile away the scene was very much less dramatic. Liore had been with the Lang family as they chased the departing *Andromeda* south in their carriage, waving and cheering, then they had turned inland to go home. Martha had laid the table for lunch, and in Daniel's place a framed photograph of him stood between his neatly laid cutlery.

Lunch was not free from drama. Mrs Lang burst into tears when the roast was served, because roast beef was a favourite of Daniel's. After that the conversation took a turn for the worse. Emily began telling the company what she thought of artists in general and French artists in particular.

'Muriel Baker, French?' Mrs Lang asked.

'She's living in Paris and she's an artist, so that makes her French,' said Emily.

'All that French frippery, that made her what she is!' added Mrs Lang. 'All that art and frilly French underwear, it isn't decent.'

'And it – it isn't British,' Mr Lang managed.

'I don't like that French impressionist painting style,' said Emily. 'It's like looking through a telescope out of focus, it's all blurry.'

'British art is sharp and accurate, like a photo,' said Mr Lang, turning in his seat to wave at a large painting. It featured a young woman asleep on a couch with a bible open in her hands while angels hovered above her.

'It's so much better than that French rubbish!' snapped Emily.

She pointed to a painting above the sideboard. It depicted some women dressed in white having a picnic on a rocky beach, with red cliffs in the background. It was definitely impressionist in style.

'I'm not having it in my house!' cried Mrs Lang.

'I'll have John take it to the gallery to be auctioned this very afternoon,' said Mr Lang.

'And have that French immorality corrupt some other innocent young soul?' gasped Mrs Lang. 'Oh, no, no, no, onto the fire with it at once!'

Mr Lang stood up so abruptly that he knocked his chair over. Snatching the painting from the wall, he carried it into the living room and hurled it into the fireplace. Mrs Lang and Emily followed, then stood clapping as the painting burned. Mr Lang folded his arms in triumph. Liore watched in silence from the doorway, her arms folded as well. Once the painting was ashes and the frame was well alight, they returned to the table.

'Oh, look at Daniel smiling,' said Mrs Lang, gazing at the photograph of her son on the table. 'He approves of us burning that horrible painting.'

After dessert was served, Mrs Lang suggested that Emily and Liore go out to the bower at the back of the house for lemonade. Here they could be watched from the upstairs smoking room, yet talk in private. Mrs Lang, who thought Liore was a boy from an aristocratic family, was very hopeful about what they might discuss. Her very worst fears could not have approached the truth.

'You keep talking in battlespeak,' said Emily sharply, unconsciously transferring her need to dominate someone from Daniel to Liore.

'Problem?' asked Liore.

'Yes! My parents are used to hearing you speak plain English.'

'In future, plain English, reserved language, is courtly. Speaking courtly . . . difficult.'

'But you are eleven decades into your own past. Battlespeak makes you stand out. Do you really want to attract attention to yourself?'

'On target,' Liore conceded. 'By your leave, speaking courtly.'

'Well then, what did you think of the dramatics over lunch?' said Emily as she poured the lemonade from a pitcher.

Emily's question was loaded, as was her way when speaking with Daniel. Whatever Daniel answered, Emily had a criticism ready. In this way she made him accept that she was always right, and that he should do whatever she ordered. She had forgotten that Liore did not think like any other girl on Earth.

'The painting on your dining room wall is *Dreaming of Paradise* by Thomas Brooks, painted in 1855,' said Liore.

'I think it is ever so elevating,' said Emily, who had been expecting a strong opinion either way, but countered by a neutral remark of her own. 'I wish I could dream of angels.'

'It sold for twenty thousand pounds in a special war effort auction in 2009.'

'As much as that!' gasped Emily. 'I mean, that's more than our house is worth.'

'The painting that your father burned was *Red Cliffs, White Dresses*, a lost painting by Tom Roberts, dating from the 1880s.'

'Oh!' exclaimed Emily. 'You mean he was not French?'

'No.'

'Well it must have been painted in France.'

'The cliffs in the background are about eight miles south, along the coast.'

Faced with evidence of a truly monstrous blunder on her part, Emily tried frantically to justify what she had done.

'Well it was in a French style,' she muttered.

'A similar painting by Roberts, *Slumbering Sea, Mentone*, was sold for nine hundred and seventy thousand pounds at the same auction.'

The sheer size of the figure stunned Emily into silence. Liore sipped at her lemonade. For a winter's day it was unseasonably mild, but Emily suddenly shivered.

'Do you want to go inside?' asked Liore.

'No, absolutely not. Here we can talk in private, even if we have no privacy.'

Emily looked up at a window where Mr Lang was smoking his pipe and holding a book up to the light. She rallied herself for another attack.

'The day will come when Father invites you into his study and demands to know your intentions regarding me,' she pointed out, deliberately choosing a difficult subject. 'What will you tell him?'

'I have not thought about that.'

This was just the answer that Emily had hoped for.

'Well, you can hardly tell him that you are a girl warrior from a hundred years in the future, and that you have travelled into the past to kill fanatical British patriots who are trying to start a war with Germany.'

'If I did, he would certainly lose interest in having me as a son-in-law.'

'Be serious! What will you do?'

'The Lionhearts that were sent to Australia are probably all dead, but there are more of them in Britain. I must go there and wipe them out before they start the war.'

'But we stopped the Century War. Twice. Once when parliament opened, and again when you blew up the wagon at Albury.'

'I thought so, too, but then I started to get new memories.'

'I don't understand. When did you get them?'

'I have no idea.'

'But you must have noticed.'

'Have you thought about what you did last Christmas lately?'

'No.'

'So if the past had changed, and you had thrown a cake in Daniel's face at the Christmas dinner, you would not know when that memory changed.'

'I suppose so. But how could I know that the past had changed at all? How do you know the future has changed?'

'My past is in the future, and it overlays what is happening here. I no longer remember being taught in the Imperial War Academy that Australia's first parliament had been bombed, but I remember what I did to prevent it. Now I come from a future where the Century War was triggered by a third incident. Time seems to heal itself. Time apparently wants a century of war. In September, a single British ship, the *Millennium*, will go up against the entire German fleet at Wilhelmshaven. Using a very advanced but unknown weapon it sinks the battleships *Brandenburg*,

Siegfried, *Frithjof*, *Hagen*, and *Kaiser Wilhelm der Grosse*, along with nine cruisers. The *Millennium* signals that Britain has a new, invincible weapon, and that unless Germany scuttles its entire battle fleet they will sink it anyway. Some torpedo boats attack the *Millennium*, but they are picked off one by one. The T97 is set on fire, but does not sink completely because it is over a sandbar. As the *Millennium* steams past the burning wreck of the T97, some very brave men launch a single torpedo. It scores a direct hit on the *Millennium*'s ammunition store. The explosion annihilates the *Millennium*, and the weapon is never found.'

'I think I know what happens next,' said Emily. 'The Germans panic, and decide that they should strike Britain before it builds any more wonder-weapons.'

'Yes. It was called the Guillotine Campaign, because the head was removed from the British chicken, leaving the body to run about without any coordination. Acting out of sheer fright, the Germans brought down a total embargo on all news, mustered every soldier, sailor, ship and gun within a matter of days, and sailed for Britain. The British had no idea of what had happened, and were not expecting anything like this because there was always a build-up before any war. The British government soon found itself under lock and key.

'The British fleet put up a fight, but it was

caught dispersed and off guard. Many ships were captured at their moorings. Britain had more large ships thanks to the *Millennium*, but they now had to operate from Canada, and the waters around Britain were soon heavily mined. The royal family escaped through France, and gradually the empire organised a government in exile. That all took time, and in the meantime Germany was building replacement warships in British shipyards as well as in its own. Yet again there is a century of war between Germany and the rest of the British Empire.'

'But – but if the British developed a weapon like that, surely that was inevitable.'

'I do not think they did,' said Liore softly, leaning forward and shaking her head. 'That super-weapon has all the characteristics of my PR-17 assault rifle.'

Emily gasped in alarm, then noticed that Liore was staring at her with a disturbingly curious intensity. *She thinks I will steal the weapon!* thought Emily automatically before she managed to get a grip on herself.

'You mean *you* sink all those ships and start a war?'

'No, but it seems that someone will steal it in the near future.'

'Who would do that?'

'If I knew, they would already be dead.'

Liore's answer had been in courtly, yet it was as blunt as battlespeak.

'You can't solve all your problems by just killing people,' said Emily, yet again trying to take control of the conversation.

'Why not?'

Emily finally admitted to herself that Liore was not as easily manipulated as Daniel. *This is like a conversation between a vicar and a cannibal,* she thought, *and I am the vicar. Things that make sense to her are totally lost on me.*

'Liore, when I asked what we were going to do, I meant about us,' she said, deciding that trying to manipulate Liore was a lost cause. 'My parents want us to marry.'

'But we are both girls.'

'Precisely. What do we do about it?'

'What worked for Daniel and Muriel will work for us. I shall go to Britain in a few weeks, then I shall write back that I have married some English girl. Your parents will think I am a faithless bounder, and that you are lucky to be rid of me.'

'That sounds plausible,' said Emily. 'What will you really be doing?'

'Killing Lionhearts.'

The cannibal is talking to the vicar again, thought Emily as she cast about for a suitable reply. Somewhere in the distance someone began blowing a whistle.

'Police whistle,' said Liore. 'Distance, half mile.'

'Whatever it is, it is far away,' said Emily, glancing

up at the window where her father was still watching them. 'There is to be a family concert once lunch has settled, I hope you don't mind. Father has been practising Sir Arthur Sullivan's "The lost chord" on the harmonium for weeks. It's been driving me mad. Mother and I are to sing Bach's "Sheep may safely graze" as a duet, and then you will be expected to sing something.'

'I am not sure that I know anything suitable. Sullivan's music is considered frivolous in my time, and Bach was a German. We only learn patriotic songs like "Rule Britannia" and "Heart of oak".'

'I can play "Heart of oak" on the piano.'

'Then that is what I shall sing.'

The family concert was a great success, but as is the way in show business, the reviews left something to be desired. As Martha brought in the tea and scones, both Mr and Mrs Lang had remarked that Daniel's piano playing was so much better than Emily's. While Emily had managed to keep her temper under control, the grinding of her teeth said more than could have ever been expressed in the King's English. They had, of course, just been showing how much they were already missing Daniel, for Emily's playing was cool and precise while Daniel was at his best when playing for dances or accompanying singers.

All through afternoon tea Emily had tapped a fingernail softly against her cup, and it was not until the seventeenth repetition that Liore realised that she was rapping out a sentence in Morse code. Daniel knew Morse code, his father had taught it to him because he thought it was something that modern boys needed to know. Inevitably, Emily had been hiding behind the sofa, taking notes, because no brother of hers could ever be allowed to know something that she did not.

It was five in the evening before Liore finally got away from the Langs, and even then she had to refuse an invitation to dinner. By now Emily had tapped out, 'I shall get them for that' four hundred and ninety-one times, and Liore suspected that an outburst could quite possibly happen when she reached five hundred. As she walked down Bay Street, Liore noticed that people were standing about in groups and looking uneasy. The further east she walked, the more nervous the people seemed. Finally at North Brighton Station she noticed the police and police wagons.

Instantly Liore's mind went into combat alert, but she kept a blank, outwardly calm expression on her face. *By your leave, speaking courtly,* she thought as she went up to one of the bystanders.

'I was hoping to catch a train to Flinders Street,' she said. 'Is there something wrong with the trains?'

'The trains are fine, mate, but there's two coves shot deader than a doorknob a couple of hours back.'

'My word!' exclaimed Liore. 'Was it a robbery?'

'Nah, nobody knows what went over. Harry Luker caught one between the eyes, and Porter the stationmaster got shot in the signal box and fell through the window to the platform. Then this cove takes a shot at Pete Lurker. I mean, you wouldn't think he could miss someone as fat as Pete, but he did.'

'Have the police caught the murderer?'

'Nah, and there were four of them. Two coves and a woman what did the killing, and another minding the carriage they scarpered in. Lurker and Porter's kid, Barry, shot off in the other direction on the station bike, so I reckon they're involved. Stole something from a big-time push, that's what I think. Not that I care. Crims killing crims just saves work for the police.'

Suddenly a lot of unconnected facts fell into place for Liore.

'Which way did Lurker and Barry go?' she asked.

'North, up Asling Street. Oi, do you know something about this?'

But Liore had already vanished into the crowd. Mrs O'Brien's house was a full mile away from the station, but she ran the distance in under six minutes. Dashing past Wellington and up the side path, she found that the door to her room was unlocked. She entered and looked around. Everything seemed to be in order, but she reminded herself that sensible spies did not leave a mess behind them. Liore tried her key in the padlock on the trunk. It did not fit. Going to her chest of drawers, she found that her Bergmann pistol and clasp knife were missing.

Liore always moved in near-silence, and thus it was that she heard the soft creak of the back door to the house being opened. She flattened herself against the wall beside her door. The barrel of a shotgun pushed it open, then began to enter. Liore seized the barrel with her right hand and wrenched the owner into the room, where she lay sprawled on the floor.

'Yourself, explain!' demanded Liore, pointing the gun between the eyes of her landlady.

'Don't shoot,' quavered Mrs O'Brien.

'What happened?' said Liore with an edge on her voice that could have scratched glass.

'Some ratty little boy tried to burgle your place, but I saw him off with my shotgun while he was still picking the lock. I thought he'd come back.'

Liore turned, pointed the shotgun at her trunk's padlock and fired. Mrs O'Brien shrieked and backed away. The lock was reduced to a dozen or so fragments. Liore opened the trunk. As she suspected, it was empty.

'Robbed,' said Liore. 'When?'

'It was about three hours ago. Wellington tried to chase him, but his legs aren't what they used to be. Then I saw Mrs Miller, who'd come out to see what all the fuss was about so I says to her, says I, "Is your Jack up to a trip to the police station?" and she says –'

'What time?' demanded Liore.

'Don't you speak to me like that!'

Liore grasped her by the neck and began to squeeze. Mrs O'Brien finally realised that although her tenant was a little young to be Jack the Ripper, he was probably no less dangerous.

'Crushing throat, is easy,' prompted Liore, then she eased the pressure a little.

'No, no, spare me, please,' wheezed Mrs O'Brien.

'What time?'

'I was having me après-lunch snooze, when Wellington started barking. I didn't look at the clock.'

'Afternoon sleep, yours, 1.30 pm to 3 pm. Regular. Correct?'

'Well, I suppose.'

Barry Porter burgled my room while Emily kept me occupied, concluded Liore. *The Century War has found another way to start.*

'Am leaving,' declared Liore, releasing Mrs O'Brien.

'Oh no you don't!' said Mrs O'Brien, her courage suddenly rallying. 'There's been a crime here, and the police will be wanting to talk to you, even though you're the victim – and anyway, you owe me a pretty penny for that damage from the shotgun to my floorboards.'

By way of answer Liore brought the shotgun down across the edge of the trunk, breaking it in two. She opened the door, only to find that a policeman who had been questioning the neighbours about the burglary had arrived to investigate the gunshot. He had a pistol in his hand, but he had spent his career threatening criminals with it, rather than doing any shooting. By contrast, Liore had spent her life acting before other people could make up their minds to shoot.

Liore raised her hands as if surrendering, which immediately made the policeman think that he had nothing to worry about. She was watching his eyes, and saw his attention flick from her to the interior of the room where Mrs O'Brien still knelt on the floor. Liore brought both hands down on the policeman's wrist, and twisted her body as she forced the gun upwards. He fired a shot into the ceiling before she slammed his hand into the frame of the doorway. He cried out and dropped the gun. She twisted his arm around to bend him over double, then drove her knee up into his face. As the policeman collapsed, Mrs O'Brien crawled for the fallen pistol, but the heel of Liore's boot came down on the back of her hand, breaking three metacarpus bones. She shrieked with the pain and backed away. Liore scooped up the fallen pistol, then removed the policeman's badge and papers before flinging his body onto her landlady as if he weighed no more than a child.

'Behave morally,' she said before pulling the door shut and locking it.

Wellington recognised Liore and wagged his tail as she wheeled the policeman's bicycle down the path beside the house. Soon she was pedalling away as fast as she was able. The sun was already down, but the moon was high in the sky so she was able to see where she was going.

Daniel leaves for Britain, so I was sure to be there to see him off, she thought as she rode. *Eleven am to 1 pm accounted for. Emily keeps me at her house for social chit-chat for the afternoon. One pm to 5 pm accounted for. Burglary between 1.30 and 3 pm. Police whistles blown about 3 pm, while I was in the garden with Emily, so that was when the shootings took place. Barry and Lurker seen going north after the murders. Conclusion: Emily had an involvement because she went to so much trouble to keep me occupied. Target: destination of Barry Porter and Peter Lurker.*

Hiding the police bicycle in a laneway near North Brighton Station, Liore muttered 'By your leave, speaking courtly,' to herself, then began a tour of the local pubs. At the third she found her quarry.

'Did anyone see the shootings?' she asked the barman, placing a sixpence on the bar.

'Yeah mate, Stevo was on the platform,' he replied, pointing to a short man wearing a cloth cap and a patched overcoat. 'He saw the lot.'

Stevo had been telling the story to whoever would buy him a drink for quite some time, but was still coherent when Liore confronted him. She flashed her stolen police badge at him and gave him a slow wink.

'Now then, Stevo, I'm Constable Clarke of the Secret Plain Clothes Division,' she explained as everyone else who had seen the badge drew back in silence.

'Ain't heard of 'em,' Stevo said nervously.

'That's because we're secret, aren't we?' replied Liore. 'Here's the deal. You answer my questions, and I'll leave so these folk can buy you free beer and listen to your story. Give me a load of nonsense, and you will spend the rest of the night in a cell with nobody buying you anything.'

'Yeah, yeah, ask!' exclaimed Stevo, suddenly anxious to please.

'You know Barry the Bag and Lurker the Worker?'

'Yeah, don't everyone?'

'Were they on the platform during the murders?'

'I seen 'em on the platform when old man Porter got shot and fell through the winder. Barry boy says

"Oh frig, it's me dad", or somethin' like that.'

'What else did he say?'

'I already told the coppers that.'

'This is what is known to crime investigators as a double check, Stevo. Tell me what you heard.'

'Barry the Bag says to the Worker, says he, "We gotta go west on the fastest wheels in Australia", then they rode off north instead on the station bike. I tell yer wot, they definitely weren't the fastest wheels in Australia.'

The drinkers laughed, and even Liore allowed herself a smile. She flipped a shilling into the air and caught it.

'What else did you hear, Stevo? There's a shilling's worth of beer in it for you.'

'Nothin' that made sense. Like Barry says he gotta tell King important stuff, that's all I can remember.'

'King?' exclaimed Liore. 'Did he say *King* or *the king*?'

'Jeez mate, um, constable, since when's little Barry the Bag gonna have somethin' to say that the king wants to hear? He musta meant Jim King at South Melbourne Market.'

Liore flipped the shilling to Stevo, landing it squarely in his glass of beer. By the time Stevo had wiped the beer from his eyes and everyone else had stopped laughing, Liore was gone.

In 1901 the fastest wheels in Australia are the wheels of

a train, thought Liore as she pedalled away up Asling Street. *If Barry is going west, it will be on the Adelaide Express. If he has my weapon and intends to sell it to the King of Britain, he will be catching a ship in Adelaide.* A new and unexpected thought now crossed her mind. *Daniel's ship calls at Adelaide tomorrow.*

Liore made good progress, for it was dinner time and the dusty, dimly lit streets were almost free of traffic. She had plenty of time to think as she rode, and her thoughts were bleak and deadly.

Deserted by Muriel and Fox? she thought. *Lovers are known to betray the empire for each other, that is why they are shot when found even kissing during a mission. Guilty of desertion. Sentence, death.*

Liore reached the Nepean Highway, wondered if she was taking a risk by continuing to ride a stolen police bicycle, then decided that it was too dark for people to notice.

Betrayed by Barry? It was only a matter of time. After all, he was more obsessed with the PR-17 than Daniel was with Muriel. Guilty of desertion, conspiracy, treason and espionage. Sentence, death.

She reached Inkerman Street, turned left, and headed for the city.

Betrayed by Emily? Her adoration of me was sure to become resentment because I am a girl who has freedoms that she does not. She manipulates people to get what she wants. She must have conspired with Barry to steal the PR-17, but he will betray her as he betrayed me. Guilty of conspiracy, treason and espionage. Sentence, death.

Only on Clarendon Street, when she was crossing the Yarra River and within sight of Spencer Street Station did Liore finally face up to the betrayal that she had not expected.

Betrayed by Daniel? Now that is a surprise. How does he fit into this whole web of lies and duplicity? Ah, but of course! Barry has the social graces of a pig in a garbage bin, but Daniel is well-spoken and has perfect manners. If Barry does the stealing, Daniel could convince some very important people to take them seriously. And here I was, sorry for Daniel because of Muriel and Fox. Guilty of conspiracy, treason and espionage. Sentence, death.

I am Liore BC, and am I guilty of betrayal? Oh no, I was developed to be perfect, so I could never be disloyal to the empire. My revolt was to save the empire, and save it I shall. Not guilty on any charge.

I am disappointed in all of them, but then what better weapon to use against the Lionhearts than one's own traitors? This is all working out very well indeed. Sentences are to be suspended until the mission is accomplished.

To Barry's relief, Wreder the Writer was in his office at Spencer Street Station when they arrived. He was, however, strangely hostile.

'What you been up to, little bagman?' asked the

elderly railway clerk, peering over his glasses as Lurker and Barry entered. 'Your bloody line 'as trouble on it. All trains stopped at Gardenvale Station. Trouble at North Brighton, that's the big word.'

'We don't know nothin' 'bout that,' said Barry. 'We just want a couple of tikkies on the Adelaide Express.'

'Trouble at North Brighton, an' suddenly the bagman wants a day off in Adelaide?'

'Both of us, like,' said Lurker.

'Lurker the Worker likes his days off, I'll give that a concede, but Lurker the Worker travellin' all that way for a day off, that's a suspicion.'

'There's a fiver in it for ya!' insisted Barry.

'Oh yeah, little bagman, and this Wreder does like readin' *Five Pounds* on a note, but this Wreder don't like readin' *Wanted: Jim Wreder* on a bloody poster.'

'No tikky, no fiver,' said Barry, as calmly as he could.

'Tell you what, then. Fat Lurker gets a tikky today, and the little bagman gets a tikky tomorrow,' said Wreder.

'How's that work, then?' asked Barry.

'It's my instinctives that whatever the coppers are sniffin' for in North Brighton was masterminded by a certain little bagman, and that Fat Lurker was only involved for transportation of goods.'

'The coppers don't want neither of us!' exclaimed Barry.

'Then ya can wait another day in Melbourne, *then* go over on the next Express and meet up with Fat Lurker. Final word from the Wreder, fatman and bagman.'

'Yeah, well we're innocent. We just got a matter of commercials in Adelaide, an' you're not gettin' no slice of it now.'

'I takes me chances, bagman. Now, show the fiver, and I'll scribe a tikky for a fat Lurker.'

A minute later Barry and Lurker were on the platform where passengers were boarding the Adelaide Express.

'Well I got a tikky to Adelaide and a cousin in Adelaide to stay with,' said Lurker, fiddling nervously with the ticket. 'What's your out, Barry boy?'

'I'm on the bleedin' train, aren't I?' said Barry.

'What train's that?'

'The Adelaide Express, Worker Man. There's more ways onto a train than wi' a tikky from Wreder the Writer. Now get on that train.'

Now that he was alone, Barry made himself think as those who were hunting him might. The Lionhearts were after him. Liore would be, too, once she discovered that her weapon was gone.

Stupid bleedin' Luker! thought Barry. *He didn't contact someone workin' for the king, he called the bleedin' Lionhearts. Now Wreder the Writer's getting' in the way, but this might be a positive. Liore's gonna break his door down and check his records. She'll see Lurker's gone to Adelaide, but not Barry boy. She'll think we split up, and I went somewhere else.*

Barry went straight to the station's locker room, picked the lock and hurried inside. Two minutes later he emerged as a conductor in an ill-fitting but convincing uniform. He boarded the Adelaide Express.

'Joe Smith, apprentice,' he said to the conductor.

'Nobody told me about you,' the man replied.

'I'se supposed to help and learn, like,' said Barry, his nervousness genuine.

'Well, follow me about and try to stay out of the way. You go as far as Ballarat and get off with me, got that?'

'Yeah, sir.'

The Adelaide Express had already pulled out of the station when Liore arrived. She checked the timetable poster, checked the station clock, checked the time on her radiocomm, then went to the ticket window. There she was told that the names of passengers on the Adelaide Express were in the office, and that the office was closed for the night. She asked where the office might be, so that she might go straight there in the morning. She was given directions.

Two shots from the stolen police pistol shattered the lock on the office door. She walked in, keyed the light on her radiocomm into life, and cast about for the register she wanted. Peter Lurker was indeed aboard the train, in second class, but not Barry Porter. *They must have split up,* she thought. *Yet why split up? Why put Lurker on a train to Adelaide under his own name? To make me think they have split up? Lurker is going to Adelaide, and Barry is apparently plotting with him.*

Liore concluded that Barry also had to be going to Adelaide because he was colluding with Daniel. Deep in thought, she left the office, then paused in the luggage area where she had left her stolen bicycle. There was no way to catch a fast steam train like the Adelaide Express on a bicycle. Her only option was to wait for the next Express, the following night.

'Yeah, I seen one of these,' a voice insisted off to her right. 'It don't need steam, it runs on spirits.'

'Git aht, all them engine things run on steam,' said someone else.

'Well looky in 'ere. There's spirits in this tank.'

'And whaddaya think this thing is 'ere, if not a boiler?'

'So where's the furnace?'

Liore saw that two baggage porters were arguing about a moped. This particular moped was no more than an ordinary bicycle with a small petroleum motor bolted on. It had a ticket attached, and was probably being shipped to somewhere in the countryside. She did some quick mental calculations, whispered 'By your leave, speaking courtly,' to herself, then walked over to the porters.

'Gentlemen, that is indeed an internal combustion engine, it does not need steam at all,' she said.

Because she was well spoken and confident, the two porters deferred to her at once. She explained how the petroleum engine differed from steam engines, then about how one had to pedal to gain the momentum to start the engine. When she offered to demonstrate for them, they were delighted. The platform was crowded, so they took the moped out into Spencer Street. Liore mounted it, primed the engine, pumped the carburettor, pushed the choke lever right over, and engaged the coil. She had pedalled just a few yards down the road when the engine caught and rattled into life. The porters cheered. They stopped cheering when she vanished amid the jumble of horses and carriages on Spencer Street.

The moped had no headlight, but Liore was able to use moonlight and the light from her radiocomm torch to navigate her way along the dimly lit Spencer Street as it curved to the west and became Dynon Road. Turning up Moore Street, she soon found herself at Ballarat Road. There were now only seventy miles between her and Ballarat, the provincial city where the Adelaide Express would stop.

Liore found that by running the engine until it nearly overheated the moped could be nursed along at thirty-one miles per hour. This was not as fast as the Adelaide Express was travelling, yet it still made her the fastest traveller on the road. The train would stop for a while in Ballarat, and that delay might just allow her to catch it.

The moped's speed brought its own problems. It was late July, and while the day had been fairly mild in Melbourne, the further west Liore travelled, the colder it became. Patches of mist blanketed the road here and there, clouds covered the moon, and drizzle came and went. She was not dressed for a trip on the open road, even at such a slow speed. By the end of the first hour she was wet, shivering, and stiff with cold.

At the little town of Bacchus Marsh she decided that money would solve some of her problems. At the first pub she came to she bought four bottles of the strongest rum on the shelf, and from the drinkers was able to purchase a ragged oilskin coat with a rain hood, and a pair of heavy leather gauntlets. Having persuaded the engine to start again, Liore rode a mile further west, stopped to empty the first bottle of rum into the tank, then continued on her way again. The engine developed a more ragged note once the rum and fuel mixture reached the carburettor, but it continued to power the moped along.

Wearing the oilskin and gauntlets, Liore was a lot more comfortable, even when it began to rain. The light from the radiocomm glowed steadily, and even after four bottles of rum the engine continued to operate, although at reduced power. Another hour passed, and a milestone told her that Ballarat was now just ten miles away. Suddenly a washaway appeared across the road. Liore slammed on the brakes, but the moped went over the edge and hit the bottom very heavily. She had been trained to fall without injury, but the moped was not built for that sort of treatment. A single glance at the mangled front wheel told her that she would now have to walk. She set off at once, but after only one mile her radiocomm torch lit up an alternative form of transport, grazing in a field.

'Nice horsey,' she said as she climbed over the fence.

Even though the horse was not entirely happy about trotting through the dark with only a strange blue-white light to guide it, she still made better time than she could have on foot. The inland city of Ballarat was quiet as she arrived, and the railway station was deserted. Going into the Railway Hotel, Liore learned that the Adelaide Express had left a quarter of an hour earlier. It had been delayed, but it was still long gone.

Liore went back outside, led the horse a short distance from the hotel, then turned it loose to graze in someone's front garden. She then returned to the Railway Hotel, took a room for the night, and asked for a fire to be lit. After arranging her damp clothing to dry in front of the fireplace, she counted out her money. It was infuriating that while she had enough money for a passage to Britain and back, there was no way to catch up with the train. She checked her radiocomm unit. There was no polling signal from Fox's radiocomm, which told her that Barry had enough sense not to play with it, and that it was still switched off.

I shall catch you, Barry Porter, she thought. *Even though you are a day ahead of me, I shall catch you. I shall then show you what a cadet officer of the Imperial War Academy does to spies and traitors.*

Barry and the conductor left the train at Ballarat. He followed the man until he entered the Railway Hotel, then ran back to the train, got back aboard, and introduced himself to the relief conductor as the new apprentice.

'Well then, may have to settle in for the night,' said the relief conductor.

'Wot ya mean?' exclaimed Barry.

'We've got a report of a bridge being washed out

up ahead at Beaufort.'

'Wot? Ya mean we're stuck 'ere?'

'Nah. The report came on the telegraph from Melbourne, so what does Melbourne know about Beaufort?'

Barry suspected that Liore was at work. It was seventy miles to Melbourne. She could ride that distance in three or four hours if she could change horses at that time of night. Knowing Liore, she would not be above stealing a fresh horse whenever she needed one.

'So how long we 'ere for?' asked Barry.

'Oh, half an hour. There's a freight train on the line up ahead. If it gets to Beaufort that proves the bridge is okay. The stationmaster there will telegraph us when it arrives.'

Barry did some hurried sums in his head. A half-hour delay was not much. On horseback Liore could not catch up with the train, even with that delay. On a bicycle she would be even slower. The minutes seemed to drag. Barry strained to hear the sound of a galloping horse, but he heard nothing. In the distance there was singing in one of the pubs. People got off the train to ask about the delay, then got back aboard. Finally the driver blew the whistle, then another minute passed. Still there was no sound of a horse being ridden to death. Finally, the whistle was blown again, the engine chugged laboriously, and the train began to move. For the second time that night Barry almost collapsed with relief.

Chapter 4

BYSTANDER

Adelaide was under clear blue skies as the Express arrived at Adelaide Central Station. Barry was the first out of the train, and he quickly melted into the crowd waiting for the travellers.

'Where's that Lurker?' he muttered as he waited at the back of the crowd. 'Lazy sod's probably asleep in his carriage.'

Minutes passed, but Lurker the Worker did not appear.

'All these folk, but Liore and the Lionhearts are only after the bagman,' Barry whimpered as he waited. 'Now there's an inspirational.'

Barry scanned the crowd for someone about his height with a suitcase and the general look of a traveller. As luck would have it, there was indeed a very short young man on the platform, and he had a suitcase. Taking Liore's weapon from his bag, Barry crouched behind a pile of heavy luggage, touched the security pad with the ring of hair, aimed at a distant water tower, and fired. The water tower exploded in a splash of charred, shattered slats, boiling water and superheated steam.

Nearly everyone on the platform rushed forward for a better view. Barry merely hurried across to the short man's abandoned suitcase, picked it up and walked briskly for the rest rooms. Here he changed out of his conductor's uniform and into the clothes from the suitcase. Leaving the uniform in a rubbish bin, Barry walked back out onto the platform. Someone began blowing a whistle. By reflex Barry assumed that the owner of the suitcase he was carrying and the clothes he was wearing had found a policeman and pointed at him. He was deciding just where he should flee when someone appeared at the door to the carriage in which Lurker the Worker had been travelling. His shouts told Barry that extreme danger was still uncomfortably close.

'Murder! Bloody murder!' the man was shouting over and over.

Suspecting that Liore had done the impossible and caught up with his train, Barry quickly left the station and vanished out into the streets of Adelaide.

Unknown to Barry, two men had been watching him from a distance, and had begun to close in just as he had unpacked the weapon and fired on the water tower. At the sight of the explosion, they had immediately dived for cover behind a luggage trolley.

'So now what?' said Garrick, who had a garrotting wire in his hands.

'Best to telegraph Lady Conrad and tell her Barry the Bag's story about the heat ray weapon is true,' said Lyle.

'Why not just choke the little devil when his back's turned. I mean that's what we've been ordered to do.'

'Listen, that thing he's got doesn't even look like a gun. What if we kill him and he's the only one who knows how to work it?'

'Yeah, suppose you're right. So what's to do?'

'Like I said, I'll go telegraph Lady Conrad for orders.'

'But she's in Melbourne.'

'When she finds out that Barry boy's got a real wonder-weapon she'll jump on the next Adelaide Express and be on this very platform tomorrow morning. Meantime you follow Barry, and telegraph the den every couple of hours.'

'But what if he points that thing at me?'

'Then you die heroically for the British Empire.'

For once Barry found that luck was on his side. Stopping to rest on a public bench, he checked some papers he had found in the stolen suitcase and discovered that his victim had arrived from England only a day earlier. His name was Barold Chalmer, and all of his travel papers and documents were in his luggage. There was also ninety pounds in English money. Against his better judgement, Barry now asked a policeman where he could find the offices of the P&O shipping company. Arriving at the offices, Barry enquired about a cabin on the next ship leaving for England.

'So, you are Barold Chalmer and you want to go back to England already?' asked the clerk pleasantly.

'Er, yeah, it's sorta urgent.'

'But you have only been in Australia one day.'

'Well, like, me old man sent me out 'ere to make me fortune, but I just got a telegram from England, like, sayin' me grandma just died an' left me a fortune so now I don't need to make one.'

The clerk stared intently at Barry, trying to make up his mind about him. Barry looked about as suspicious as mice look fluffy, yet most suspicious-looking little thieves did not dress respectably and want to buy tickets to England.

'Please accept my condolences, Master Chalmer,' said the clerk, although he sounded doubtful rather than sympathetic. 'When were you planning to sail?'

'Er, there's a ship called the Andro-something arrivin' from Melbourne today. Can I get a tikky for that one?'

'I think you mean the *Andromeda*. There are only a limited number of berths available, and they are all first class.'

'Well, I got money. Write me a tikky.'

'The *Andromeda* sails tonight at 8 pm. Is that enough time to put your affairs in order?'

'I haven't had any bleedin' affairs, I only been 'ere one day. Now where's me tikky?'

'Will you be paying by bank cheque?'

'Ya don't have to check with no bank, I got cash.'

After another half hour Barry walked out with his ticket to Britain and hailed a horse cab to take him to the docks. It was the first time he had ridden in a cab, and he felt strangely guilty for some reason. He would have also felt frightened if he had known that another cab was following his.

Barry was waiting on the pier, bag in one hand and stolen suitcase in the other, when the *Andromeda* docked in the late afternoon. He hurried aboard, locked himself in his cabin, and then laid out on the bunk, able to relax at last after two days of life on the edge. He had not slept on the entire trip to Adelaide, but now when he closed his eyes he still could not sleep.

'Wot if that Chalmer cove tells the coppers he had his papers 'alf inched?' Barry muttered fearfully to himself. 'Wot if they check if some cove's been tryin' to use his papers . . . but nah, no crim's gonna want papers. Relax, Barry boy, you're goin' to England, an' big bad Liore and them Lionhearts will never find ya there.'

Being a thief, Barry was well aware of the danger

of theft. Taking a beeswax candle that he had stolen from the shipping office, he lit it and poured molten wax into the keyhole of the padlock on his bag. Now there was no danger that anyone else could do to his bag what he had done to Liore's trunk.

Back ashore, Garrick had telegraphed Lyle that Barry had boarded a ship bound for London. Lyle in turn telegraphed Lady Conrad in Melbourne, and their orders soon came through. It was sunset when Lyle joined Garrick on the wharf.

'What's to report on Barry the Bag?' asked Lyle as they stood watching the *Andromeda*.

'Barry went aboard and stayed there. Mind, with the light fading, it's going to be hard to tell it's him if he gets off again.'

'He's only five feet tall. Whatever disguise he wears, his height's the same.'

'So what's orders? There's only a couple of hours before the ship sails.'

'Ladyship says leave him aboard the *Andromeda*. That way we know where he is. He's calling himself Barold Chalmer, I got that from the P&O office. They also said that the *Andromeda*'s next port is Colombo.'

'Colombo! We got Lionhearts in Colombo?'

'No, but we have the *Millennium* at anchor, right over there,' said Lyle, pointing across the water. 'Even with a couple of days' delay she can be in Colombo before the *Andromeda*.'

Barry did not leave his cabin until he heard the ship's horn booming out, announcing that they were ready to sail. He only ventured out of his cabin once he saw that the lights beyond his porthole were moving. Going out on deck, he was in time to see the last of the waving and flower-throwing, and the weeping of the dozen or so girls and women who had boarded at Adelaide.

'Barry?' said an astonished voice behind him.

Barry's mind was already racing as he turned to face Daniel. In the frantic scramble to stay alive and get aboard the ship, he had not thought through a plausible story to tell his friend.

'Danny boy, how's prospectives?' he asked casually.

'What are you doing on the *Andromeda* – and in a suit, and on the first-class promenade deck?'

'Well, what's good for Danny boy is good for Barry the Bag.'

'What do you mean?'

'If you gotta reason to go to England, so have I.'

'I'm going to an English preparatory school so I can pass the Oxford entrance examination. You can't even *spell* examination.'

'Yeah I can – er, well maybe I can't, but there's

other stuff the bag boy can do.'

'Like what?'

'Oh, secret stuff.'

'Secret stuff? You mean Liore's sent you to spy on the Lionhearts in Britain?'

Barry was by now floundering for a good excuse for being on the ship, but Daniel's suggestion was absolutely perfect.

'Yeah, well, secret spy Barry Porter an' all that. Look, er, I – she's given me a new name, Barold Chalmer, so I can be secret.'

'Barold?'

'Yeah, and that's on me papers.'

'Barold?'

'Yeah, so ya gotta call me that when we're with other people.'

'Barold?'

'Yeah, Barold!' snapped Barry.

'And you're travelling first class. Didn't she think that someone with your accent, elocution, education, manners and background would look less suspicious in steerage?'

'Yeah, well I got a story that me rich uncle died, leaving me a fortune, but like I can only get at it if I gets better manners, so I'm off to learn manners in a manners school. An' anyway, Liore said you were sad, 'cause that Muriel baggage dumped ya for Foxy boy and ran off to Paris, so why not send Barry the

Bag along for company?'

'Liore said that?' exclaimed Daniel, blinking in surprise. 'How sweet of her.'

'So I'm 'ere.'

'Yes, here you are, as unlikely as it seems.'

Something had been playing on Barry's mind for most of the day. This was that ships travelled on water, and that ships were known to sink. Were this to happen, he could not swim. It was time to raise the subject with Daniel. While Daniel could not pick a pocket to save his life, he did know just about everything about everything else.

'Er, Danny boy?'

'Yes?'

'Wot if the ship sinks?'

'Modern ships hardly ever sink, Barry, that's why they don't bother having enough lifeboats for everyone.'

'They don't?' gasped Barry.

'Of course not. The lifeboats are just there to reassure nervous people like you.'

'But –'

'You have a better chance of being run down by a horse-drawn carriage than drowning on a sinking ship.'

'Yeah? I bet there's no horse-drawn carriages at sea.'

'You see? That's how safe it is.'

Barry was not sure of what to make of that reply, and it did not stop him worrying. An hour later, alone in his cabin, he took the beeswax candle that he had used to block up his padlock and melted wax into the seams of his bag to waterproof it. Were the ship to sink, and were he not allowed in the lifeboats, he now had something to help him stay afloat.

Although Liore never left home without such necessities as false papers, her radiocomm and plenty of money, she had set off after Barry without taking a change of clothing, toothbrush, comb, or even a bag. As Ballarat's shops opened for what was a typical Friday morning in winter, the cadet from the future set off to equip herself for a long chase. First she bought a carpetbag with a shoulder strap, then spread her other purchases over a dozen shops so as not to draw attention to herself. These included a ticket to Adelaide, a bag of dried fruit, a bread roll, a box of .32 calibre ammunition, and a small telescope.

When the newspapers arrived at the stationers at noon, she bought the *Adelaide Advertiser* and the Melbourne *Age*, and took them to a café. She was not surprised to read of a double murder at North Brighton Railway Station. She also read that a youth called Liore Besay had assaulted his landlady and a policeman, and stolen the policeman's gun, badge and bicycle. In the shipping notices she saw that the *Andromeda* was due to dock in Adelaide in the late afternoon, and was offering passage to Colombo, Port Said and London. It would only be in port for a few hours. Liore thought about the way Daniel had fallen apart when Muriel had jilted him, and of how Fox had deserted. Love was apparently involved. Those in her old academy squad had been absolutely loyal to her, so why had Fox changed? Clearly love was nothing like loyalty, and was possibly a form of mental illness.

'Pardon me, sir, but can I get you anything else?'

The waitress was standing before Liore's table. She judged her to be about seventeen, and saw that she was a little more stylishly dressed than most girls in the provincial city. *By your leave, speaking courtly,* thought Liore.

'Another hot chocolate, if you please,' said Liore, more to make her go away than because she wanted the drink.

Now Liore looked around the café. Sketches of customers were pinned to the walls, all done in a startlingly accurate and acutely observed style. Certain points were emphasised, points that highlighted something special about each face. Liore's impression was that the subject would be easier to identify from such a sketch than from a photograph.

On a corner table were a pad and pencils, along with napkins to be folded. On the pad was a sketch. Liore stood up as if to stretch, took a few soft paces across to check the face, then walked back and sat down again. It was her face, partly sketched. The girl returned with Liore's hot chocolate.

'You did the sketches on the walls, perhaps?' said Liore, letting the hint of a French accent into her voice.

'Yes, they're mine,' she said. 'How did you know?'

'There is a sketch pad beside the napkins you are folding at the corner table. Are you wishing to make a career in art?'

'Oh, sir, I haven't got any talent for art,' said the girl, blushing.

'You should let others judge that. What are your plans for the future?'

'My plans are all dreams, sir.'

'Then what are your dreams?'

'I want to go to London and be like Sherlock Holmes, but that's never going to happen.'

Liore blinked in surprise, then scanned the sketches again. The girl's powers of observation were very sharp.

'Female police are not being employed, so this is not a realistic career. If you wanted to run away to Paris and be an artist I would be more likely to believe you.'

'More crimes are committed against women than men, and I think that women would be more comfortable consulting me. My father is a policeman. He taught me lots of things about how to catch criminals.'

'Yet here you are in a café.'

'Mother wants me to marry Gerald Heath, so she had me taught art, piano and French to make me seem refined. Mother is ashamed that she married a mere policeman. She made herself rich by opening a lot of cafés and cake shops, then she divorced Dad. Now she pretends we are from a rich English family with a title.'

'So Master Heath is refined, too?'

'Hah! He's at boarding school in Melbourne, because his parents want to keep him away from his lout friends in Ballarat. His father is the Heath of Heath's Drapery.'

'A big store. He must be rich.'

'He's such a drone.'

'Why not go to London, as you dream of doing?' said Liore, tapping the shipping notices. 'Twenty pounds will pay for a second-class berth on a ship. Perhaps another ten pounds will allow you to eat and have somewhere to sleep until you can find a job. You know waitressing, and waitresses are needed everywhere. Gradually you can make a name for yourself, tracking down rogues who take advantage of women. I know London, it is a city of opportunities, and it is packed with rogues.'

'You make it sound so easy.'

'Ah, but it is.'

'Then why don't more people do it?'

'Because they do not know how easy it is.'

They laughed for a moment, then the girl glanced about to make sure that they were not being watched.

'I have fourteen pounds saved, but mother doesn't know that. I really want to go to London, I dream of just getting on the train to Melbourne, then boarding a ship and never coming back here. The money helps me believe that it is not just a dream. Do you like my sketch of you?'

Liore was instantly on alert, and very nearly replied in battlespeak.

'How do you know I have seen it?'

'You walked softly, but from the kitchen I heard a floorboard creak near the corner table.'

'Well done,' said Liore, although shaken by the girl's powers of observation. 'Finish it, and I shall give you a good price.'

'Oh, sir, I didn't mean to –'

'Not another word – and I am Leon, not sir.'

'And I'm Madeline. Madeline Drake.'

Liore continued to scan the shipping notices as Madeline sketched. She had originally wanted to get the sketch so that there would be no image left to mark her stay in Ballarat, but seeing the hope and brightness that was now in Madeline's face made her feel genuine sympathy for the girl. She had talent, she worked hard, she was trapped by her circumstances, yet she dreamed. Other customers came and went, and the afternoon began to darken into evening. At last the sketch was complete.

'It is a very fine and accurate rendering,' said Liore, exchanging the sketch for a ten pound note. 'My thanks to you.'

'Ten pounds!' exclaimed Madeline. 'But – but this is more than I have ever earned for all my sketches.'

'Then you should go somewhere your talent is better appreciated,' said Liore, standing up. 'And now I must go.'

'Oh sir – Leon, please wait! I mean, I should close the café now and clean up, but – but will you stay and tell me about London? I meet so few people like you.'

The request suited Liore. She had seen the twisted remains of the moped brought in on a dray, while one of the local police had been leading the horse that she had stolen and was asking people in the street if they knew of it. Once the café was clean for the next day, they went out into the street and wandered past the shop windows for a time, chatting. The light was dim, and the streets were almost deserted. Laughter and raucous singing came from the hotels.

'There are some men following us,' said Madeline, suddenly pressing close to Liore.

'Fear, show none,' said Liore crisply in battlespeak. 'Victims, they want. Not fighting.'

'But they're miners, and drunk.'

'Have scanned,' said Liore. 'Three men, bearded, no guns. Closing. Intercept, fifteen seconds.'

'Ho there, missy!' called a deep voice behind them.

Liore and Madeline turned. Two men were approaching them along the boardwalk, the third was in the street, walking in a curve to cut them off. Liore was desperate not to become embroiled in any incident. One thing would lead to another if she had to account for herself to the police.

'No screaming, stay close,' she whispered.

'Dark night, you shouldn't be out with a boy,' said one of the men that they now faced.

'Yeah, ya need a man on a cold night, missy,' said the other.

Liore heard footsteps that told her where the third man was treading, and that he was close behind. Twisting her head for a moment to take aim, she kicked straight back, driving her heel into the man's stomach. The other two stood in astonishment for a moment, then the man on her left aimed a much clumsier kick at Liore while his companion groped for his knife. Liore twisted slightly to dodge the kick, then gracefully swept an arm under his foot and pushed up sharply. The man rotated upon his centre of gravity and fell backwards, striking his head on the boards.

A knife gleamed in the dim light as the man on Liore's right lunged, but she already had her two hands spread wide and descending to where his wrist was moving. Liore twisted outwards under the man's arm, spun right around and drove the knife up under his ribs. By now the third man had regained enough breath to stagger forward to help his mates, but he was still partly doubled over. Liore stepped into his outstretched arms, twisted his head and slammed her knee up into his temple. There was a loud snap.

'Stealthmode, leave, now,' hissed Liore, taking Madeline by the arm.

'Those men,' began Madeline.

'All dead. Crushed skull, stabbed heart, broken neck.'

Nobody had yet come upon the bodies by the time they reached the café. Madeline took out a key and they hurried inside.

'You killed them!' gasped Madeline, sitting down heavily on a chair in the darkened café.

'On target.'

'But –'

'Violating you, their intent,' said Liore coldly, looking back out into the street. 'Myself, killed, would have been.'

'Your voice, what is wrong with it?'

By your leave, speaking courtly, thought Liore. 'I have a tendency to slip into battlespeak.'

'Battlespeak? What is that?'

'Best not to ask.'

Out in the street someone began shouting for the police, then a whistle was blown over and over again. People came running with lanterns.

'You killed them with your bare hands.'

'Yes.'

Madeline put her fingers to her lips.

'You are not as you seem.'

'Correct. I am . . . a type of spy.'

'You are also a girl.'

Liore turned away from the street and stared at what was visible of Madeline in the gloom of the shop.

'Why do you say that?' she asked warily.

'Your hands are too small for a boy, your neck has no Adam's apple, you show no sign of shaving, and the features of your face are too fine and rounded.'

There was a sudden tapping at the door of the café. Liore backed away into the shadows, but Madeline made straight for the door and unlocked it. A policeman entered.

'Maddy, Maddy, are you all right?' he asked.

'Dad, of course. What's all the fuss out there?'

'Drunks, rioting. Three are dead. I get so worried

about you being here alone.'

'Not for long, Dad. I have been meaning to tell you, I'm leaving.'

'Leaving Ballarat? I – I know you want to, but your mother, the café!'

'Mother can run the café herself if she wishes. She can also marry Gerald Heath, seeing she thinks he is such a suitable match. I have made arrangements to support myself, and I have friends.'

'Friends?'

'Trust me, I am your daughter. Tomorrow I shall be gone without trace, but don't worry. I shall write when I can.'

'Tomorrow? Just like that? Can't you wait until I've cleared those bodies out there to the morgue and I'm off duty? We need to talk about your plans.'

'It would take too long to explain, but believe me when I say I must go, and it must be now. The chance may never come again.'

'How long will you be gone?'

'Until I'm old enough to be legally free of Mother.'

Liore watched in silence as Madeline's father gave her fifteen shillings and a button from his uniform to remind her that she was the daughter of a policeman. Madeline took a self-portrait of herself from the wall and presented it to him. They embraced in awkward silence, saying nothing because there was too much to say.

'I'll worry about you,' he said, 'but I suppose I've already taught you all I can, so what better time than now?'

Then he was gone, and Liore was alone with Madeline again.

'Thank you for saying nothing of me,' said Liore.

'You were right, there is nothing to keep me here,' said Madeline. 'Do come upstairs. I shall make dinner for us, and you can tell me what to pack.'

'But I am leaving in two hours.'

'Only two hours?'

'Yes.'

'What a pity. So much to ask you about, but so little time.'

'I am sorry, but trains run on strict schedules. I am on an important journey.'

'What is it about?'

'I am not at liberty to discuss it.'

'You say so little about yourself,' said Madeline, 'yet I know so much about you now.'

'You do?' asked Liore with a trace of amusement. 'Tell me more.'

'The right pocket of your coat is weighted heavily, just like my father's coat when he carries a gun. When you walk there is the rattle that loose bullets make in a pocket. You are armed, Leon.'

The girl misses nothing, thought Liore, but she held her features neutral.

'Go on.'

'You have perfect manners and a military bearing. The scar over your eye marks you as someone who sees action. Girls seldom have scars like that. You must be travelling to Adelaide, for the Adelaide Express is the only train that leaves in two hours. You have also been studying the shipping notices, and know the fare to London. You bought my sketch so that your image would not remain in Ballarat, yet you gallantly paid far more than you needed to. You are a gentleman spy, even though you are a girl. I had hoped to charm you into taking me with you, at least while I still thought you were a boy.'

For a moment they both sat absolutely still and silent, then Madeline gestured upwards.

'What do you want from me?' asked Liore as they climbed the stairs. 'I cannot take you with me. I lead a very dangerous life.'

'Just tell me how to travel as you do, fast and light. What clothes to wear, what to take, what not to take, how to hide money, how not to draw attention to myself, and how to seem what I am not.'

'That is easy,' said Liore. 'When you leave here, wear three sets of clean underwear and two dresses. That will get you a long way without having to worry about laundry or carry a large bag. It will also make you look a bit stout, and less likely to catch the eye of annoying rakes. Never look about in wonder in new places, always try to seem like a local who is familiar with everything. Carry only one bag.'

Madeline lit a lantern and made notes, then began dressing in the multiple layers that Liore had prescribed. Liore supervised as she packed a large knitting bag.

'When you flee, try to look as if you are only going for a day trip to Melbourne, and say as much to anyone who asks. Arrange for someone else to open the café, so it will be longer before the alarm is raised. Tell the man at the station that you are buying the ticket for a friend or aunt. Walk onto the platform as if you are only seeing someone off, and wave at the train windows a lot. When the whistle blows, step aboard the train briskly. That will confuse people, they will wonder if they saw correctly. You will be more dumpy with the extra clothes, they will think you might be the very relative you came to see off.'

'So much detail,' said Madeline, who was scribbling furiously.

'After a while it becomes a way of thinking. Never carry all your papers and money in your bag, sew a pocket into your underwear and keep enough to get by in there. Bags can get stolen, but underwear is harder for strangers to search.'

'You're right, Leon, or whoever you are. I have to learn to think ahead.'

'No, no, you have to learn to think like a criminal.

Criminals go about as people they are not. Remember that, it will keep you out of trouble.'

For Liore the Adelaide Express seemed to pull out of Ballarat very slowly, and then settle down to something not much above walking pace. For a time she sat working out the train's speed by timing the distance between milestones, and she was not at all happy with the results. She stopped the conductor as he walked past and asked if they were on time, and if anything was wrong. He replied that the train was on time, and would arrive in Adelaide right on schedule.

Liore tried to distract herself by checking her bag, checking her gun, and checking the shipping pages of the newspapers yet again. Barry was going to London, she was increasingly convinced of that. It was only a matter of when, and on what ship. There was only one ship scheduled to leave before the Adelaide Express arrived in Adelaide, so he would still be in that city unless . . . unless he had gone straight from the station to the docks and caught the *Andromeda*. Daniel's ship.

Suddenly a nightmare of paranoia descended on Liore. Was Daniel going to London to provide an escort for Barry, or was he tempting her to chase after the *Andromeda* while Barry stayed behind in Adelaide and sold the PR-17, perhaps to the Lionhearts themselves? Emily had kept her at the Lang's house all afternoon so that Barry could burgle her room and steal the weapon, that was absolutely obvious. Fox and Muriel had run away to Paris when she needed them most . . . but was that all part of a plan to give Daniel an excuse to be sent to England? Although she remained in firm control of herself, Liore felt isolated, deserted and very severely betrayed.

Time for coldness, time for death, she thought, her teeth grinding. *They have all been tested, and they have all failed. Time to break Barry Porter's scrawny little neck.*

Liore imagined herself flinging Barry to the ground, pinning him down with a knee between his shoulderblades, then placing one hand on his forehead and another on the back of his head. She twisted. There was a very satisfying snap. She felt her mouth watering.

Time to drown Emily Lang.

Liore's imagination conjured the Lang's house in Melbourne, late at night. Everyone else was asleep as Emily crept into the moonlit backyard of the Bay Street house, as she had been instructed in a note, supposedly from Barry. Liore crept up behind her, dropped her with a foot to the back of her knee, then plunged her head into the lily pond and sat on her as she drowned. *Listening to your breath bubbling away into death will be far more pleasant than putting up with your lies,* thought Liore.

Time to choke Fox on a tube of his oil paints, time to hang Muriel by her own frilly knickers.

Liore thought of Fox tied to a chair in an artist's garret, gagged with strips of Muriel's petticoat, while Muriel kicked and struggled at the end of a rope made of her underwear tied together. Fox had two tubes of paint jammed into his nostrils. Liore was painting the scene. *I always wanted to run away to Paris and become an artist,* she was telling them. *I rather fancy the symbolist school. This is very symbolic, don't you think?*

Finally, what to do with Daniel? He might well be an innocent bystander, but I think not. Time to beat the tall and handsome Daniel until he is unrecognisable, then strangle him with my bare hands.

Liore did not think of any specific setting for her fantasy of thrashing Daniel into a bloody pulp. She was into the second minute of planning what to do to him when she heard the voice of the conductor in the distance.

'Now then, I think your brother is in the next compartment, mademoiselle,' he was saying. 'The boy in there has a French accent.'

'Oh, merci, monsieur, then it must be him.'

In an instant Liore was sitting up straight and whispering, 'By your leave, speaking courtly.' The conductor opened the door and Madeline swept in and embraced her.

'Oh Leon, Leon, I thought I had lost you!' she cried as she flung her arms around Liore. 'I had not my ticket, and I was so frightened.'

Thinking quickly had kept Liore alive on many occasions, so her answer was both prompt and appropriate.

'Thank you so much for looking after my sister, monsieur,' she said, pressing a shilling into the conductor's hand. 'I shall make sure that she does not wander off again.'

The conductor smiled broadly, then left without bothering to ask for Madeline's ticket. Liore closed the door to the compartment.

'Well, how do I look?' asked Madeline, spreading her arms. 'Is this convincingly dumpy?'

'Madeline –'

'I bought a ticket to Melbourne so that nobody would know that I was on this train.'

'But –'

'I thought about what you said about thinking like a criminal. Mother will think I've gone to Melbourne. Why would I go all the way to Adelaide instead?'

Liore considered this carefully, and suddenly remembered what Emily had once said about Muriel. *Some girls can get things from men by just batting their eyelashes, but a boy would need a loaded pistol to do the same.*

'I agree to take you to Adelaide and get you booked onto a ship to London on one condition,' said Liore, folding her arms and glaring sternly at Madeline.

'Oh, yes. What am I to do?'

'*You* must teach *me* how to dress and act like a girl.'

Liore and Madeline arrived in Adelaide to find the police at the station, still investigating the murder of the previous morning. Liore bought a newspaper as they left the station, then they stopped at a café.

'"The murder of Peter Lurker, also known as Lurker the Worker, is being linked to the murder of Harold Luker and James Porter, and the disappearance of James Wreder in Melbourne",' Liore read as they sat drinking coffee. 'One little sentence, so many mysteries.'

'Four murders,' said Madeline uneasily. 'You were telling the truth when you said your life was dangerous.'

'"Police are anxious to interview a youth named Liore Besay, suspected to be a Norwegian seaman, in connection with the murders. Mr Besay is armed and considered to be exceedingly dangerous. He is also wanted in connection with an assault on a police officer and Mrs Agatha O'Brien of Brighton, theft of a police firearm, theft of a police bicycle, theft of a motorised bicycle, destruction of property, and breaking and entering".'

Madeline gazed steadily at Liore. Liore shrugged.

'So you are Liore?' Madeline asked.

'Yes.'

'How much of that report is true?'

'I am not Norwegian, and I did not kill those men.'

'But everything else?'

'Is true.'

'Have you killed others?'

'Since arriving in your, ah, country, I have killed twenty-one men, but that was war, not murder.'

Madeline took some time to think through what she had just learned, and to make her judgement.

'At the risk of becoming your next victim . . . I believe you,' she said at last.

'Thank you.'

'Well then, what about your disguise? It would certainly be easier to hide you if you were dressed as a girl.'

'Not so,' said Liore, feeling strangely uneasy. 'Having a girl's body is not enough. I walk, talk, behave and react like a boy, and I have never worn a dress in my life. You need to teach me everything about being a girl. That will take days, perhaps weeks.'

'Well, we at least need new names,' Madeline suggested. 'Who will you be?'

'I have not used Leon before. Leon I stay.'

'Perhaps I could be Muriel?'

'Muriel could be very complicated. What about Monique?'

'Monique, yes. Monique and Leon. What about a surname?'

'Cluny.'

'So I am Monique Cluny, and you are my brother Leon. But we have no papers.'

'I can forge papers. All I need is lemon juice, lampblack, some thick paper and a device that I carry. We also need a strategy. You want to go to London, I want to . . . to find someone.'

'And kill him?'

'None of your business. I shall leave on the next ship for London, while you stay here and practise being a detective. We shall communicate by telegraph. I would like you to locate someone, a small and furtive youth named Barry Porter. If you find him, inform me at once.'

'Barry Porter. Is he related to the murdered James Porter?'

'Barry is his son. I am not entirely sure what is happening, but as you may well guess, it is very, very dangerous to be involved. Do you still want to help?'

'Oh yes. I brought the old Webley revolver my

father gave me in case anyone broke into the café while I was alone there,' Madeline said, patting her knitting bag.

'Can you use it?'

'Yes. Dad treated me like a son and taught me a lot of things that boys do. My mother hated him for that.'

'You are not typical of the girls of your time.'

'Of my time? Don't you mean my age?'

'Ah, yes, of course. A girl of your age. A girl who does not have a background like mine.'

There was an uneasy silence. Liore wondered if she might have just lost her only ally in all the world. Words had so many meanings when spoken in courtly. In battlespeak it was much easier.

'Do you think I am mad for running away to become a detective?' asked Madeline.

The question was not one that Liore had expected.

'I was surprised,' she said guardedly. 'I thought you might spend months, perhaps years, packing and planning, then not run away at all. Most people prefer to dream of freedom rather than leave their cage.'

'Liore, I ran away because I am sure I shall never meet any other girl like you. Two or three days of learning from you will be worth two or three years of planning and dreaming.'

'You may be disappointed.'

'Let me be the judge of that. What now?'

'We visit the shipping offices and ask about someone answering the description of Barry Porter, also known as Barry the Bag.'

'Do you have a photograph of him?'

'No, but I can show you his face with this little black box. Do not ask what it is or where I obtained it.'

Madeline proved to be very useful in the shipping offices. While Liore would have got what she needed by threats, intimidation or armed robbery, Madeline used charm on the clerks. She even persuaded one of them to show her a list of passengers who had boarded the *Andromeda* at Adelaide. Madeline had made a sketch of Barry from the image on Liore's radiocomm, and it was this she showed to the clerk.

'The only man who boarded in Adelaide was named Barold Chalmer,' said Madeline as she and Liore walked out into the street. 'I showed my sketch to the clerk, but he did not recognise the face. Mr Chalmer wore a straw boater hat pulled right down to his eyebrows, and the clerk never got a clear view of his face.'

'How tall was the clerk?'

'Taller than you. He said that Mr Chalmer was no taller than my shoulder.'

'Which was why he did not get a proper view of his face. Barry is only four feet eleven inches tall. What else did the clerk say?'

'Only that he had an accent better suited to steerage than first class.'

'Then we have him, Madeline. Barold Chalmer is Barry Porter. We need to be aboard the next ship for London.'

'We?'

'Yes. If my stolen property is aboard that ship, there is no point in you staying here.'

By the afternoon Liore and Madeline had booked into a second-class cabin on the *Seabird*, which was the next ship scheduled to sail for London. Liore chose a hotel near the docks, and they took a double room together. They settled into the room quickly, washed their clothes and dried them by the fire. Madeline let Liore try on a dress, and Liore spent half an hour learning to take short steps like a girl wearing the high heeled slippers that were currently in fashion, rather than striding. The results were promising rather than successful. They went on to training her to flash a winsome smile. This proved to be even harder. Finally Liore began changing back into her own clothes while Madeline looked over some lists that she had compiled.

'The *Seabird* sails for London via Colombo and Port Said on Monday. Another ship sails later tonight, but that one is not taking passengers.'

Madeline looked up, caught sight of Liore with most of her clothes off, and gasped.

'Problem?' asked Liore at once.

'Your body, your – your muscles. How did you come to look stronger than a champion boxer?'

'Training, in Academy, since five.'

'And all those scars and burns?'

'Fighting, did cause.'

'You're using that strange accent again.'

'By your leave, speaking courtly,' muttered Liore.

'Liore! What is that meant to mean?'

'Sorry, part of my – my training. It is reflexive, like a man raising his hat to a woman in your society.'

Once she was dressed as a boy again, Liore began servicing the pistols. Madeline sat on a chair, using her bed as a desk as she studied lists of ships, train timetables and other documents.

'Unless there is a reason to stay awake, we should make sure that we get plenty of sleep,' said Liore. 'Tired soldiers make mistakes.'

'Mother says the same about getting sleep, but she says it is to stay beautiful and avoid wrinkles,' said Madeline. 'And speaking of feminine matters, tomorrow we must definitely go shopping to buy you a dress, proper underwear, a hat, a parasol –'

'Stealthmode!' hissed Liore, making a chopping motion with her hand.

Madeline considered saying something about bad manners, then decided that Liore was incapable of being deliberately rude. A tiny light was flashing on the smooth, flat, black case that lay on the desk. Liore brushed her fingers over various images on the screen. A compass bearing and range was returned a moment later. More brushing of fingers on the screen conjured a little map with a flashing red dot at the centre. Liore blinked with surprise.

A ship, Liore realised. *The radiocomm is on the same ship as the PR-17.*

'What is that thing?' asked Madeline.

'Hard to describe. Someone has activated the only other such unit in the world, and it is aboard the *Andromeda*, with my other property. Nobody knows how to do that except someone named Fox. From what I know of shipping schedules, he would have arrived in Paris two weeks ago, so it is not him.'

'Could someone else turn it on by accident?'

'No. It must be held in the hand at a certain angle, then the activation stud must be pressed and a keyword spoken before a message can be transmitted, but . . . but what am I thinking? A radiocomm can be activated but not enabled. Activation does not need a password. Once active, the radiocomm puts out a polling signal, looking for the nearest British unit.'

'Are you speaking that funny language again?' asked Madeline.

'No, no, I am thinking aloud. *Anyone* can merely turn the unit on, but why just turn it on?'

'My father attended a very sad incident in Ballarat last year,' said Madeline. 'A little boy of three had found his father's revolver, and was playing with it. He had gripped it by the barrel and was using it as a toy hammer when it went off. He died.'

'You are saying that Barry Porter is playing with the radiocomm without knowing what he is doing?'

'Perhaps. Is he intelligent enough to work it out?'

'Barry is cunning beyond belief, but not well educated. He knows that the radiocomm can also record sound and motion pictures, then play them back. He may be trying to learn how to use it so he can impress important people when he reaches London. He may also play about with my other property, and that could be very dangerous. The *Seabird* does not sail until Monday, and that is too long to wait. You said that there is a ship sailing tonight?'

'Yes, but it is not taking passengers.'

'No matter, I can stow away. You will follow on the *Seabird*. When does the other ship sail, and what is the name?'

'Just before midnight tonight. It's called the *Millennium* –'

'The *Millennium*?' exclaimed Liore, suddenly leaping across the room to Madeline, twisting her arm and pinning her down. 'Full details, present! Now!'

'Liore! Stop it, you're frightening me.'

'Sorry,' said Liore, standing back, mortified, with her hands held apart and her fingers splayed. 'By your leave, speaking courtly. Please accept my sincerest apologies.'

'Of course. Just try to remember that I am on your side.'

'Thank you. Now may I ask what you know of the *Millennium*? It is a very, very important ship. I should have realised that it might be in Australian waters because of – but never mind. Please tell me of it.'

'Here are the notes I made at the shipping office. Seven thousand tons, twin quadruple expansion engines, can cruise at nineteen knots, launched two years ago. It arrived in late April from Colombo, but has been lying at anchor because of some legal dispute.'

'And now it sails before midnight. I *must* get aboard that ship, for more reasons than I can possibly explain. Time for me to go.'

'But Liore, remember that the *Millennium* is not taking passengers.'

'It is taking me.'

'What about me?'

'As I said, you must follow on the *Seabird*. It will be too dangerous aboard the *Millennium*.'

'So you may have to fight your way aboard?'

'Perhaps.'

'Yet you want the *Millennium* to carry you in pursuit of the *Andromeda*?'

'Yes.'

'Well, London is five or six weeks away, and you cannot run a ship all by yourself. You need officers, sailors, stokers, engineers and other people like that. You will have to sneak aboard, and that is where I can help.'

Chapter 5

ENGINEER

On the second night after leaving Adelaide there was a music hall concert for the first and second-class passengers on the *Andromeda*. Some of the maids, waiters and stewards were also musicians and singers, and knew the latest popular songs and dances from around the world. Items ranged from 'A bird in a gilded cage', to 'O solo mio', to 'Hello! Ma baby'. It was the first music hall concert that both Daniel and Barry had attended.

After the show they went out on the promenade deck. For a time they chatted, looking out into the blackness of the ocean. With the surface calm and the stars gleaming brightly, it seemed like the *Andromeda* was steaming through the sky itself, like some enormous flying machine.

'So wot's all the fuss I've heard about seasickness?' asked Barry. 'Bein' on the ship's no problem for me.'

After his first bout of nausea Daniel had recovered quickly, then learned to tolerate the ship's motion. He was secretly disappointed that Barry had not suffered as he had.

'I can't say either,' he replied casually. 'Some people must have very delicate stomachs.'

Daniel began humming the tune of 'Hello! Ma baby' to fix it in his mind.

'So what ya think of the music, Danny boy?' asked Barry.

'I liked the ragtime songs and piano pieces. They have lots of energy.'

'They're not like the stuff that yer family sings.'

'Music has to be boring and dead before my family likes it,' said Daniel. 'I must take the opportunity to learn some ragtime piano on the voyage. What about you?'

'Ya know, I really liked the song that tart with all the lace and frontage were singin',' said Barry wistfully.

'She sang six songs.'

'The one about the girl wot was like a bird in a cage, 'cause she was married to some rich cove wot she didn't love.'

'"A bird in a gilded cage"?'

'Yeah. That's a bit like me, I reckon. Caught by me circumstantials.'

'You're not in a gilded cage. You're not in any sort of cage.'

'Yeah I am. I got no prospectives.'

Daniel was at once suspicious. If Liore had put Barry aboard the *Andromeda*, then he was being trusted with very important work. Now he was complaining about having poor circumstances and no prospects. It did not make sense.

'Liore got you a position with prospects,' said Daniel guardedly, 'but you gave up on the third day.'

'Danny boy, that was too . . . er . . . intersomething. Not the rude word, the other one.'

'Intellectual?'

'Yeah. That was too intellectual for me.'

'Apprentice fireman on the Sandridge steam train is hardly intellectual.'

'Yeah, but I had to study stuff.'

'One night a week at the Mechanics Institute?'

'Well, I'm more of a practical cove. Where would it get me?'

'In five years you could have been an engine driver. If you worked really hard you could have been a goods yard manager by the time you were your dad's age.'

At the mention of his father Barry fell silent. Daniel decided not to prompt him.

'That's not me style,' said Barry eventually.

'Well, that's probably why Liore has made you a spy.'

'Whaddaya mean, spy? I – oh, yeah. She did. That's more like wot I'm good for.'

Daniel was glad of the darkness, because Barry could not see him frown. There was definitely a lie in there somewhere, he was sure of it.

'So, you are going to do some spying in London while you seek your fortune.'

'Yeah, yeah. I might even get made mayor.'

'Mayor of London?' exclaimed Daniel. 'You?'

'Yeah, like that Dick Whittington cove, the one wot had a hat.'

'He had a *cat*, Barry, and . . . look, the only way you are going to make your fortune in London is to steal it from someone else.'

'Yeah, well, why not? I saved the world when them Lionheart coves tried to bomb parlyment and wot did I get? An afternoon gettin' yelled at by your batty sister, twenty pounds from sellin' some stolen dynamite, an' a job shovellin' friggin' coal on a train. I deserve better, an' I'm gonna get it. I reckon the king will be more generous when he knows wot I done.'

Suddenly a whole collection of fragments began to sort themselves into a very alarming mosaic for Daniel. Liore would not have sent Barry first class. Liore would never have changed his name to Barold Chalmer. Barry could only make his fortune by stealing it from someone else. Barry talking about meeting the king. Most suspiciously of all, Barry was currently without his bag. Why? Perhaps is was now too heavy to carry everywhere. Heavy with what?

'Well, there are a few privileges for travelling first

class,' said Daniel. 'Have you discovered the smoking saloon yet?'

'The wot?'

'It's a place where gentlemen from first class can go to smoke their pipes and cigars, and drink port wine from Madeira.'

'Wot's it cost?'

'Nothing.'

'Nothin'?' gasped Barry.

'Well we *are* meant to be rich gentlemen. You are, anyway. I'm just registered as a schoolboy.'

'Where abouts is it?'

'I'll show you.'

With Barry safely settled in an armchair, listening to the captain telling shipwreck stories to other first-time passengers, Daniel returned to his cabin. He opened a copy of *Treasure Island* which he had borrowed from the ship's library, and left his door open as he began reading. He had read just over fifty pages when he heard distant cries of outrage. This was Daniel's cue to hurry down the corridor to the first-class infirmary. Moments later the master-at-arms appeared carrying Barry, who was trying to sing something about a ratcatcher's daughter and was smelling of port wine and vomit.

'I say, Master Lang,' said the master-at-arms.

'Yes, sir?'

'Do you know this young wretch? I have seen you speaking with him.'

'I, ah, met him when he boarded the ship in Adelaide. His family is newly wealthy, so I was trying to coach him in polite behaviour.'

'Well he certainly needs it. He got himself beastly drunk in the smoking room and was sick over himself, a costly Persian rug, a rosewood table, and a box of the captain's best cigars. He is going to spend the night in the infirmary. When next you see him, tell him the captain said that one more display of such revolting conduct will see him spending the rest of the voyage in steerage – if they will have him.'

'Yes, sir, I'll be sure to.'

Daniel held Barry upright while the officer got out his keys and opened the door. Barry was dragged inside and put on a bed.

'Should I stay with him while you fetch the nurse?' Daniel asked.

'Thank you, but don't bother. He's not going anywhere.'

While Daniel did not know one end of a pickwire from the other, it had taken no real skill to remove the key to Barry's cabin from his coat pocket while the master-at-arms opened the infirmary door. Daniel now went straight to the cabin and let himself in. Barry's bag was chained to the bed and held shut by a single padlock. Daniel noticed that the lock appeared to be solid inside, and there was something waxy around the keyhole.

Beeswax, thought Daniel. *He's filled the lock with wax to deter other thieves with picklocks.*

A search of the cabin yielded several candles and a silver case of matches engraved with the name Barold Chalmer. There were also several sets of electroplated knives, forks and spoons, stolen in the belief that they were real silver, and three stolen milk jugs featuring the ship's name. Daniel returned to the bag and examined it again, then took out his pocketknife.

Why break the door down when the window is open? he thought as he slit a side seam of the bag. Putting his hand inside, Daniel encountered the unmistakable shape of Liore's plasma lance rifle.

'You little worm, Barry Porter,' muttered Daniel as he drew out the weapon. 'You despicable, greedy, devious little worm.'

The weapon appeared to be undamaged, but no lights were glowing. Liore had said that only an authorised person could turn it on. Daniel pressed his thumb against the security pad. Nothing happened. *Why did Barry steal it?* he wondered. *Does he have a means of switching it on?*

The very tricky question of what to do next now presented itself. If Daniel were to keep the weapon it would certainly be in safe hands, but that would also imply that he had plotted with Barry to steal it. If Liore caught up with them, she would think the worst. He thought about presenting it to the ship's purser, but that would involve a lot of impossibly improbable explanations. There had to be another way.

Daniel left the cabin with the contents of Barry's bag in a pillowcase. Back in his own cabin, he thought about what to do as he laid out the contents of the bag on his bed. There were two uniforms, both with battle damage from a fight a century in the future. There was also Liore's weapon, Fox's radiocomm, a clasp knife, a strange pen, some coins from the 1990s and 2000s, a German pistol called a Bergmann, a little medical kit, and some notes in code. Barry's own possessions included two gold coins, fifteen keys, eleven rubber prophylactic devices, two dozen postcards featuring women wearing very little or nothing at all with captions in French, two tins of tobacco salvaged from discarded cigarette butts, a silver whiskey flask, a gold tooth, a rather battered copy of *A Scientific Guide to Human Reproductive Biology*, a false moustache, a pair of spectacles with plain glass lenses, a pair of grubby silk gloves, and a sketch of Muriel by Fox that Barry had somehow contrived to steal. At the bottom of the sketch was a smudge where Barry had tried to erase Fox's signature. Across the smudge was written 'Dar Vinchy 1650', in an attempt to make it seem like an old masterpiece.

'Oh, Muriel, Leonardo da Vinci would have made your image into a greater work of art than the Mona Lisa,' sighed Daniel as he gazed at the sketch.

Beneath the false bottom of the bag were seventeen pounds in banknotes, two gold coins, two pocket watches, five gold rings, a list of names and addresses, a false beard, a wig, and a spare pickwire set.

Daniel picked up Fox's radiocomm unit, then hesitated. Were he to switch it on, Liore could track it down with her own radiocomm. Drawing Liore's attention to the stolen goods was about as dangerous as jumping into a pit full of scorpions, yet it would definitely tell her where she could find the ship carrying Barry and her weapon. She would need her weapon to do whatever was still needed to save the world. Alternatively, he could telegram her from Colombo, but that would give Barry a start of another two weeks.

Daniel examined the smooth black box. There were several little depressions with studs at the bottom. He tried to remember what Liore did when she activated her own unit, and recalled that she used her thumb to make it work. Holding it as she did, he noted what studs were within reach. Then he remembered that she held it differently when starting it. She only shifted to another grip when she was doing things with it.

Daniel changed his grip and pressed a stud. Nothing happened. He pressed another with the same result. The third stud caused a small green light to come on. *Green probably means the thing is working,* Daniel thought hopefully as he slipped the radiocomm into his pocket. Liore would find him first. If she did not kill him on the spot, he could direct her to Barry. Barry would then have the difficult task of accounting for the weapon in his bag.

'Well, what have I got to live for anyway?' Daniel said to the black radiocomm. 'I'm not even sixteen and my life is already ruined.'

The prospect of Barry still having the weapon did not appeal to Daniel, however. Had he found a way to activate it? If so, what might he do with it, if and when Liore caught up with them? If Barry could activate it, he might kill her with it.

'Liore, dead?' said Daniel. 'No, never. Not Liore.'

Daniel pondered the problem of activating the weapon. A part of Liore's body could activate it. Any part, alive or not. It was something to do with what she called DNA, and that had not been discovered yet. What to do? Any part of Liore would probably be good enough, but he had nothing of her. He had been obsessed by Muriel alone, even to the point of keeping a strip of her petticoat that had been used to bandage him. He had kept it, never washing it because it had once belonged to his lost sweetheart. His dried blood was still on the cloth, and the cloth was in his luggage . . . but there was also *another* strip of her petticoat with it! Liore had been bandaged on that same day, also by Muriel. In his obsession with Muriel, Daniel had kept both strips of petticoat.

Daniel went to his own suitcase and sliced the lining of the lid open. The folder with Fox's sketches of Muriel and the two strips of petticoat was hidden inside. Dried blood was on both strips. He pressed one strip against the security pad. Nothing happened. He pressed the other strip against the pad. A faint red light came on. *The cloth is stained with Liore's blood,* he thought, *and it once brushed against Muriel's legs.*

The symbolism of the two strips of cloth was all too much for Daniel. He burst into tears and collapsed across his bed, the strips of Muriel's petticoat clutched tightly in his hands. Presently he remembered that he had duties to perform, duties involving the fate of the world. He rubbed his eyes and sat up, then pocketed Barry's money and postcards, put Liore's weapon, uniform and medical kit aside, and began to pack everything else into a cloth lace-up bag that his mother had given him to carry trinkets and souvenirs that he might buy in Colombo and Port Said. He hesitated over the book on human reproductive biology, then decided to keep it as well. After all, Fox had borrowed the book, and Daniel did not want to be Fox's inferior in any way that could be helped. Weighting the lace-up bag with the German pistol, he went out onto the promenade deck, checked that he was alone, then heaved it into the ocean.

Daniel now returned to his cabin and sat on the edge of the bed for a long time. He felt wretched, yet in a strange and warped way this suited him. He was sure that he had nothing to live for, so despising himself justified his death. His only wish was to make sure that his death would be in a good cause. Daniel stared at the PR-17. Getting it back into Liore's hands might save the world, and that was surely a good cause. He also wanted to protect Liore, and to let her know that he had deliberately signalled the weapon's location to her. If he could not have Muriel's love, he would have Liore's approval. He picked up the PR-17.

Barry had stolen it, so Barry quite probably knew how to make it work. He probably had fingernail parings or hair from Liore's place. *How to mess it up a little so it cannot be used against Liore?* he wondered. It was hard to know what to do. Daniel could keep the weapon, but Barry might tell the master-at-arms about it and have Daniel's cabin searched. If Barry demonstrated its power, the master-at-arms would confiscate it and hand it over to the authorities when the ship reached London. It was currently in Daniel's power to throw it over the side, but Liore might need it to fight the Lionhearts.

Daniel knew that guns came apart easily so that they could be cleaned and serviced, and he assumed that the PR-17 was no different. After some experimentation he managed to get a cover off by pushing down on one edge then rotating it. He peered at the internal workings, but not much made any sense to him. On closer examination he found that one tiny switch had writing on it: *CAUTION: FIREW DISABLE*. It was in a box that also enclosed a little glass tube and some complicated, delicate-looking thing that resembled a honeycomb trailing tiny wires as thin as hairs. At one side of the switch was a black cross, on the other a green tick. *FIREW is to do with firing the weapon,* Daniel guessed. *It must mean FIRE WEAPON, and flicking the switch disables the weapon's ability to fire, like a pistol's safety catch.* With the end of a pen Daniel pushed the switch across to the green arrow.

Now the thing will not fire if Barry tries to use it, thought Daniel smugly.

He examined the cavity further. There were other switches here and there, but the tiny letters on them were cryptic and made no sense to Daniel. One of them had the word TRACE on it. *TRACE,* thought Daniel. *What does TRACE mean?* It appeared to be off. He decided to flip it on. Another switch was labelled BC, and it was off. *Battle Commander?* wondered Daniel. *Does this switch have something to do with the Battle Commander?* Not knowing what else to do, Daniel flipped this switch as well.

After flipping two more switches that looked promising, Daniel thought about test-firing the weapon. It seemed like a dangerous idea, but then Daniel reminded himself that he was expendable. If he died, it would be to defend Liore. Liore was definitely worth dying for. She was his commander, she was perfect, incorruptible. He opened the porthole of his cabin, aimed at where he thought the water was, then hesitated. If he died now, Liore would never know that he had died for her.

'What is more important?' he hissed to himself. 'To die defending Liore, or to brag about it? Would you die for your queen?'

Perspiration trickled down the side of Daniel's face. The weapon might explode like a little bomb.

'Is Liore my queen?' Daniel asked himself.

Liore was above courtship, and was absolutely dedicated to her mission into the past. Liore was safe to die for.

'Yes!' Daniel concluded breathlessly. 'Liore is my queen, so I *can* die for her.'

Before some new twist of logic materialised to stop him, Daniel squeezed the firing stud. Nothing happened. Daniel staggered back from the porthole and collapsed across his bed, the PR-17 still in his hands. He had done it! He had disabled the weapon so that Barry could not use it against Liore. Daniel lay still for two entire minutes, trying to comprehend that he was still alive, then sat up and wrote down all the changes that he had made to the switches so that Liore could reset everything properly when she got the weapon back. Even if she failed to catch Barry, and the little thief got as far as the king, he would be seriously embarrassed when he tried to demonstrate the weapon.

Finally Daniel pushed the cover back onto the switch recess and rotated it until it clicked into place. He did not notice a very small pressure switch on the edge, a safety switch that prevented the weapon from being fired if the cover was not in place. Now that the cover had been put back, the weapon was most definitely ready for use.

Daniel's father was one of those men who thought that they should be absolutely self-reliant if they ever found themselves cut off from the services of a wife, daughter or maid to do the sewing. Thus he had given Daniel a little sewing kit with ARMY stamped on it to give it a masculine look. The kit contained needles, buttons, a little blade and waxed thread. Mr Lang's theory was that waxed thread was so strong that you would not need much of it to sew a button on a shirt or mend a tear.

Daniel took the kit with him as he returned to Barry's cabin with the weapon in the pillowcase. After pushing the PR-17 back into Barry's bag, Daniel began to sew up the slit that he had made in the side seam. It was slow work, for the seam faced inwards and he was working blind most of the time, but the bag had other repairs, so Daniel reasoned that once some more wax was melted onto the seam Barry would not notice. With the cabin restored to the way he had found it, Daniel locked the door and went to the infirmary.

The nurse opened the door when he knocked.

'I came to see how Master Chalmer is recovering,' Daniel said, going across to the bed where Barry was lying on his side with his mouth over a bedpan.

'Are you a friend of his?' asked the nurse.

'No, we only met yesterday, on the ship. There are no other boys of fifteen in first class, so we have been keeping each other company.'

'Fifteen!' exclaimed the nurse. 'He told the steward in the smoking saloon that he was twenty-two, but that smoking had stunted his growth.'

'I think that was just one of Master Chalmer's

amusing little stories,' said Daniel.

'The little pig is certainly no charmer.'

'Is this his coat?' asked Daniel, reaching over to the coat draped over the back of a chair. 'What a mess.'

Daniel slipped Barry's key back into his coat pocket, promised the nurse that he would try to keep Barry out of trouble in future, then left. Returning to his own cabin, he lay down on his bed fully clothed, too keyed up to even close his eyes. Within his pocket was one of the two most advanced communication devices in the world. Now aware of his location was the deadliest killer in the world, and she had probably set off after him already.

Daniel curled up tightly, emotions and contradictions pouring through his head. Muriel had run off with Fox, who was Daniel's superior in every way, so his love for Muriel was entirely without hope. All he could do was die, but if he died heroically, there was a chance that Muriel would think the better of him when he was gone. He wanted to die at the hands of Liore, that was one thing he was certain of. It would be like being executed by Napoleon or King Arthur.

'I'm going to die,' whispered Daniel, again clutching the strips of Muriel's petticoat in his hand. 'Muriel, Muriel, will you ever know that I died for love of you?'

Daniel stroked the strips of petticoat, wishing that they were Muriel's cheek. Eventually he fell asleep.

Within a few minutes of leaving the hotel, Liore and Madeline were on the docks. The *Millennium* was getting steam up, but had very few lights burning. Liore examined it through her small telescope.

'Three men on guard, one visible at the gangway, the other two flanking at forty feet apart. All three will be armed, and they have the bearing of trained guards rather than stewards. I cannot get aboard without a very visible fight.'

'They would not shoot at a girl,' said Madeline.

'Explain?'

'We must make you look harmless.'

'No target.'

'Sorry?'

'*No target* means I do not understand.'

'We need a disguise for you.'

'Disguise?'

'A dress.'

'But it is nearly midnight, the dress shops are not open, and there is no time to return to the hotel for one of your dresses.'

'Since when has that stopped you? Come along, I'll point you at a dress.'

A minute later Liore had her target acquired.

Madeline stayed back in the shadows as Liore walked up to a woman leaning against a gas streetlight.

'Hullo sailor, you just off your ship?'

The woman was elaborately dressed in lace and frills, and was somewhat fuller of figure than Liore.

'Your clothes, I want them.'

'Cor, now that's a first. Sorry luv, the wrapping's not for sale.'

'Take them off. Now.'

The woman suddenly looked uneasy.

'Horace, I got a bad swell!' she called.

A heavily built man swaggered out of the nearby shadows. He was used to intimidating people with his sheer size, and he knew that few could punch hard enough to harm him seriously before he could beat them senseless. Liore's foot came up to her knee like that of a ballet dancer, then drove straight out into his abdomen. As Horace doubled over Liore seized his head and slammed her knee into his face. Horace collapsed. Liore seized the woman by the arm, twisted it and pressed a nerve. The pain was so great that the woman only wheezed rather than screamed.

Liore wished that she had had more experience with wearing female clothing and footwear as she teetered up the gangway behind Madeline. The deputy master-at-arms confronted the pair. He was not sure what to make of them. Madeline had been assigned the role of negotiator.

'Hullo luv, you might remember us from the trip from Colombo,' she said cheerily.

'I've only just joined the ship,' replied the man suspiciously. 'What do you want?'

'I forgot a bag in me cabin when I left the ship, I'd just like to get it back.'

'You will have to see the purser for the key.'

'Oh. Well we know where pursey lives. You just stay here.'

'Hurry up, the ship is about to sail.'

Liore and Madeline made for the second-class cabins. Those that were unoccupied were unlocked, so they were soon out of sight.

'The ship definitely has almost no passengers,' said Liore. 'This is very unusual.'

'What do we do now?'

'I become a boy again and join the crew.'

From somewhere nearby there was a scream of outrage. Liore's victim had finally been discovered and set free from the strips of Madeline's petticoat that had been used to bind and gag her. People began to gather on the wharf.

'Some filthy young deviant stole my clothes,' she shrieked, but the rest of her words were lost as the *Millennium*'s horn announced that the ship was casting off.

'I can't go ashore with all that going on,' said Madeline.

'Agreed,' said Liore reluctantly. 'Best you hide in a cabin while I arrange identities for us. Prepare to cut your hair.'

'My hair?' exclaimed Madeline. 'Cut it? But –'

'While we are aboard this ship you must be a boy. It is one of many prices for living as I do.'

The ship was about a hundred yards from the shore when the master-at-arms came in search of the two women his deputy had allowed aboard the ship, and the two stewards who were meant to have seen them off. Liore was dressed as a saloon steward and standing where one of the real stewards had been.

'Boy, did you see two women wandering about here?' the master-at-arms demanded. 'I've been looking everywhere for them.'

'Yes, sir, and they waved to me and went down the gangway. They were carrying three bottles of spirits.'

'What? Why didn't you stop them?'

'Your deputy let them aboard, sir.'

'The young idiot! They were harbour trollops, sneaking aboard to steal liquor.'

'One of them said she had bought the bottles in Colombo, sir.'

'Those three bottles will come out of his pay! Now

remember, you are a patrol steward, which means you are meant to keep the ship secure, not stand about looking decorative. What is your name?'

'Kingsley, sir.'

The master-at-arms held a clipboard up to a lantern.

'Albert Kingsley, patrol steward,' he said, nodding. 'Perkins was meant to be flanking the gangway with you. Where is he?'

'George Perkins, patrol steward, reporting, sir!' said Madeline behind him.

The master-at-arms turned.

'Now that's a better attitude – but aren't you two a little young to be patrol stewards?'

'We are cadets, sir.'

'Cadets? We have no cadets.'

'With respect, sir, we do indeed,' said Liore firmly. 'There is a secret Lionheart training school for cadets in the mountains near Adelaide.'

'Is there indeed? What sort of training have you had?'

'Sufficient training to know not to stop the two women,' said Madeline. 'They would have created a fuss, so it was more prudent to let them escape with the stolen bottles than draw attention to the ship, especially with police on the wharf attending that woman whose clothes were stolen.'

This had not occurred to the master-at-arms. He smiled after a moment.

'Good work,' he said. 'I must learn more of this new cadet programme when I get back. Carry on.'

Once they were alone again, Madeline whispered to Liore.

'Where did you get our clothes and papers?'

'They were superfluous to the needs of the previous owners.'

Madeline looked over the side, but there was nothing to be seen but glints on the waves from the distant lights.

'Does that mean what I think it means?'

'I am a warrior, and this is war. Now repeat our names to me.'

'I'm George Perkins, you are Albert Kingsley.'

'Remember that until we reach Colombo, our lives depend on it.'

'What now?'

'We go to their cabins and go to bed.'

Some time later, once she was off duty and alone in Kingsley's cabin, Liore checked her radiocomm again. The signal from the radiocomm aboard the *Andromeda* was still clear and strong. There was now a tiny red circle beside it.

The trace signal from my weapon, thought Liore. *I have you where I want you, Barry Porter. Very soon I shall have everyone else where I want them as well.*

Two days after the *Andromeda* had left Adelaide, the weather was clear and calm. This was unusual for that time of year and latitude. The ship was turning out of the Southern Ocean. Soon it would be heading north on the Indian Ocean, and there would be nothing between the *Andromeda* and Colombo but open water. Daniel was out of bed early, and he had a leisurely breakfast in the first-class saloon. Barry was nowhere to be seen, which was hardly surprising to Daniel, as well as quite a relief. His friend had learned a little about how polite people behaved at table from visits to the Lang house, but there was no solid foundation to his knowledge. Barry could do a few things correctly, but he had no idea *why* he was doing them. Sooner or later he would come up against a situation that required understanding, and then there would be another disaster.

Daniel was lying back in a chair on the promenade when a very seedy-looking Barry finally appeared. By now it was time for morning tea, and deck stewards were out and about with trays. Daniel cringed a little lower in his chair as Barry sat down not far away, snapped his fingers for a steward, and called for a tray. When the tray came he tried a cup of tea. He did not like it. He added sugar. That did not seem to improve the taste for Barry. He poured in some milk, but even this did not measure up to his standards. By now Barry had attracted an audience of children, who were laughing at his version of morning tea.

Barry did like an audience, and he began to parody what the first-class adults were doing. The children laughed even more. By now Daniel was hiding behind *Treasure Island*, but no longer reading it. Barry did a napkin trick and a teaspoon trick, then he performed spin-the-saucer. The children clapped and laughed. In the distance Daniel could see adults glancing Barry's way and looking uneasy. *Only a matter of time,* thought Daniel. *Who will strike first?* Barry picked up a little milk jug decorated with blue and gold cornflowers and drained it. *Too late, Barry is loading for his first shot.*

The audience of first-class passenger children had never seen anyone spray milk through their tear ducts, and Barry was rewarded with squeals of delight and applause. Because thin streams of milk were not visible at distance unless one knew what to look for, the adults did not notice. He did it again and again. The children joined hands and danced around him.

Should I flee before Barry runs out of milk? wondered Daniel.

Barry ran out of milk. Daniel watched as he stood up, made his way through his adoring audience, and walked over to a group of older but very fashionably dressed women. *I can't watch, but I can't help myself,* thought Daniel. Barry seemed to be politely asking the women for their little jug of milk. One of the women smiled nervously, but apparently said yes. Barry picked up the jug, drained it, and blew the liquid out of his tear ducts, splattering milk over Lady Matindale, Lady Scott-Bugden and Baroness Featherington. The three women screamed, leapt to their feet and fled. The large group of children behind Barry shrieked their approval. Barry performed an elaborate but clumsy bow.

Please, please don't notice me, thought Daniel as angry parents began to retrieve their children and drag them away. *The angel of doom hovereth above thee, Barry, surely thou canst feel the beating of his wings.*

The angel of doom took the form of the master-at-arms, who soon appeared in the distance, flanked by Lady Matindale, Lady Scott-Bugden, Baroness Featherington, and four deck stewards. Fingers were pointed at Barry. Barry suddenly comprehended that he had probably gone too far with something. He turned to flee, but ran straight into the deputy master-at-arms. Daniel watched in relieved silence as Barry was borne away shouting, 'I didn't do nothin'!' Realising that Barry was in serious trouble, what remained of his audience of children scattered.

Daniel waited until mid-afternoon before visiting Barry. Because first-class passengers were expected to need incarceration only rarely, one of the cabins had to be set up to double as a brig. The lock on the door was modified so that it could not be opened or picked from the inside, the luxuries were removed, and Barry was bundled in. A steward was assigned to sit outside.

'You actually know the little wretch?' asked the steward when Daniel came to the door.

'I only met him when he came aboard,' replied Daniel.

'I can hardly believe he has a first-class ticket.'

'New money,' said Daniel knowingly. 'Very new money.'

'There should be a test of manners before one can travel first class.'

'Quite so, sir. Now then, I have a note from the master-at-arms permitting me to visit Master Chalmer.'

'Really? What for?'

'A scheme to get him out of the brig, but isolate him from the other first-class passengers, sir.'

'Ah, I see. Well, go ahead.'

Daniel was admitted to Barry's new cabin. Barry was not coping well with being isolated. He was an exceedingly social person, and needed things to do and people to interact with, sell to, and steal from.

Here he had nothing to do but stare out of the porthole at the sea.

'Danny boy, am I glad to see you!' he exclaimed as soon as the door closed behind Daniel. 'That toffy steward cove locked me in 'ere just for not speakin' proper to some hoity old bat.'

'Don't lie to me,' said Daniel firmly. 'You are in here for doing your milk trick all over the three most important ladies on the ship.'

'No I didn't!'

'I was there.'

'You were?'

'Barry, that was the most disgusting thing I have seen since Nigel Tromper stuck a smoked oyster up his nose at the Middle Brighton Dancing Academy's annual ball and asked my sister if she had a handkerchief.'

'Cor, I gotta remember that one. Wot happened?'

'She screamed. Then he pulled it out and ate it.'

'Didn't think old Nigley was that brave. Bet she weren't too pleased.'

'She wasn't. She slapped his face.'

'That's a logical.'

'With a plate of cucumber sandwiches.'

'Oh jeez! I wondered how he got his nose broke.'

'Getting back to yourself, the master-at-arms tells me that you are to be confined here for the rest of the voyage.'

'Bleedin' hell, I'll go mad.'

'The alternative is to toss you off the ship at Colombo.'

'Oh. So I gotta stay in this place for a week until London?'

'Five weeks and two days to go, Barry.'

'But – but can't I get out and about? There's nothin' to do. This is awful. Can't I get out and, er, learn respeccyble deck games or somethin'?'

'It may not be as bad as that. Firstly, you are meant to spend a few days in here to learn the errors of your ways.'

'Wot?'

'The captain wants you to suffer, so do some suffering. After that, he wants you to reform yourself through hard work.'

'Work? But I'm –'

'A first-class passenger, I know, but you are also a first-class passenger who has been behaving like a pig in a pastry shop. It's either five weeks of solitary confinement or five weeks of hard labour.'

'Five weeks?'

'Actually five weeks and two days. The choice is yours.'

'Choice? I don't call that much of a choice.'

Four hundred miles astern, the *Millennium* was slowly reducing the lead of the *Andromeda*. Liore and Madeline were now sharing a second-class cabin, and were performing well in their personas as patrol stewards. After their rounds of the decks they reported to the bosun about damage or shoddy work, then they worked as saloon stewards. The combination of Madeline's experience as a waitress and Liore's background as a cadet a century in the future soon had most senior officers very impressed. The standard of the service in the first-class saloon did not please everyone, however.

'This sort of thing is what is dragging the empire down,' said the master-at-arms, as the officers finished their main meal on the third night since leaving Adelaide. 'Cadets should be martial youths, not little White Star dandies who could just as easily be serving aboard the *Oceanic*.'

'Be easy on them, Tom,' said the captain. 'They are supposed to be convincing as saloon stewards.'

Liore and Madeline were clearing the plates away as they spoke, and both remained respectfully silent.

'All on a warship should be fighting men,' replied the master-at-arms, taking an orange from the fruit tray. 'I mean were this orange an enemy assassin, how would they defend us from him?'

The master-at-arms tossed the orange at the

purser, who put out his hand and caught it a few inches from his face.

'Oh, fine catch, sir!' exclaimed the second officer, and the others applauded.

The purser tossed the orange back to the master-at-arms, who caught it easily. He held it up again.

'I wager that there's not a man at this table who could not defend himself against this orange,' he continued, 'but what about our new cadets?'

He had raised his hand to throw the orange at Madeline when Liore's free hand flickered. A knife embedded itself in the orange, which was still in the hand of the master-at-arms. He froze. Every man at the table froze.

'With respect, sir, the only way that an enemy would know that there is a Lionheart cadet in the room would be the knife in his back,' said Liore.

'This – this is *my* knife,' said the master-at-arms, whose face had lost all colour.

'I took it from you as I cleared your plate away because I anticipated what you were leading up to. We cadets are very good at anticipating the moves of opponents.'

The master-at-arms lowered the orange and stared at the blade that was protruding from between his fingers.

'You could have injured my hand,' he said angrily.

'Not unless you were the enemy, sir.'

'Bravo!' cried the captain, suddenly breaking the mood and signalling that his approval was with the two young stewards. 'If these fine lads had been in Melbourne or Albury, the result would have been very different, what?'

Across the saloon Liore's performance was being observed by those at another table. These were the ship's only passengers, and among their number were Lady Conrad and Sir Bernard.

'I did not know there was a Lionheart cadet scheme,' said Bernard.

'There isn't,' replied Lady Conrad. 'Not that I know about, anyway. Find out everything about them, Bernard. I want a full report two days before we reach Colombo.'

'And after that?'

'I want them over the side.'

Madeline and Liore were back in their cabin before they spoke of the incident in the saloon.

'Twelve more days of these fools,' said Liore quietly. 'I have seen better displays of discipline and security from the Imperial War Academy's guard dogs.'

'Liore, what you did with the knife,' said Madeline.

'Yes?'

'I could never do that.'

'With a few months of training, I am sure you could.'

'But I can't do it now, and I'm meant to be as good as you.'

'Then you had better stay close to me and let me do any fighting,' said Liore as she stretched out on her bed and closed her eyes. 'This ship is important. Very important.'

'In what way?' asked Madeline.

'It is very dangerous, and the Lionhearts have been granted use of it. Just being aboard puts you in danger.'

'Liore, I deal in facts like all detectives should,' said Madeline, 'but you give me no facts that I can work with. The ship is important? Perhaps. We are in danger? Perhaps. What does all this tell me? Nothing. I am your ally, yet you treat me like the enemy.'

'Very well, Madeline, then here are some details. Beneath this ship's bridge is a pair of six-inch cannons. At the rear of the ship is a saloon that is supposedly closed for renovations, but it conceals two more such cannons. There are also torpedo tubes on the foredeck and poop deck, hidden beneath hatch covers. This ship is a light cruiser disguised as a luxury passenger liner.'

'I don't understand. Why disguise a warship?'

'Because it can sidle up to a battleship, then open

fire at point-blank range with four guns and four torpedo tubes.'

'Would that sink the battleship?'

'Oh yes, but there is more. The engine hall is particularly well guarded, but I suspect that the engines in there can drive the *Millennium* along at as much as thirty knots. I have made some sightings on the sun and stars with a sextant that I improvised, and checked them against the figures from my radiocomm. At our current speed we shall arrive at Colombo half a day before the *Andromeda*, and we are burning a lot of coal to maintain that speed. What does that tell you?'

'These Lionhearts must want to kill Barry.'

'Kill Barry? They could telegraph ahead to Colombo, and have some petty thug slit his throat. No, they must know about the thing Barry stole from me. There are some people aboard that everyone defers to, even the captain. My feeling is that they are the Lionheart leaders, and that they know what my stolen property can do. They want it.'

'So your property must be a weapon?'

'Good guess, but do not ask about it. You would not believe my answer.'

'Very well, but what are we to do? We are two girls against an entire warship. What chance have we?'

'We are two girls in disguise among five hundred crewmen, pursuing the *Andromeda* on a very fast warship.' Liore held up the radiocomm. On its screen two little red lights were pulsing. 'We also know precisely where the weapon is located. The advantage is with us, and we must keep it that way.'

'Advantage? I see no advantage.'

'At Colombo I can get to my weapon first. Once I do that I shall use it to sink this ship and prevent a war.'

Chapter 6

MUSICIAN

With Barry safely confined to the brig Daniel felt a lot more at ease, yet his problems were not yet over. At first he tried to read on the promenade deck, but he quickly learned that people on long voyages were a lot more affable and outgoing than in their day-to-day lives. This was because everyone travelling first class assumed each other to be genteel company, so they had no reservations about needing to be introduced before opening a conversation. Worse, the stewards were always on the lookout for people to drag into deck games. Daniel was a prime target because as far as they were concerned, someone reading a book was doing nothing.

Tuesday was the sixth day since leaving Melbourne, and the weather was already warmer. A steward told Daniel that they were only a few hundred miles from the tropics, and to celebrate there would be a ball. This was yet another problem for Daniel: there were a dozen girls of about his age travelling first-class, but only four boys. One of those boys was in the brig, however, leaving three girls for every boy. Two of those boys were only twelve years old, meaning that Daniel was the boy of choice for any girl in search of male company. All that Daniel wanted to do was pine for his lost love, yet he was pursued by girls wherever he walked, and surrounded by girls when he stopped.

The ball was the second of the many diversions planned for the voyage. Unlike the music hall concert, this was for first-class passengers only, and was entirely formal. People were announced and introduced as they arrived, so that they were not entirely unknown as they began to mingle.

'Daniel William Lang, travelling to Britain to do a preparatory year at Harlingford, prior to studying law at Oxford,' declared the steward as Daniel entered.

Every mother of every eligible daughter instantly gave Daniel their undivided attention. Going to Harlingford meant that Daniel came from a family that was either rich or at least prosperous. Oxford and law meant that Daniel had very bright career prospects. Daniel was also tall and handsome, and his suit disguised the fact that he weighed only a hundred and forty pounds. His name and school were written into twelve little notebooks trimmed with gold.

The dancing started with sedate waltzes, but as people became a little more relaxed in each other's company the band moved them on to livelier dances like the 'Champagne gallop' and the 'Railway steam gallop'. Daniel had learned all the latest dances at the Middle Brighton Dancing Academy, and his dancing created a very good impression with nine mothers and twelve eligible daughters.

Daniel was naturally shy, but he did have a little experience with girls in his past. There were eleven two-hour lessons at the Dancing Academy in the company of two dozen girls who were no better at polite social banter than himself, and fifteen years of being dominated and ground down by his sister Emily. His three months under the command of the deadly Liore did not really count, because Daniel classed her as more of a goddess than a girl. Thus his month with Muriel had given him his best experience of polite flirtation, and he now did this very well. Everyone was thoroughly charmed by Daniel's manners and modesty, even though he was not interested in trying to make a good impression with anyone.

In the breaks between dances Daniel sought out the musicians, who were employed as assistant stewards and actually worked in the saloon most of the time. While associating with servants in preference to supposedly respectable people was not quite as outrageous as squirting milk through one's tear ducts, it did at least signal to the mothers present that Daniel might have a dangerously Bohemian streak. The pianist was an American named Lewis, and he had travelled widely even before getting a job as a ship's musician.

'I first heard ragtime at the Chicago World Fair back in 1897,' he said as Daniel stood beside him at the piano. 'It started among us blacks, but it's quite a craze everywhere now.'

'So it was named after the syncopated, ragged rhythm?' asked Daniel.

'Yeah, you got it. I'll play you the "Maple leaf rag". It's by a guy named Scott Joplin, and when it comes to ragtime he's the best.'

Daniel was soon joined by several girls. He was invited to play a few ragtime pieces from the sheet music, and Lewis complimented him on his sight reading. Seeing him on familiar terms with the musicians did dampen the enthusiasm of several mothers and daughters, but other girls merely thought him more clever and desirable. He stayed on with the musicians after the ball was over to avoid unwanted approaches and invitations on the way to his cabin, and ended the night learning new tunes until after 2 am.

The following morning Daniel decided that he had to take drastic action if he wanted some peace and quiet in order to be heartbroken and to wallow in misery. While at breakfast he asked one of the steward-musicians to introduce him to the chief engineer.

'So you want to look at the engine hall?' said the engineer. 'Aye, I suppose I can have Alderson give you a tour later today.'

'Please sir, you misunderstand,' said Daniel. 'I want to *stay* down in the engine hall.'

'Stay there? Why?'

'Just to – to get a feel for it. I always liked looking at the steam trains in Melbourne, and I thought the engines of a ship would be a lot more impressive.'

'That they are. Very well then, come along with me now. Mind though, stay with me and don't touch anything unless you have my say so.'

The ship was new, so the engine hall was freshly painted and clean. Massive machinery gleamed as it moved, pumped and rotated, and the shadowy stokers at the furnaces seemed like demons stoking the infernal fires of the underworld.

'You do seem to like this place, laddie,' said the engineer after Daniel had stood quietly watching the routine of the engine hall for a full hour.

'I like engines, sir,' said Daniel, who had actually been thinking about a picnic with Muriel. 'Without the engines, those ladies and gentlemen up above would be going nowhere. Engines are what make the world work.'

'Spoken like a true Scot.'

'I'm afraid I'm English.'

'Nothing wrong with that, they led the Industrial Revolution once we showed them what to do.' The engineer pointed to one of the engines. 'So, what do you know about this fine lady?'

'This is one of two triple expansion steam engines driving twin screw propellers.'

'Ah, but do you know what that means? Lots of brainless goats up above have memorised words from the brochures, just to impress the ladies.'

'The hottest steam is used in the smallest cylinder, but is still warm enough to be useful as it is expelled. It gets piped to a bigger cylinder, one that works at a lower pressure. After that it goes to the biggest cylinder, and is used one last time. All that saves fuel, because it makes the most efficient use of the steam.'

The engineer was impressed. 'That's splendid, young man. Where did you learn that?'

'My best friend's father worked in the railways, so I've spent years having steam engines explained to me.'

'Are you planning a career in engineering?'

'Not unless I can run away to sea, sir. My father wants me to study at Oxford, then go into law.'

'Does he now? What say I make you something of an apprentice while we steam to Colombo? That way you can get a real taste for engine-hall life before you decide to run away to sea.'

'Sir, do you really mean it?' asked Daniel eagerly.

'That I do. I have some books in my cabin that you can borrow as well.'

For the next two days Daniel spent all his waking hours in the engine hall. On the first morning he followed the greasers as they lubricated the enormous joints and pistons of the twin engines, but all the while he fantasised about doing nude sketches of Muriel. In the afternoon he watched the stokers shovelling coal, making air channels in the furnaces and breaking up slag, yet he was pretending that Fox was a stoker and was too stupid to do anything else. The following day he even ate in the engine hall, avoiding the saloon altogether. He made notes on what the readings on the gauges should be, the roles of all the people, and the meanings of the signals from the bridge, all interspersed with love poetry dedicated to Muriel. By the end of the second day he was feeling like a brokenhearted engineer instead of a lovesick schoolboy, and for some reason Daniel was rather proud of this.

On the third day Barry was released into Daniel's supervision. Daniel found himself acting as Barry's chaperone because he spent all his time in the engine hall. This was a place where Barry could not offend anyone important, and in the words of the master-at-arms, 'With luck he might even get himself killed.'

'Dunno why ya wanna look after these friggin' engines all day,' muttered Barry as Daniel went about with him, explaining what the greasers had to lubricate, and why.

'Engines are like Liore,' Daniel replied.

'Eh? Wotcha mean?'

'They are powerful and reliable, as long as you serve them faithfully.'

The subject was clearly one that unsettled Barry, and he failed to come up with an amusing or even annoying reply.

'Ya sound like ya keen on that daft bat,' was all that he could manage.

'She is not a daft bat, and she is above mere human emotions,' said Daniel firmly.

'Wot's that mean?'

Daniel decided that this was the time to unsettle Barry very seriously. Liore would run him to earth eventually, and when that happened Barry needed to know that Daniel would neither help him nor even offer sympathy.

'Liore is my queen, beautiful and terrible. I am barely worthy to serve her or die for her. I love her like I love the British Empire. Both are much greater than I am.'

Knowing what was in his bag, in his cabin, chained to his bed, Barry was suddenly anxious to change the subject.

'Thought ya loved Muriel,' he said, delicately steering Daniel onto another topic.

'I did love Muriel, and I still do.'

'Ya can't mean it!' exclaimed Barry, genuinely shocked. 'I mean ya was holdin' hands and kissin' her for three weeks, but all the while she was posing nude for Foxy – *and* probably doin' things like in them piccies on page thirty-seven of that educational book of mine.'

Daniel sighed. 'Probably.'

'Yeah, no wonder he kept it for a week. Hope ya don't mind me lendin' it to him, like.'

'Mind? No. I just hate myself for not . . . for not living up to Muriel's expectations. I failed Muriel by being such a prude.'

'Yeah. If she'd whipped her dress off for me I'd have tried to draw something, even though I can't draw.'

'I also failed Liore, and she is my queen. I shall die with her despising me. She thinks I am a foul betrayer, a traitor and a cad.'

'Wot happened? Did she strip off for ya, too?'

'Barry! How dare you?'

'But I only –'

'No she did not, and she never would.'

'Then wot?'

'I deserted her.'

'Wot? By goin' to school in England?'

'You could not understand. She hates me, and that's an end to it. All I can wish for is that her hand is the one that ends my life.'

'Danny boy, get a grip!' cried Barry in alarm. 'Listen to what yer saying. That sorta talk gets ya locked in the looney bin an' tied up in one o' those white jackets.'

Daniel looked at Barry very intently for a moment, then gazed up at the engine beside them.

'You are right, Barry. For now I must distract myself by caring for these engines.'

'Yeah, but what about me?'

'The chief engineer thinks you should be a goonya man, clearing slag out of the furnaces.'

'Ya mean one of those poor bastards wot wears wet sacks over their heads 'cause it's so hot where they gotta work?'

'That's right.'

'But I'm a first-class passenger.'

'You are a first-class passenger who stole first-class crockery and cutlery, got drunk in the smoking room, vomited into the captain's cigar box, then squirted milk through his tear ducts onto Lady Matindale, Lady Scott-Bugden and Baroness Featherington. You must behave and work hard if you want to sail on to London.'

'And if I don't?'

'You will be thrown off the ship at Colombo.'

The prospect of being alone in a country where they did not speak English was for Barry much the same as solitary confinement. Wearing a goonya sack over his head, and under instruction from the other firemen and stokers, Barry learned to prod at the glowing slag in the furnaces with an iron rake until it broke up, then progressed to building channels for the air amid the glowing coals.

Daniel continued to work alongside the chief engineer. To his surprise, he found himself thinking about Muriel less often, because he actually liked to operate and maintain engines that were bigger than the average house. Games on the promenade deck and social events for the amusement of bored and jaded rich passengers were of no interest to him, but he could not entirely avoid all that.

'Please explain to me again why the ship's engineers have to attend a fancy dress ball,' said Daniel as he met the chief engineer and several other officers in the room behind the bridge.

'Passengers like to see the human face of the crew, my lad.'

'They see the stewards.'

'But the stewards don't steer the ship, tend the engines, predict the weather, and know where to steer on an ocean that looks the same in every direction.

Dinner at the captain's table is all very nice, but there's nothing like mingling with the officers to inspire confidence on a ship.'

'So what am I tonight?' asked Daniel.

'While your mask is on, you are whoever you like. If you take it off, you are a passenger.'

Once again Daniel was alone, and he was not happy about it. He did not even have Barry to talk to, because Barry was definitely not welcome at the ball. This time the announcements were made for the costumes rather than the people wearing them. Among the women there were three overdressed Cleopatras, an elderly Josephine Bonaparte, a Queen Elizabeth and two Britannias. Male characters included five Sherlock Holmes, one Dr Watson, a Captain Nemo, and three Lord Nelsons. Eleven passengers came as Romans wearing togas, as these costumes were easy to improvise from bedsheets. The remaining dancers were just wearing masks with their ordinary clothes or uniforms. Daniel wore his academic gown and a mask, carried the cardboard dagger his mother had packed, and had himself announced as Mr Smith, Master Spy. He was recognised and set upon instantly by several mothers and their daughters.

'We were so worried about you,' said one girl breathlessly. 'You have not been seen for over a week. Mother asked one of the stewards if you might have fallen overboard, but he said that you were all right.'

'Thank you for your concern,' said Daniel. 'I have just been in the engine hall.'

'The engine hall! Whatever for?'

'I like big engines. My intention now is to become a ship's engineer instead of following a career in law.'

The girl's mother took her aside and whispered to her. Daniel caught something about not marrying a man who shovels coal, then the girl was whisked away into the crowd. The next girl presented for Daniel's attention asked whether he had been seasick. Daniel made the same reply about being in the engine hall for the week past, but this time her mother thought he was embarrassed about being seasick, and was lying. She presented him with a small bottle of seasickness pills.

The dancing consisted of the usual mixture of waltzes, polkas and gallops, but with several folk dances added to loosen up the mood. Loosening up was certainly achieved when one of the Romans had the hem of his toga trod upon during the 'Waves of Tory' and was left wearing his sandals, mask and nothing else. After this excitement there was a display of Morris dancing by four of the stewards. Daniel spent as much time as he could with the band, and was even allowed to play the piano while the pianist toured the dance floor, supervising during the folk dances. Now Daniel noticed that some girls, and even some women, were loitering near the band. Some were smiling boldly at the players.

How can I nurse a broken heart and prepare to die tragically when there are all these girls swarming around me? wondered Daniel yet again as he played.

A break in the dancing meant that the singer had ten minutes to fill in. She sang a selection of songs from Gilbert and Sullivan operettas, and because Daniel had spent years playing the piano in the living room while his father and sister sang songs from the same shows, he continued to play. As the musicians returned for the next bracket of dances, Daniel felt a hand on his shoulder. It was Julia, the singer. She was about ten years older than Daniel and had what his sister called a wanton manner.

'Daniel, you've been playing for two hours,' she said. 'Come away, take a break.'

'I don't mind playing on, miss.'

'I've been watching you, luv. The girls and their mothers have been trailing after you all night, and you look unhappy about it. Did you leave a special girl behind in Australia?'

'A special girl left me, miss. I've been sent away to forget.'

'Was it for someone else?'

'Yes, and he is above my station.'

'Thought so. Come along, we're going for a walk.'

❇

Out on the promenade deck they found themselves alone and looking out over the dark ocean. The night was warm and balmy, for they had just crossed the Tropic of Capricorn.

Daniel had found Julia a bit unsettling from the moment he had first seen her. Having quite large breasts and hips but a relatively narrow waist, she could easily have been one of the women posing in Barry's French postcards. She was also quite pretty, but with more suave grooming than the teenage Muriel. Her general manner suggested that she would probably have been quite willing to disrobe and pose for the cameras herself. Thoughts of Muriel taking her clothes off entered Daniel's mind. *Julia and Muriel are very similar*, he decided. *This might be a good chance to practise being sophisticated, so I'll not be such a fool when I meet Muriel again.*

'It's a beautiful night,' said Julia, looking up at the sky. 'I wonder what those two pretty stars are.'

'They are the planets Jupiter and Saturn,' said Daniel.

'If there were a moon it would be just so romantic.'

'The moon will rise in about three hours.'

'Goodness! You seem to know the sky as well as the ship's navigator.'

'I like the sky. It's very reliable, not like people.'

'Poor Daniel. You look like an eligible young bachelor, you talk like a world-weary old man, yet all the while you are a schoolboy.'

For a time they walked slowly in silence. A steady wind from the ship's motion played over them, but the air was warm.

'Why do they have so many social things so early in the voyage?' said Daniel presently.

'That's so shipboard romances can start early,' said Julia.

'Truly?'

'Truly. Romance is why a lot of people take a voyage. In London or Melbourne you are just another face in the crowd, but on a ship you are part of a sort of exclusive club. People talk to strangers more easily, and you know where that leads.'

'So people start courting without being introduced?'

'Oh yes, it's a big adventure. Nothing is arranged or predictable.'

'But strangers might well be rogues!' said Daniel. 'Even I might be a rogue, yet girls and their mothers set upon me whenever I emerge from the engine hall.'

'I've met a lot of rogues. Believe me, Daniel, they are not like you. Ever wonder how I ended up here?'

'You auditioned for a shipping company?'

'No, I ran away with an exciting rogue. After a few

weeks my money was gone. I woke up one morning to find that he was gone too, and that the hotel room was not paid for. I was lucky. I couldn't go home, but the hotel manager let me work in the kitchen, washing dishes. One day the singer in his restaurant was sick, so I borrowed a good dress and sang in her place. A man in the band started recommending me to music halls and other hotels, and soon I was able to stop washing dishes and sing for a living. One thing led to another, and when I decided I wanted to see the world I got a job on a ship.'

'It sounds like a wonderful life,' said Daniel. 'I envy you.'

'Oh, it was not all good times. I did a lot of things to survive that were a bit horrible, but I had a lot of luck, so here I am: twenty-five, a thousand pounds in the bank, and around the world seven times. What about you?'

'I'm a schoolboy for one more year, then I'm at Oxford, then I'm a lawyer.'

'Yet you want to run away to sea, you are good on the piano, and you know about things like planets.'

'And I also depend on my father for all my money.'

'So did I, yet here I am. How old are you?'

Daniel took out his pocket watch and glanced at it.

'In about half an hour, sixteen.'

'Truly? Tomorrow is your birthday?'

'Yes.'

'I was sixteen when I ran away, it's easy. All you have to do is let go. Why not start running in half an hour?'

Daniel shook his head.

'Death is behind me, Miss Julia. There is no point in running.'

'Death?' exclaimed Julia. 'What do you mean?'

'Death is my only escape. Leave it at that.'

'I think I understand,' she said, reaching across to take his hand. 'Do you know what I find? Bad times don't last. Just do your best and get your mind onto other things until life improves.'

'You wouldn't believe how bad the bad times are.'

'Then let me distract you until we reach Colombo, so that you don't jump over the side.'

'Distract me?' asked Daniel nervously. 'How?'

'Not how, why. Being distracted gets you two days closer to the good times. After that, I can't help. I'm leaving the ship at Colombo and going to China.' Julia squeezed his hand. 'Promise you will not kill yourself.'

'But why bother with me?' asked Daniel, turning to look at her at last, his face haunted but puzzled. 'I'm just a schoolboy, and in two days you will never see me again.'

'Because I may be able to save you. Remember the hotel manager who let me wash dishes and sleep in a broom cupboard instead of throwing me out into the street? I can be that person for you.'

'But if Muriel found out –'

'Then it serves her right for leaving a lovely boy like you!' said Julia, stamping her foot in exasperation. 'Come on, Daniel. People will talk if we're alone together for too long. Besides, it's getting cold out here and the band needs us.'

Aboard the *Millennium*, Sir Bernard was conducting his investigations slowly but thoroughly. The supposed Lionheart cadets did nothing at all that seemed suspicious. They asked no questions about the ship or Lionheart plans, and a search of their cabin uncovered nothing that they would not be expected to have. The days passed, and he reported to Lady Conrad every morning, yet there was never anything significant to mention.

The cadets trained openly in the ship's gymnasium, although they always wore heavy jumpers, even when the ship entered the tropics. It was clear that Kingsley was by far the superior fighter, and much of their time in the gymnasium was spent teaching Perkins to throw knives, fence and wrestle.

For a military cadet, Perkins was even more of a problem than Kingsley. His service in the saloon was perfect for a steward, in fact Kingsley looked clumsy by comparison. Perkins knew everything about laying out the service for meals, never spilled a drop or crumb when serving, and could balance an astonishing amount of crockery on his arm when clearing away. Stewards liked to draw attention to their good service, to flaunt the skills that they were so proud of, but Perkins was as discreet and self-effacing as . . . a waitress!

Eleven days after Liore had impaled the orange held by the master-at-arms, Sir Bernard had finally uncovered something significant. Perkins was a girl in the clothes and role of a boy. All the clues came together: the small hands, the shape of the throat, and a voice that was rather high for a boy of that age. Kingsley was a youth who was well trained as a fighter, but Perkins was a girl who had a lot of experience serving in saloons and restaurants. Together, they distracted the observer from each other's shortcomings. Kingsley was deadly with a knife, so everyone assumed that Perkins was, too. Perkins was a very accomplished saloon steward, and so the diners paid less attention to Kingsley.

The question of how and why they were aboard the *Millennium* remained. Two women had been reported boarding the vessel just before it left Adelaide. Sir Bernard wondered if this was significant. He asked the master-at-arms for his journal.

'Is there a problem?' asked the master-at-arms

as Sir Bernard turned to the entry for the twenty-seventh of July.

'No, no, just checking some facts,' replied Sir Bernard.

Ten minutes before embarkation Barnsley reports that he allowed two women aboard in search of lost property, he read. *Barnsley should have known better. The ship had been idle for several weeks, and had not carried paying passengers on the voyage out. Barnsley said that Perkins and Kingsley had seen them leave just before the ship cast off. They were carrying three bottles of spirits . . .*

'Thank you, that is all I needed,' said Sir Bernard, handing the journal back.

Now he knew the truth. Kingsley and Perkins had not seen the women leave, Kingsley and Perkins *were* the women. The real Kingsley and Perkins had probably been killed and dumped over the side twelve days ago.

Sir Bernard knew that the pair did some deck patrols together and some alone. Because he had been watching them for eleven days, he knew their movements as well as they did. He also knew precisely which shadowed recess on the poop deck to stand within. Perkins always paused on the poop deck and leaned on the railing to gaze back the way they had come, as if already missing Australia. The distant rumble of the engines and the rushing of the air were enough to smother Sir Bernard's footsteps as he walked forward.

Sir Bernard wrapped his arms around Madeline and pinned her against the railing with his body. Although a little past his prime as an active soldier, he was a big man and very strong. Caught by surprise, Madeline screamed.

'Cadet Perkins, you scream like a girl!' said Sir Bernard. 'Anyone would think you *were* a girl.'

'Let me go, or I'll report you!' gasped Madeline as she struggled in his grip.

'Oh, but I'll report you first. I can hardly believe I took so long to see through your disguise, but better late than never. You're coming to my cabin, where we are going to –'

Five talons slashed down Sir Bernard's back, laying his coat, shirt and skin open all the way down to his buttocks. He turned more out of surprise than pain, lashing out backhand with his left fist, but his blow was deftly deflected upwards as the fingers of the taloned hand slashed across his ear, eye, cheek and throat. Luckily for Madeline's sanity, it was too dark to see what Liore did for the next two minutes.

'By your leave, speaking courtly,' panted Liore in the shadows.

'Liore?'

'Come with me, down the steps to third class. We must go the long way to get to our cabins unseen.'

'But there are no lights in steerage.'

'I can see in the dark. When we get to the cabin, I am going to strip off and wash. Take my clothes and throw them over the side, there is too much blood to wash off. After that, continue your deck patrol to the bow.'

They reached their cabin without incident, but Madeline made the mistake of switching the light on before Liore could tell her to close her eyes. Madeline was confronted with a creature with half-inch talons protruding from beneath her fingernails, and pupils twice as large as those that should have been in human eyes. She was also drenched in blood.

'You're hurt,' Madeline managed in a whisper.

'Do not insult me,' said Liore as she unbuttoned her shirt. 'His guards were easy, they were dead before they even knew I was among them. When I saw that he was bending you over the rail I thought the worst and – and I do feel very protective toward you. I broke into vasder mode before I could stop myself.'

'Vasder mode?'

'Vascular Dilation Mode, a type of near-mindless berserker fighting frenzy. Some doctors have been experimenting with improvements to the human body: different blood, better muscles, retractable talons, night vision, a taste for raw flesh, and a lot more. My mind was also changed in ways that would give you very bad dreams, but the result is that I am the perfect officer for leading a squad of humans. They know that I am superior to them, so I am never challenged. I was one of the prototypes, but they made one big mistake. I was configured for independent thought on missions.'

'Who are these doctors? They sound terrible.'

'You would not believe me if I told you. Now take my clothes and pitch them over the side. I'll try to wash and change before someone raises the alarm.'

As she accepted the reeking bundle of clothes, Madeline put a hand behind Liore's head and kissed her on the forehead.

'Thank you for caring for me,' she said as she stuffed the clothes into a pillowcase. 'You are my guardian angel. A very frightening guardian angel, but an angel nonetheless.'

The bodies were discovered ten minutes later. Four of Sir Bernard's guards had died of snapped necks or slashed throats. Two others were missing, presumed overboard. Most of Sir Bernard was found on the poop deck.

The immediate conclusion was that some deadly animal had been turned loose aboard the *Millennium*. The crew was ordered to go about in groups no smaller than three, and the lights were left on day and night for the rest of the voyage. All passengers and off-duty crew were to lock themselves in their cabins. The strategy seemed to work – almost. When the ship reached Colombo, the cadets Kingsley and Perkins were found to have vanished, but so too had the creature. A thorough search of the *Millennium* by the Lionhearts and members of the harbour police failed to find any trace of it, but even so it took a lot of persuasion and the promise of a bonus to convince the crew to return aboard.

The next morning Daniel rose from his bed too late for breakfast, and was two hours late for collecting Barry. The air was warm and humid, for the equator was very near. He threw back the bedsheet, and remembered that he had slept naked for the first time in his life because of the heat. Mortified, he bounded out of bed and pulled on his trousers.

On the dressing table was a note that read, NEVER LET GO UNTIL TOMORROW. Julia had written it for him the night before, and told him to keep it where he could see it first thing every day. Daniel smiled down at the note, nodding, then he locked his cabin and set off to collect Barry from the brig.

'Bit late today,' commented Barry, who was used to Daniel being absolutely punctual.

'The fancy dress ball went rather late,' replied Daniel.

'So how was it last night?'

'No worse than the previous ball. How was the brig?'

'Ha ha ha, but not so bad. The cove wot's supposed to be guardin' the door come in and we had a chat about ships and things.'

'That was nice of him.'

'He said three hundred ships hit icebugs in the last twenty years.'

'I think he probably said icebergs.'

'Yeah, an' thirty of 'em sank. Wot if we hits one?'

'Barry, we are at the equator, there are no icebergs for thousands of miles. They're made of ice. They melt when they reach warmer waters.'

'Yeah? Well wot about near England? It's colder there.'

'It's colder in Melbourne, too. Have you ever seen an iceberg in Port Phillip Bay?'

'Er, no.'

'Well then, don't worry about hitting an iceberg.'

'Look, wot if we did hit one that didn't melt proper? I mean, I can't swim.'

'The *Arizona* hit an iceberg in 1879. Its bow was crushed, but it didn't sink.'

'Yeah? Why not?'

'Because big, modern ships have things called collision bulkheads. That's a watertight wall just behind the bow of the ship. If the ship hits something, only that compartment gets water in it.'

'So a ship's unsinkable if it's got one?'

'I suppose so, yes.'

'Does this ship have one?'

'All big ships have them, I read about them in a book.'

'So is the *Andromeda* a big ship?'

'Yes!' shouted Daniel, growing exasperated. 'Trust me, Barry, there are no icebergs within thousands of miles, and even if there were, they can't sink a ship as big as ten thousand tons.'

Suddenly a very unexpected sight confronted them.

'Oi!' exclaimed Barry in astonishment, pointing in front of them. 'There's three coves in grass skirts. One's got a pitchfork.'

Daniel gazed calmly at the approaching men.

'It's a trident, Barry. The master-at-arms is dressed up as King Neptune. I imagine the other two are Davey Jones and Capricorn.'

The three men encircled Daniel and Barry.

'Good afternoon, young fellows,' said King Neptune. 'Do you know who I am?'

'You are King Neptune, your majesty,' said Daniel politely.

'Do you know why I am here?'

'You are in search of pollywogs who have never crossed the equator before.'

'Well then, you know what is to come.'

'With respect, your majesty, not for me,' said Daniel, drawing a scroll out of his coat pocket.

Davey Jones read the scroll, then showed it to King Neptune.

'Two years old, but you definitely crossed the equator,' said King Neptune, nodding and smiling. 'What about your little friend?'

'This is his first time out of Australia.'

'Oh, splendid. Seize him!'

Davey Jones and Capricorn immediately took Barry by the arms and lifted him from the deck.

'Oi, wot's all this then?' cried Barry as they bore him away.

Daniel and several hundred other passengers from all three classes watched as those who had admitted to never crossing the equator before were subjected to equatorial initiation by King Neptune and his courtiers. The girls and women had their cheeks smeared with wet flour, and sugar was sprinkled in their hair. The men were stripped to their trousers, sprayed with seawater from a hose, and then pelted with little packets of flour. Finally it was Barry's turn. Orders had been given that he was to receive special treatment.

Daniel watched in great amusement as Barry was doused with buckets of bilge water, made to eat a raw egg whole, and dangled upside down over the side by a rope tied to his ankles. After having chutney poured down his shorts and being sprayed with seawater, Barry was set free. He ran straight back to the brig and refused to come out or see anyone, including Daniel.

Daniel met Julia as he returned from knocking on the door of the brig.

'So you are still alive this morning,' she said as they paused to look out over the water. 'How do you feel after our little talk last night?'

'Um . . . peculiar. As if I've done something bad but not been caught.'

Julia slipped something into his coat pocket.

'Happy birthday.'

'Thank you.'

'Don't take it out until you are in your cabin.'

'Why not?'

'Just don't. Are you going down to the engine hall today?'

'Yes. It keeps my mind off things I should not think about.'

'Then you should stay in the engine hall after I leave at Colombo. I'm working as a saloon stewardess for the rest of the day, but there's a rehearsal with the band between five and seven. Do you want to come along and help? Being able to play in hotels and bars is good for earning a bit of money anywhere in the world.'

'You mean if I run away from school?'

'I mean if you don't even bother going to that English school. I'm almost tempted to take you to China, Daniel, but you have to learn to do things alone.'

'Thank you, I'm touched. I'd like to go to China, but I have something important to do. Something very dangerous.'

'Like jumping overboard?'

'No, I promised not to. Remember?'

'Then what?'

'I have to deliver something important.'

'Well then, back to getting you through today. Will you come to the rehearsal and play while I sing tonight?'

'Thank you, I'd love to.'

The following morning Barry was still quite nervous about leaving the brig. Daniel gave him a bread roll that he had taken from the saloon after breakfast.

'I been molested, humiliated, an' subjected to inhuman practices,' muttered Barry as he attempted to fish out a fragment of eggshell that was still stuck between his teeth.

'Life at sea can be very hard,' said Daniel.

'Yeah, but I'm a first-class passenger.'

'To King Neptune, all men are equal.'

'Yeah, an' I been thinkin' about that, Danny boy. I thought ya was born in Melbourne.'

'I was indeed.'

'An' ya never been to England?'

'No.'

'Then how come ya crossed the equator? I mean England's on the other side.'

'My father told me about the King Neptune business years ago. I forged that scroll.'

'Wot? Why didn't ya do one for me?'

'It must have slipped my mind.'

'I'm tellin' that Neptune cove!'

'I'll say you are lying, and it's your word against mine. Who do you think he will believe?'

Barry muttered something about hoity snobs looking after each other as he stared out over the sea. Presently, he pointed to the horizon.

'Is that England?' he asked.

'It's Ceylon, Barry. We're not even halfway to England.'

'Oh. Bleedin' stupid ship, I'm sick of it. Why'd they pick on me yesterday?'

'Because since you have been in the brig nobody in first or second class has had a pocket picked or a cabin robbed, neither has anything been stolen from the first-class saloon.'

Barry had no answer for that. 'So we're not even halfway there?' he said instead.

'About three more weeks.'

'Bleedin' hell! With trains ya get from Melbourne to Adelaide in one night.'

'England is a lot further away than Adelaide.'

'Stupid ship,' muttered Barry again. 'Why can't it go faster? That ship over there's goin' faster.'

Barry pointed to a ship that was slowly overhauling the *Andromeda*. Daniel raised his telescope and drew it out to its full length.

'The *Millennium*,' said Daniel, reading the name on its bow. 'Yes, it certainly is faster, judging by the way it's passing us. I remember the *Millennium* being in Adelaide harbour when we sailed. It must have steamed really fast to catch up with us.'

Liore! thought Barry as he experienced a spasm of pure terror and jumped to the worst possible conclusion. *Liore's taken over a whole bleedin' ship and come after me. Sure as the king's got a bum for sittin' on his throne, she's on that ship. She's gonna take her weapon back an' burn me so friggin' bad with it that even a bleedin' cannibal wouldn't bother takin' a bite.*

Daniel lowered his telescope and turned to Barry. Barry's face had gone chalk white, and his mouth was hanging open.

'Er, when d'ya reckon we dock, Danny boy?' he asked in an unsteady voice.

'Another two hours, according to the notice board, but I think it will be earlier than that.'

'Er, yeah, thanks. Well, I orta go get cleaned up in the brig.'

'Barry!' Daniel called after him.

'Yeah?'

'Don't bother trying to hide. Liore knows where we are.'

'Wot!' exclaimed Barry. 'That is, like, wot ya mean? Liore's back in Melbourne, studyin' to be a doctor.'

Daniel drew the radiocomm from his pocket and held it up.

'You are not the only thief aboard the *Andromeda*, Barry. I burgled your bag on the second night and switched on this radiocomm. Liore knows where we are, and she is almost certainly aboard the *Millennium*.'

With that Barry turned and ran.

'Barry, you're not meant to be out of the brig unless I'm with you!' Daniel called after him.

Chapter 7

CASTAWAY

Barry ran straight to his cabin, instead of the brig. He still had his own key, and once inside he locked the door, lit a candle and held it under the padlock attaching his bag to the bed. After the wax had melted and dripped out he opened the padlock and looked into his bag. The weapon was there, but everything else was gone. He removed the false bottom. The space below was empty as well.

'Only Danny knows about that bleedin' false bottom,' said Barry. 'Danny boy, I thought we was mates.'

Barry looked for his hidden caches of money, but found nothing. He put the weapon back in the bag along with a pad of the ship's notepaper and a pencil, then went to the door and inserted his key — but something had been inserted from outside, jamming the keyhole. He rattled at the handle. It did not open. His pickwire was no help because of whatever had been jammed into the keyhole.

'Danny boy!' he shouted. 'Ya can't do this! She's gonna murder me!'

There was no answer. He ran to the porthole and looked out. The ship had entered the port of Colombo and appeared to have stopped. A steam launch was approaching. In the distance was the *Millennium*.

Barry took out the weapon, groped for the ring of Liore's hair in his coat's inner pocket, then used the hair to activate the weapon. *If this can sink a bleedin' ship it can clobber a lock,* he thought, then fired at the lock on the door. There was the usual squeal of the weapon firing, then a flash of light and a puff of smoke. Barry batted at the smoke, and saw that the lock had burst apart. What was left had melted. Barry noticed that the shot had gone through the door on the other side of the corridor.

In his haste to pack away the PR-17, Barry forgot to deactivate the weapon. He checked his pockets for change, but found only five shillings.

'That's not gonna get me a tikky on another ship,' he decided.

He now hurried down to the engine hall, talking his way past each member of the crew who tried to stop him, insisting that Daniel had gone on ahead. Once alone he went to the stokers' quarters and stuffed a goonya hood and some stokers' clothes into his bag. On the way out he scooped up some coal dust in his handkerchief. Back on the deck, he discovered that the passenger tender was already returning to the wharves. However, a tender was now alongside and loading coal through doors in the side of the ship. Barry dashed down to the engine hall again, found a quiet corner and changed into his stolen stoker's clothes. Taking the notebook and pencil from his bag, he approached one of the Ceylonese supervisors at the door in the side of the ship.

'Ha ha, my man, I'm the inspector of bags, an' I gotta take a bag tally on yer boat,' said Barry confidently.

The man looked at him with surprise. The youth was English and he had a bag, notebook and pencil, therefore he had to be someone official. After all, who would want to get aboard a coal tender, except for official reasons? Barry was waved past. Once aboard the vessel, he hid until the unloading was finished and it was steaming back to the docks. He now rubbed his cache of coal dust on his face, then approached the tender's master.

'Excuse me, mate, but I gotta be put on me ship,' he said politely.

'Young sir, I was not aware that you were aboard,' said the Ceylonese master. 'Who allowed you on my vessel?'

'It were the seaman's mission cove, mate. He said you'd get me aboard me ship, like.'

'Oh, I see. Well if the holy man from the seaman's mission said it is all right, then it is my obligation to obey. What is your ship?'

Barry looked about the harbour. A grubby looking ship with a single funnel was belching smoke into the calm air. Barry concluded, correctly, that it was about to sail.

'That one,' he said, pointing.

'Oh my goodness, that is the *Ajax*, and it is imminently sailing!'

The tender master ordered his steersman to change course and blow the steam whistle. The anchor of the *Ajax* was being raised as Barry clambered through the loading door. Once he was in the ship, he was confronted by a man who was covered in coal dust and carrying an armload of empty sacks.

'Ha ha, my man, I got a telegram wot said me poor dear mother's gonna drop off the perch pretty damn soonish, so I gotta go 'ome urgently.'

The man did not understand English, but he did understand the five shillings that Barry pressed into his hand, so he let him past. Barry furtively explored the ship until he found the engine hall. It was not on the same scale as that of the *Andromeda*, but it also had huge pistons, cylinders and furnaces. In the privacy of a toilet Barry dripped more candle wax into the lock on his bag, then hid the bag under a pile of coal sacks and reported for duty. To his dismay, he discovered that the superintendent of stokers spoke English.

'You are very, very small boy to be a stoker,' said the burly Egyptian, looking down at Barry in the glow from the furnace doors. 'You will not usefully shovel coal.'

'Yeah, well, that's because I'm a slagger, aren't I?' replied Barry, waving his stolen goonya man hood.

Yet again Barry's confidence and unlikely story wove their spell and allowed him to pass. Breaking up the slag inside a hot furnace with a long metal rake was not popular work, and Barry spoke as if he knew what he was doing, so he was assumed to be genuine. He soaked his goonya hood and shirt in water, then put them on, but the furnaces were only newly fired, so no slag had yet built up. The men of the engine hall quickly settled into their routine, and Barry was soon just another anonymous body tending the fires that drove the ship forward.

The *Ajax* began to roll gently as it reached the open sea, and Barry relaxed as he realised that he had escaped both the *Andromeda* and the port of Colombo. The Egyptian superintendent turned out to be quite friendly, and was keen to talk with Barry to improve his English. From him Barry learned that the *Ajax* was bound for Port Said, which was at the head of the Suez Canal. Barry asked whether he could find a ship going to London from there. The superintendent replied that nearly every ship from Port Said was going to London. Barry would be paid at Port Said, and that would be enough for a ticket.

Nothing can go wrong now, Barry thought as he hefted his rake and began to break the slag apart.

Some miles away, ashore, Liore activated her radiocomm and discovered that the other radiocomm was not on the *Andromeda* at all, but on a passenger tender on the way into Colombo. Daniel had left the ship with several other adventurous passengers. Julia was also on the tender, but Daniel did not approach her. The people were crowded closely together on the little vessel, and what he wanted to say to Julia was for her ears only. He had planned to surprise her once they were ashore.

Daniel stayed out of Julia's line of sight as they disembarked, then he approached her on the pier. She certainly was surprised to see him, but she did not look at all pleased.

'Daniel, what are you doing here?' she exclaimed.

'I decided to see the sights in Colombo,' he said cheerily. 'I might even go on to China.'

'But you have no luggage.'

'I'm sure my luggage will like it in England.'

'How will you live? You need money to travel.'

'I did bring money.'

'Oh. I see.'

Daniel had already noticed the change in Julia's

attitude. Two days ago she had been encouraging him to abandon Harlingford, Oxford, and a career in law. She should have been overjoyed to hear that he was following her advice, but instead she looked worried.

'You said you had something important to deliver,' she continued.

'I left that where the owner is sure to find it,' said Daniel.

His hand slipped into his coat pocket, where he had put the radiocomm. It had been his intention to toss it into the water so that Liore could no longer trace him, but now he hesitated.

'Well, ah, do enjoy China,' said Julia nervously. 'I'm only travelling there, then sailing on to, er, Alaska. There's a gold rush there, I thought I'd look at the people rushing about, looking for gold.'

'What ship are you sailing on?'

'Oh my ship is all booked, no room left. You need to go to a shipping office, and ask about berths. You should do it right away, there may be a ship about to leave.'

Daniel was not surprised when an officer from another ship approached them. Introductions were made. The man's name was Harry.

'I say, so you're a schoolboy on a real schoolboy adventure, what?' said Harry in an annoyingly cheery tone.

'I'm going to Britain to study,' said Daniel. 'Compared to some things I've done, that's hardly an adventure.'

Daniel had flagged that he was not going to make a scene. Out of the corner of his eye he could see Julia go limp with relief, even though she did not actually smile.

'Daniel is a wonderful pianist,' she said, suddenly sounding like her old self again. 'He played with the *Andromeda*'s band during the voyage.'

'You played with the band?' said Harry. 'You should have been on the floor, dancing with the girls.'

'Oh, leave him be, Harry. Danny is still very shy when it comes to girls.'

'So, just in from Adelaide on the *Andromeda*? Nice ship. Ever been on a ship before?'

'No, sir.'

'Lots of fun when you crossed the line, ha ha?'

'Fun is just the word, sir.'

'Well, can't stand about chatting, got a ship to sail, what? Julia darling, where are your bags?'

'Still on the tender.'

'I'll get them aboard the *Zephyr*. We sail in three hours.'

Harry set off, calling orders to the men on the tender.

'Is he really one of the people in charge of your next ship?' asked Daniel.

'I know what you mean, but it's all right. He's the chief steward, he doesn't steer it or run the engines.'

'So he only organises the entertainment.'

'Entertainment is very important, Daniel. Always be nice to the people doing the hiring.'

Daniel had by now realised that he had made a complete fool of himself, and desperately wanted to get away before Harry returned, realised what was really going on and laughed at him. The pain that he was feeling already had Daniel close to tears. Add humiliation to that, and he would go over the edge. He took a step back and gave a shallow bow in Julia's direction.

'I'd best be away to see the sights,' he said coldly. 'Enjoy China.'

'Daniel, wait!' hissed Julia, stepping forward and taking him by the arm. 'I feel bad about this and, well look, I have three hours before sailing. I can send Harry off on some errand and I know a club where we can have some privacy to, well, sort things out.'

'I think we are rather well sorted out already,' replied Daniel, who had grown up considerably over the past five minutes.

'Daniel, please! Don't be like that. I'm serious.'

'As you once said to me, all you have to do is let go.'

Julia released Daniel's arm and he hurried away. For Daniel the world suddenly became darker in spite of the bright sunlight and clear sky. The radiocomm was in his pocket, so if Liore was nearby, then he was being tracked. A ship from Adelaide had caught up with the *Andromeda*. Knowing Liore, she would have been on it. Liore, who would be tracking whoever had stolen her weapon. Liore, who killed as easily as Barry stole. Liore, who believed that Daniel was also a thief, and had stolen from her. Liore, who was better at everything than even Fox.

I am worthless, Daniel told himself as he walked. *Julia pities me, Barry lied to me, Emily despises me, I am not the son my father wanted, and Mother is disappointed by everything I do. Liore is sure to think I am conspiring with Barry, so she hates me, and that's the worst of all. I worship her, I adore her . . . and I wish that the last thing I ever feel is Liore's hands on my throat.*

Daniel found a post office, and there he bought a notepad. He scribbled out a note to Liore. *She is out there,* he thought. *Death is tracking me, I am already in her gunsights.*

The minutes passed. To his surprise, Daniel remained unmolested. He passed the time by writing and posting a letter to his parents and sister. Still nobody tried to kill him. *Perhaps Liore does not like killing in public places,* he decided.

He left the post office and explored the nearby streets, taking several photographs as he wandered. Colombo had a strangely British look to it, and few of the buildings would have been out of place in Melbourne. The people in the streets had dark skin, but many were dressed like Europeans. The smells, background sounds, heat and humidity were what was really different, but none of that would come across in a photograph. His family would be disappointed with his pictures, but then his family was disappointed with whatever he did.

Daniel soon lost track of where he was. After all, he would never have to find the docks or his ship again. He turned down an alley. Providing a discreet venue to kill him was the least he could do for Liore.

'Feelthy postcards?'

The speaker was a swarthy man in brownish robes, with a headdress that shadowed his face.

'No speak your language,' said Daniel, attempting to walk on.

'Feelthy postcards!' insisted the man, following after him.

'I only speak English, French, German and Latin,' said Daniel, who then told the man to go away in the latter three languages.

'Feelthy postcards,' responded the man.

'Go away, I'm trying to die tragically,' said Daniel.

The intruder seized Daniel by the arm.

'Feelthy postcards!'

'Oh very well,' said Daniel, taking out the French postcards he had stolen from Barry's bag and holding them up. 'How many do you want?'

The astonished man stared at the postcards for a moment, his mouth wide open and eyes bulging, then he pushed the cloth back from his face and began to examine them carefully. He muttered something that Daniel did not understand.

'Do hurry up,' said Daniel. 'I'm expecting someone.'

The man looked up, his mouth still hanging open.

'Sixpence each,' he said.

'Look, just take them and go away. I'm going to die in a few minutes so I don't need money.'

The man did not understand much English. He also had no concept of being given something for free.

'Shilling each!' he bargained.

'Keep them,' said Daniel, turning to leave.

'Shilling each and postcard of mine,' said the man, thrusting one pound four shillings and a postcard at Daniel.

Daniel accepted. The man hurried away before Daniel could change his mind. Evidently erotic French postcards were in demand in Colombo. Daniel thrust the money into his pocket and examined the card. It featured a girl wearing a costume of beads and spangles that covered a total area equal to one rather small handkerchief. He put it in his pocket and glanced about. Nobody else was in the alley. Daniel checked that he still had the note for Liore.

Where is she? he wondered. *I'm all prepared to die and she doesn't show up. Some people just don't think.*

Someone pushed Daniel in the back and slammed him into a wall, then seized him by the arm, spun him around and punched him in the face. Blood gushed from Daniel's nose as he staggered backwards and struck the wall again.

'Fight back,' ordered Liore.

Daniel raised his hands, but a foot flicked out and kicked him in the groin. Daniel doubled over. A hand seized him by the hair and drew him up straight. Another hand slammed into Daniel's stomach, and as he doubled over again a knee rose up to strike him in the left eye. This time Daniel collapsed and lay in the dust as he was kicked repeatedly in the ribs. For some moments there was an unexpected respite.

'Is he dead?' asked an unfamiliar female voice.

'Comes next,' said Liore.

Daniel felt Liore's knees pressing against his sides, and his cracked ribs blazed with pain. Both of his arms were swept together then pressed down in a double arm lock by her chest. Strong, hard fingers sought a spot on his neck.

'Pressing carotid artery,' said Liore. 'Dying, you are.'

'There's a paper in his hand,' said the other girl.

'Annoyed, I was, by Barry,' Liore continued. 'Hurt,

I was, by you.'

Daniel's vision began to blur as Liore squeezed his life away. His world had gone dark as the other girl began to read.

'Dear Liore, I locked Barry and your weapon in First-Class Cabin 37 aboard the *Andromeda*. He cannot fire it because I disabled . . . '

Daniel woke lying on his back. A girl he had never seen before was kneeling beside him, splashing rose water on his face and pleading with him to wake up. Daniel shook his head. It hurt a great deal. So did his ribs, stomach, arms, neck and testicles. The girl helped Daniel to sit up. Liore was standing back with her arms folded and her face blank. She stood absolutely still, like a machine that had been switched off. She was also wearing a dress.

'My name is Madeline,' said the girl. 'Are you feeling all right?'

'What a failure,' wheezed Daniel. 'I can't even get myself killed.'

'I am going by the name Monique Cluny, and Liore is calling herself Lucielle Chasseur. Are you still using the name Daniel Lang?'

'Daniel Lang, that's me.'

'Police approaching,' said Liore. 'Shall target?'

'No!' exclaimed Madeline. 'Let me do the talking.'

Two European men in khaki uniforms strode up the laneway, both carrying guns. Madeline stood up and confronted them.

'Are you the police?' she demanded.

'Yes, miss. Is this young bounder bothering –'

'This gallant young man just saved me and my friend from the attentions of three filthy sailors!' shouted Madeline. 'Well don't just stand there, get after them!'

Madeline had apparently hoped that they would run off in search of the sailors who did not exist. This did not happen.

'No chance of catching them now, miss,' said one of the police as he went to Liore's aid.

'Leave her!' shouted Madeline. 'Help this young man. He was hurt when he drove the ruffians off.'

Liore walked forward with smooth but mechanical elegance.

'By your leave, speaking courtly,' she said quietly. 'I have led a sheltered life, I find all this violence very frightening.'

The two harbour police made sure that Daniel was not actually dying, then they escorted them to the wharf. Madeline explained that their bags had been stolen, along with their tickets for the *Andromeda*.

'I am from the *Andromeda*,' said Daniel, playing along with their story. 'I shall explain everything to the purser.'

'We still have all our money,' said Madeline.

'So, those rotters only got the tickets and bags, what?' said one of the police. 'Don't worry, we'll take you to the ship.'

They travelled out to the *Andromeda* on a steam launch belonging to the harbour police. Liore seemed angry with Daniel, and refused to speak to him. Once they were alone together, she took out her radiocomm and studied it.

'Weapon bearing south-south-west, range five miles,' she said, and then pointed.

Daniel and Madeline turned. There was a ship in the distance, and it was steaming out of the port.

'So it's now on that ship?' asked Madeline.

'Daniel went ashore to distract us,' said Liore, giving Daniel a very dangerous glare. 'Now the weapon is on that other ship, and we cannot pursue it.'

Without any warning at all Madeline's hand lashed across Liore's cheek. From the look on Liore's face Daniel concluded that Madeline had only moments to live, and stepped between her and Liore. Madeline spun him around and slapped his face as well, then pushed him aside.

'Will you bloody well think logically, you silly cow!' she snapped, stamping her foot. 'What sort of commander are you? You told me the weapon was sending signals to you from the *Andromeda*. Why didn't you just go after the weapon, instead of wasting time going after Daniel? And anyway, how do you know what has happened aboard the *Andromeda*? The Lionhearts may have got aboard and stolen the weapon while you were chasing Daniel.'

In her blind fury and thirst for revenge, Liore had not considered this.

'Perhaps it was a bad decision,' Liore finally admitted.

She folded her arms very tightly and turned to glare at the departing ship.

'To me it looks like you were trying to trick Liore into killing you,' said Madeline, now rounding on Daniel. 'Why?'

'I – what makes you say that?' he asked, taken off-guard by the question.

'Liore told me all about your obsession with suicide, we had plenty of time to talk about Barry and you on the voyage from Adelaide. Well? I'm still waiting for my answer.'

'It's, um, so much nicer to have a friend kill you than an enemy,' said Daniel, although not very convincingly.

'That is the most twisted, revolting, perverse thing I have ever heard!' exclaimed Madeline.

'No target,' added Liore quietly.

Daniel said nothing. Being twisted, revolting and perverse made him unworthy to be alive, and so fitted in neatly with his mood and outlook. Even better, being in pain made him feel less guilty, which was actually pleasant. Unlike Daniel's sister, however, Madeline responded to problems by trying to understand them rather than by shouting at people until they agreed with her. She drew a red and black frilly garter out of her purse and handed it to Daniel.

'This was in your pocket,' she said. 'I went through your pockets while you were lying unconscious. My father says a good detective should check everywhere for evidence.'

Daniel blushed luridly red on the unbruised parts of his face as he accepted the garter.

'The note tied to it says "Happy Birthday Danny, and never jump over the side until tomorrow",' said Madeline. 'Whoever she was, she seems rather nice.'

Thoroughly mortified, Daniel seriously considered jumping over the side anyway, but then Liore was sure to jump after him and drag him back, so there was no point.

'I also found this,' said Madeline when nobody had said anything for a time. She drew another note out of her pocket and began to read. 'Dear Liore, I locked Barry and your weapon in First-Class Cabin 37 aboard the *Andromeda*. He cannot fire it because I disabled it by flipping the switches FIREW

DISABLE, TRACE, BC, AL and RC. The spare radiocomm is in my pocket. I turned it on so you could find us. Barry stole your weapon by himself. You will have killed me by now, so you have to believe what I write. Hope I was useful for a change. Daniel.'

'The BC switch activates the Command Override function,' said Liore. 'It is a training option that allows me to watch what a cadet is shooting at. FIREW DISABLE means Firewall Disable, and is hard to describe. AL and RC are only diagnostics.'

'What does all that mean?' asked Daniel.

'You did some very clever work, but . . .'

'But?'

'My weapon is still active.'

'I – ah, oh,' said Daniel. 'Another failure.'

'Not to worry. You left the TRACE function on permanently, so I have been able to track Barry ever since.'

'And now you will apologise to Liore for trying to make her kill you,' said Madeline.

'But Liore doesn't mind killing people,' began Daniel.

'Apologise!'

'All right, righto, yes. I apologise Liore,' babbled Daniel. 'I promise I'll never do it again.'

'Think nothing of it,' said Liore quietly.

Daniel now left and walked aft. After some minutes he returned.

'I asked the harbour police about that ship,' he reported. 'It's the *Ajax*, and is bound for Port Said.'

Liore turned away from the *Ajax* and smiled at Daniel.

'Thank you, that solves one of my targeting problems,' she said, sounding surprised. 'Good work.'

The arrival of Daniel, Liore and Madeline on the *Andromeda* caused a great deal of fuss. The harbour police explained how heroic Daniel had been, and how the girls had been robbed of everything but their money. While Daniel's injuries were being treated, the girls were provided with tickets and assigned a cabin. He was still in the infirmary when a steward told him that Barry was gone.

'He just burned a hole in his cabin door and vanished,' explained the steward.

'You mean he lit a fire and burned the door?' asked Daniel, with very convincing innocence.

'No, he used some sort of red-hot poker to burn through the lock. I've never seen anything like it.'

Once the nurse had finished with Daniel he went to Barry's cabin with Liore and Madeline. It did not take long to assess the damage to the door.

'The weapon was fired from inside,' said Liore to Daniel. 'You were telling the truth.'

Next they locked themselves in the girls' cabin for a private and very sensitive conversation. Daniel sat on a chair, Madeline sat on a bed, and Liore leaned against the wall with her arms folded and her eyes closed. At first nobody said anything, even though their privacy was guaranteed.

'So you are Daniel,' said Madeline, mostly to break the silence.

'Yes. I'm sixteen, and I'm a schoolboy,' said Daniel. 'You are Madeline, and that's all I know about you.'

'I'm a waitress from Ballarat, I'm seventeen, and I'm running away to London to be a detective.'

'Fifteen,' said Liore. 'Am soldier. Kill people.'

'You're using battlespeak,' said Madeline.

'Language mine,' said Liore, now trembling visibly. 'Comforting. Have left, nothing else.'

'You're looking worse than Daniel,' said Madeline. 'Please, sit down.'

Liore unfolded her arms, slowly opened her eyes, then stared at the porthole as if it were a way to escape. Walking stiffly to the writing table, she cycled through some breathing exercises, tried to speak, failed, then brought her fist down so hard that it smashed right through the tabletop. Finally she slumped in a corner with her hands over her head.

'Please, go,' she rasped. 'Near me, dangerous.'

Daniel and Madeline looked at each other, then turned back to Liore.

Daniel shook his head.

'No,' Madeline agreed. 'We stay.'

'Please!' shouted Liore.

'You need us,' said Daniel.

'Need nobody. Go! Like this, being seen, unseemly.'

'We're your friends,' said Daniel. 'You don't have to worry about how you look in front of us.'

'Battle Commander, I am!' exclaimed Liore. 'Friends, have none.'

'We *are* your friends,' insisted Madeline.

Again they lapsed into silence, none of them moving except to breathe. Finally, after more than half an hour, Liore looked up.

'You stayed.'

'Of course,' said Madeline. 'Now speak courtly, try to relax.'

'By your leave, speaking courtly.'

'Now then, where were we?'

'I . . . showed weakness,' said Liore. 'I allowed myself to hate, and it corrupted my judgement. I lost a chance to retrieve the weapon. I am furious with myself for that.'

'So?' asked Daniel. 'I make mistakes all the time.'

'Enough has been said about mistakes,' said Madeline. 'I want to move on to a petty criminal called Barry the Bag who was supposed to be on this ship. Daniel, please tell us about what happened on the voyage.'

'There's not much to tell,' said Daniel. 'As the *Andromeda* was leaving Adelaide I discovered that Barry was aboard and calling himself Barold Chalmer. He said Liore put him aboard to do some spying in Britain.'

'Did you see any pigs flying past?' asked Liore.

'Soon he lost track of his own lies, and started to talk about not being rewarded properly for stopping the bombing of parliament. That made me suspicious, so I got him drunk and locked in the infirmary for the night. I burgled his cabin and discovered that he had stolen things from you.'

'*You* got *Barry the Bag* drunk, then *you* burgled *his* cabin?' exclaimed Liore.

'Well, yes.'

'You have been spending too much time in his company – but never mind, go on.'

'I remembered you said that you could tell where the second radiocomm is when it's turned on, so I played with it until a light came on.'

'So you had nothing to do with Barry stealing the weapon?' asked Liore.

'No.'

'And the garter?' asked Madeline.

'There was a lady . . .' managed Daniel, then his voice trailed away.

'I worked that out for myself,' prompted Madeline.

'I was talking about not living for very long, so she

was worried about me.'

'I'm not surprised.'

'We saw a lot of each other.'

'All of each other, by the sound of it.'

'No! Please, this is hard enough already.'

'Continue,' ordered Liore.

'That's all. As we approached Colombo, we saw the *Millennium* overtake us, and Barry thought you must be aboard. When he went to his cabin to retrieve the weapon, I locked him in there. I thought I had disabled the gun, but I was wrong, and you know the rest.'

'So you burgled Barry's famous bag,' said Madeline. 'Apart from the radiocomm, did you keep anything else?'

'Not much. I threw most of his stolen goods over the side, but I kept what looked useful.'

'And you tried to disable the weapon before putting it back into his bag,' said Liore.

'I did disable it! I tried to fire it through the porthole. Nothing happened.'

'With the switch cover off?'

'I . . . yes. Is that important?'

'Very important. Go on.'

'That's all. When Barry saw the *Millennium* catch up with the *Andromeda*, we were both pretty sure that you were aboard. He ran to his cabin to get the weapon, but I followed and jammed the lock with a pencil in the keyhole.'

'Nice plan, if you had managed to jam the weapon, too,' said Madeline.

'Failed again,' muttered Daniel.

Madeline put her hand on his arm and squeezed it.

'Not so,' she said. 'You did well.'

'You're just saying that to make me feel better.'

'Of course, but you still did well. Why did you go ashore with the radiocomm?'

'Um . . .'

'The truth?' said Madeline.

'So . . . so Liore could track it and . . .'

'Kill you.'

'Yes.'

'Why?'

'Because I'm worthless alive, but I didn't want to waste my death.'

'Daniel!' exclaimed Madeline. 'I – never mind, go on.'

'Once I was dead Liore would find the note about how I thought I had disabled the weapon and locked Barry in his cabin. Liore, I wanted you to, well, to respect me, but only after you had killed me. Do you understand?'

'No target – I mean no,' said Liore.

'I didn't want you to think I was on Barry's side. I wanted you to kill me, then realise it was an honest mistake and not feel bad about it. It would have been perfect –'

'Daniel!' shouted Madeline.

'Sorry.'

'So, we still have to catch Barry,' Madeline continued.

'The *Ajax* is only a tramp steamer, so the *Andromeda* should catch up with it while it is taking on coal at Port Said,' said Daniel. 'The weapon is still working, so Barry will be very dangerous.'

'The soldier is more dangerous than the weapon,' said Liore. 'How did you and Barry activate it?'

'Barry must have had some part of your body.'

'Hair, most likely,' said Liore.

'How would he have got it?'

'I would say he used a broom when he burgled my room. And you? How could you have obtained my hair?'

'I have a strip of Muriel's petticoat that was once used to bandage your stomach. Your blood was on it.'

'Clever.'

'You kept a strip of a girl's petticoat that had been used as a bandage?' asked Madeline.

'Um, yes.'

'Why?'

'Because the girl I love once wore that petticoat.'

'I've heard of keeping a lock of a girl's hair, but

– but never mind. Now back to practical matters. Liore, we should see the purser about sending ashore for spare clothes for us.'

'I should leave,' said Daniel.

'Before you go, please take this back,' said Liore, holding the radiocomm out to Daniel.

'Don't you need it?'

'Of course. I need it to stay in contact with you. You are still a member of my squad.'

'Oh. Thank you. And if you want your old uniform back, it's in my cabin.'

Daniel put the radiocomm in his pocket and began to stand. The cabin suddenly spun before his eyes and went dark.

Daniel spent the next two days in the infirmary, drifting in and out of consciousness in the sweltering heat, attended by the ship's nurse. He had a string of visitors, mostly girls and their mothers enquiring after his health, or telling him how heroic he had been to defend Liore and Madeline from the sailors, whose number by now had grown to between five and ten. At some stage the ship had loaded the last of its coal and got under way, but Daniel had no memory of that. Gradually his strength returned, and he passed the time by reading the books about ships' engines that he had borrowed.

On the third day after leaving Colombo he was well enough to go back to his own cabin. On the fourth he went to breakfast in the first-class saloon, then found a vacant deck-chair on the promenade deck and fell asleep for the rest of the morning. After lunch he decided that he felt strong enough to face Liore and Madeline again. As he raised his hand to knock on their cabin door, Liore called to him.

'The door is unlocked, Daniel. You may enter.'

Daniel opened the door. The table that Liore had smashed four days earlier had been replaced, and was now covered with tools, wires, and what looked like parts of electric motors. Liore was sitting at the table, heating something in a glass tube, while Madeline sat on her bed, winding an electrical coil.

'I don't remember you bringing all this aboard,' said Daniel.

'Foraged,' said Liore.

'She stole it,' said Madeline.

'Can you tell me what are you building?' asked Daniel.

'And not in battlespeak,' added Madeline.

'It is an extension for the radiocomms.'

Daniel looked down at the thing. It had six barrels, all wound with wire, and the general shape of a gun. Liore's radiocomm was attached to it with wires and sealing wax, and there was a space for Daniel's unit.

'What does it do?' asked Daniel.

'Pull the trigger, and you set off six charges together. They shoot magnets along these barrels, generating a resonant field which is tuned and focused on the target by the radiocomms.'

'So it's a death ray?' guessed Daniel.

'No.'

'Then what?'

'Worse.'

Daniel shivered.

'Oh.'

'You can help if you like,' said Madeline cheerily. 'We need some metal brackets filed into shape.'

When one has been confined to bed for some days, one loses the proper matching between day and night. So it was with Daniel, on the fifth night after leaving Colombo. Ignoring the promise of 'A concert of tropical love songs', he went to bed soon after dinner. He awoke at two in the morning, lit a match, looked at his pocket watch, then closed his eyes and tried to go to sleep again. After what seemed to be a very long time, he lit another match. It was seven minutes past two. He lit the beside lamp before the match burned out, sat up in bed and stared at the books on his writing desk. He decided upon *A Scientific Guide to Human Reproductive Biology*, mainly because Fox had read it.

Daniel became aware of a sound like the drone of a large flying insect. He got up and checked his cabin, but found nothing. He returned to bed, and his book. After a time the droning faded. Daniel checked the time, and found that it was only two forty-five. He was now too tired to concentrate on a book full of unfamiliar bodily parts and functions, so he extinguished the lamp and closed his eyes. He soon discovered that he was too alert to sleep. For a while he tried thinking about sitting in cafés in St Kilda, holding hands with Muriel and looking into her eyes.

'I shall love you until the end of time,' said Daniel.

'I want your heart,' replied Muriel, who now had darker hair and a lean, pale face.

'My heart is yours for the taking.'

'Then I shall take it!' cried the girl, who turned into Liore as she dragged Daniel up onto the table and plunged a knife into his heart.

Daniel sat up in bed with a gasp, clutching his chest, his skin slick with sweat. He struck a match. His watch declared the time to be two fifty-five. Daniel lit his lamp again. Getting out of bed, he drew the radiocomm from his coat pocket and thumbed the studs as Liore had shown him. The screen glowed into life. He spoke the password, and with a few more taps called up the location of Barry and the weapon. The display declared Barry's ship to have just entered the Red Sea, travelling at seventeen knots. Bored, but unable to sleep or read, Daniel wondered what else he could do to pass the time.

A ragged line burst across the radiocomm's screen. Daniel felt a pang of fear, thinking that he had damaged the device. Lines began flickering across the screen in what was almost a rhythm, but which never became regular. *It's detecting radio noises,* Daniel realised. Liore had said that thunderstorms could interfere with it because they emitted radio waves. Thunderstorms were apparently like a huge, primitive radiocomm. Daniel looked out of the porthole. Stars were visible in the sky. That meant there were no clouds. *Perhaps the storm is somewhere over the horizon,* thought Daniel. *Strange that the flashes are so regular, almost like Morse code . . .*

Suddenly Daniel snatched up a pencil and began to write. He kept writing until the flickers ceased to travel across the screen. Although it was now just past 3 am, Daniel dressed hurriedly and opened the door of his cabin. The corridors were lit by dim electric lights, and Daniel glanced at his piece of paper several times as he walked to reassure himself that this was indeed important. He felt awkward to be tapping at a door at such an hour, but it was Liore's door, so that excused everything. The door opened. Daniel peered in.

'The small hours of the morning are dangerous for

visiting me,' came Liore's voice from the darkness. 'It is the preferred time for death squads to arrive, and I kill death squads.'

'Pardon me, but I think this is important,' said Daniel, holding up his piece of paper.

'Then come in. Madeline, the lights.'

Daniel handed his piece of paper to Liore. She glanced at the words for a moment.

'It reads like a telegram,' she said. 'A telegram from the Lionhearts. Where did you get it?'

'I couldn't sleep, so I thought I would check on Barry's position. The radiocomm started to pick up, um, what is the word? Inference?'

'Interference, static, white noise. Go on.'

'After a few seconds I noticed a pattern. There is a radio on this ship.'

'This is 1901. The only radios in this time are primitive devices called spark gap transmitters that generate bursts of static to transmit Morse code. Just a moment.'

Liore took the radiocomm from Daniel and pressed a pattern of studs, calling up an encyclopaedia entry.

'1901 . . . experimental spark gap transmitters were – are – being installed on ships,' Liore read from the screen. 'Someone has sent a telegram on the ship's spark gap radio.'

'But this ship has no spark gap radio,' said Daniel. 'I've talked about it with the engineer.'

Liore tapped at a few more studs. 'You are right,' she said. 'Spark gap transmitters still had a very limited range in 1901, no more than some dozens of miles. They are not yet very practical for use on ships.'

Liore handed the piece of paper to Madeline, who read it out aloud.

'IX LION CUBS ABOARD STOP SEALION RETURNING STOP SEARCH COMMENCING STOP REPORT AT MID AND HALF STOP OUT STOP. Then there's another line with just ACKNOWLEDGED.'

'How did the radiocomm intercept this?' asked Liore.

'Flickers on the screen,' said Daniel. 'The message was about half over when I realised what I was seeing and began to write the words out. The last word was a lot weaker, as if it were coming from very far away.'

'And this was in standard Morse code and plain language?' asked Liore. 'It is hard to believe that there is no security encryption.'

'We are in the middle of the Arabian Sea,' said Daniel. 'They probably think nobody could listen in.'

'What does it all mean?' asked Madeline.

'The *Andromeda* has been boarded by Lionhearts,' said Liore.

'But another ship would be visible if it got close enough for that, even on a moonless night,' said Daniel.

'Not so. All of the lifeboats on the *Millennium* had internal combustion engines fitted. One of them might have been sent after the *Andromeda*, and got close enough for someone to throw a padded grapple up to the stern rail. Nobody would have noticed, not at this time.'

'I heard a buzzing, like a very big beetle was flying nearby,' said Daniel. 'It was about a quarter hour before this message was sent.'

'A petroleum engine would sound like that. How many boarders were there, I wonder? IX. That might be nine in Roman numerals or six with the S missing. This is serious.'

Liore slipped off her dressing gown and stood naked before Daniel and Madeline. Daniel had never seen her naked before, and the contrast with Muriel could not have been greater. She looked like neither a boy nor a girl, in fact she did not look entirely human. Her skin was like silk stretched over wire rope, and her shoulders were a little too broad for a girl. The overall effect was astonishing rather than alluring.

'My shirt, trousers, are where?' she asked Madeline.

'In the ship's laundry.'

'Daniel, your clothes!' she said coldly, then remembered herself and added 'Please?'

'I – you – my – um, sorry?' stammered Daniel, staring at Liore in complete disbelief.

Madeline put a hand over her eyes.

'Take your clothes off, Daniel,' she said. 'Liore needs to dress as a boy.'

'But, but, but –'

'You can have her dressing gown to get back to your cabin. Now undress! Do it for the British Empire.'

Faced with no other choice, Daniel turned away, closed his eyes and began to strip. One by one he dropped the items of clothing behind him. Now naked and burning with shame, Daniel stood with his back to the girls with his eyes closed and his hands over his groin. Suddenly he felt something being draped over his shoulders.

'Lucky Julia,' said Madeline admiringly behind Daniel. 'Liore, how is the fit?'

'Legs, arms, slightly long, otherwise good.'

'You have dropped into battlespeak, Liore.'

'Battle, has begun. Daniel, with Madeline, stay. Protect.'

'But people will talk. I'm only wearing a dressing gown, it looks like I am here to, ah . . .'

Daniel heard the door click.

'Liore has gone,' said Madeline. 'Turn around and open your eyes, Daniel – oh, and best to tie the cord on the dressing gown first.'

Daniel turned, and saw that Madeline was holding two pistols. She held one out to him.

'Do you know what this is?'

'Webley Bulldog, it's a five-shot police pistol. My father has one on his study wall.'

'Have you ever used one?'

'No.'

'Any pistol?'

'No. Just target rifles at school sports.'

'Well then, lots to learn.'

'You must think I'm really pathetic.'

'Pathetic? No. The only person who thinks you are pathetic is you, Daniel. I think . . . I think that you have grown up into a very fine young man, but that nobody has bothered to tell you.'

'I still think we should not be alone together,' said Daniel.

'You would leave me at the mercy of the Lionhearts?'

'No.'

'Then we *should* be alone together. Here, take one of the Webleys, I'll show you how to use it.'

'You – you know how to shoot?'

'My father is a policeman. He believes that girls should be able to look after themselves because there may not always be a man handy to defend them.'

Daniel took the gun from her and examined it, checking the chambers and action. After some instructions from Madeline he felt confident that he could point the dangerous end at an enemy and look threatening. He extinguished the lamp.

'I'll take first watch,' he said to Madeline. 'Sleep with your gun in your hand, on the floor, behind your bed.'

'What?' exclaimed Madeline.

'If you were an assassin, where would you look first?'

'On the bed – oh, I see.'

'Sunrise is just before 6 am, you must take over then.'

Chapter 8

WARRIOR

Three Lionhearts made their way along the darkened steerage corridor with the purser. The purser was holding a lantern, for the luxury of electric lights did not extend to this part of the ship.

'At this rate, five days to search the ship,' said the leader, Harris, to the purser.

'This is the last of the unoccupied steerage cabins,' replied the purser.

'Are you sure that Barold Chalmer has not been seen since the ship left Colombo?'

'He was last seen on the promenade deck as we entered the harbour. After that a hole was burned through his cabin door, a hole so large that you might put your fist through without touching the sides.'

'I must see that, but it can wait for daylight.'

'Here's the next cabin. Dodgeson, mind the door. Roberts, with me.'

The purser and two Lionhearts entered the cabin and began their search, but it did not take long.

'One second-class cabin and two first-class cabins are empty,' said the purser. 'They will not take long to search.'

'We can search the cargo holds and mail rooms by day, it's the occupied cabins that will be difficult,' said Harris.

'If the weapon is not found anywhere else, I can call a lifeboat drill for two hours. That will empty the cabins.'

'There are only nine of us to search the bags and berths of nine hundred passengers. We can't do that in two hours.'

'You said the weapon is about two feet long, and resembles a stocky rifle with three barrels.'

'That is the only description we have, and the source was not one of us.'

'No matter. The point is that the thing is too big to conceal easily. With seventy seconds per passenger over two hours, you and your people can certainly do the searches. Come along, only one cabin in second class.'

They emerged from the cabin and looked up and down the corridor. The purser held his lantern up. The corridor was empty.

'Where the hell is Dodgeson?' whispered Harris.

Dodgeson woke to find himself bound and in darkness. He was not gagged, and he would have said 'Is anyone there?' but no sound came out of his mouth. He shouted for help but produced no more sound than before. Now in considerable fear of the unknown, he screamed. No scream reached his ears from his lips.

'By your leave, speaking courtly. William Henry Dodgeson, by now you should have realised that you cannot make any sound. I have a device that is generating standing waves in your mouth. It is just like a gag, but not as uncomfortable. You can speak, however, and I shall see the words on a little screen. So far you have said, "Is anyone there?" and "Help! Help! Help!"'

Who are you? asked Dodgeson.

'I am Battle Commander Liore of the Imperial War Academy operational crews. Having the rank of Battle Commander means that I have the authority to charge, assess and execute any British citizen found to be endangering the empire of his majesty King Charles the Third by an act of treason.'

What? There is no such king.

'In 1989 he will be crowned in Melbourne, and he will reign over an empire most perilously endangered by the actions of a group of traitors called the Lionhearts – eighty-eight years earlier.'

I don't understand. None of that has happened.

'But it will. I am from the future.'

Impossible.

'All too possible, William Dodgeson. There will be a century of total war between Britain and Germany because of the Lionhearts and what they did, in fact it will be called the Century War. How do you justify trying to provoke a war between Britain and Germany?'

Socialist traitors in the government are letting the empire fall apart. We need a good war to clear the air and pull the empire back together.

'Then by the authority assigned to my rank I find you guilty of treason. Do you wish to say anything by way of appeal?'

Look, even if you are from the future, you have no authority here. Your king is not even born yet.

'I follow the letter of the law. You are a British citizen, and you have committed treason by attempting to bomb the opening of parliament in Melbourne, then bomb the train carrying the heir to the British throne in Albury. You are still trying to start a war between Britain and Germany, and that endangers the empire for the century to come. Do you have anything else to say in your defence?'

I demand a proper hearing before –

'You are found guilty of treason and have forfeited your right of appeal.'

What? You have no right to do this.

'These proceedings are at an end, William Dodgeson. So, you wanted a war to clear the air? I come from over a century in the future, and I can assure you that billions are dead, Britain has been occupied by Germany, and the air is most certainly not clear.'

It was two hours after dawn when Daniel awoke. Moving only his eyes, he took in the cabin. Madeline was at his feet, crouching with the Webley in her hand.

'Good morning, miss,' he whispered.

'My first night with a boy,' said Madeline. 'A gun in my hand, on the floor, hiding behind a bed. They never put this sort of thing in romantic novels.'

'I suppose not. Have you heard from Liore?'

'Not a word, not a note.'

'So what now?'

'We stay here.'

'Here? So what am I to wear? Liore's dress?'

'Not quite your colour. Best to stay in her dressing gown.'

'If anyone sees us together like this they will think the worst.'

'So?'

'Don't you care for your good name?'

'If I get spots on my name I shall change it. You should do the same.'

'You don't have a family with expectations back in Australia?'

'I have a mother and father in Ballarat. Mother

no longer has expectations. One day Father will be proud of me.'

'Oh. Well, I suppose I care nothing for what my family thinks.'

'Then why worry about good names, yours or mine?'

Daniel had no answer for this. He stood up slowly. There was a chair jamming the door shut, and the table had been cleared of the device that Liore had been building. It had been replaced by bread, cold tea and cheese.

'You did all this without waking me?' asked Daniel.

'My father taught me how burglars move with stealth.'

'I like the sound of your father. He sounds better than mine.'

With the search of the vacant cabins complete, the Lionhearts devised a new plan for those that were occupied. As the passengers appeared in the saloons for breakfast, the Lionhearts went to their cabins with the purser's master keys and did their searches. By the end of breakfast all of the second-class and half of the first-class cabins had been searched. Part of steerage was done at lunchtime. When not searching the cabins they went through the storage areas. It was in the late afternoon that another mystery was brought to the notice of Harris.

'I swear, I only turned my back on Roberts for a few seconds!' said Moore, gesturing behind him, then to the sack of mail he had been searching.

'Was it as well lit as it is now?' asked Harris.

'Yes, yes, even brighter. I'd borrowed his knife to cut the cord on the mail sack and turned away from him for about five seconds. I said, "That's got it open", and turned back to return his knife, but he was gone. No footsteps, not a sound.'

Harris looked up and down the walkway. It would have taken a dozen strides in either direction to reach cover. The walkway was metal, so if Roberts had run, the sound of his boots would have been easily heard. Harris looked up. Behind the walkway was a crate perhaps eight feet high.

'Get a couple of trunks from storage,' he said. 'I want to look on top of that thing.'

Standing on two trunks Harris looked over the top of the crate. In spite of the tropical heat there were some drops of clear liquid on the wood. He dipped his finger in one, and found it to have the consistency of saliva.

'No mystery. Someone pulled Roberts up here while your back was turned,' he said.

'No mystery?' exclaimed Moore. 'Who or what could lift a fully grown man straight up there in a second without making any sound at all?'

'That thing from the *Millennium*,' said Harris, trying not to sound fearful.

'But – but it's an animal. You saw what it did to Sir Bernard and his guards.'

'I smell a German plot. Notice how it only kills Lionhearts. I have heard of guard dogs trained to bite people who do not speak German. Perhaps it's a trained ape being used as an assassin.'

'An ape with claws?'

'Why not? Germany has a colony in New Guinea, there are all sorts of strange things there. I wager that someone put it aboard the *Millennium* as a test, to see how much damage it could do.'

'Well, what's it doing on the *Andromeda*?'

'Probably the same as us – searching for Barry Porter and that secret weapon. We must be on our guard, and never go anywhere alone.'

Roberts awoke in some dimly lit space that was not familiar to him. He was tied spread-eagled on his back, and standing over him with a foot to either side of his chest was one of the stewards who had vanished from the *Millennium* in Colombo.

'By your leave, speaking courtly,' said a husky voice.

Who are you? Roberts tried to ask, then added helplessly, *What have you done to my voice?*

The steward held up a small, sleek, black thing.

'I am Battle Commander Liore of the Imperial War Academy operational crews. The rank of Battle Commander allows me to charge, assess and execute any British citizen who endangers the empire of his majesty King Charles the Third by an act of treason. Your voice has just been cancelled, but I can read what you say.'

Whatever you are going to do, you can't get away with it.

Liore dropped to her knees, straddling his chest. She reached out and clasped a hand around his throat.

'I am from a century in the future, John James Roberts. You Lionhearts have made two attempts to start a war between Britain and Germany, one in Melbourne, the other in Albury. That is treason. Treason draws a sentence of death. How do you plead?'

You have no authority. You're mad!

'No plea is taken as a plea of guilty, so you are guilty of treason, as charged.'

Harris paced beside one of the lifeboats as the makeshift antenna for his spark gap transmitter was rigged on the superstructure of the *Andromeda*. It was half an hour past midnight, and the ship was only dimly outlined by the lights on the upper decks. Somewhere in the distance someone was playing a piano and people were clapping in time.

'Count the men,' he said to Moore as they worked.

'I counted them only a minute ago.'

'Count them again.'

'Six,' said Moore after a moment.

'So only Roberts and Dodgeson are missing. Are you sure nobody has seen anything at all?'

'Nothing that could lift a grown man like Roberts and –'

'Enough. Hurry up with the transmitter.'

Daniel sat on Madeline's bed and dictated as he stared at the screen of the radiocomm wired into whatever Liore had been building. During the day Liore's shirt, coat and trousers had been returned from the laundry, so he was now dressed more normally. Propped up with the pillows from both beds, Madeline recorded everything in a notebook. The exchange of messages was brief and cryptic.

'They must be finished,' said Daniel after a period of silence. 'Can you read the exchange back?'

'LION SCOUT TO LION PRIDE STOP PROCEED STOP,' said Madeline. 'That's followed by, ACKNOWLEDGED STOP PROCEED STOP. Then they sent MOST CABINS SEARCHED STOP ALL MAIL AND CARGO SEARCHED

STOP FINISHING FIRSTS STOP OUT STOP. There is, ACKNOWLEDGED, then nothing.'

'The Lionhearts are going to search the last of the first-class cabins,' said Daniel. 'That includes this one.'

'They can't do that!' exclaimed Madeline.

'They certainly can,' replied Daniel. 'Maids and stewards have keys to get into all cabins to tidy up, so why not Lionhearts?'

Daniel put his ear against the door and listened for sounds in the corridor outside.

'There is a sign on the door saying we are not to be disturbed,' said Madeline. 'Liore put it there when she started building that thing with all the tubes and coils of wire.'

'That will not stop them once all the other cabins have been searched.'

'The door is jammed shut with that chair.'

'Then they will be certain that this is the cabin they want. They will take a fire axe and break in – there! I can hear them arguing with someone in a cabin down the corridor.'

'What can we do?'

Daniel thought frantically. *What would Liore do? Irrelevant, nobody can do what Liore does. Barry? He would hide under the bed and say he didn't do nothin'. Dad would call the police, but there are no police here. Emily would say something so stunningly embarrassing that the Lionhearts would cringe, not know where to look, then back out of the cabin and close the door behind them – but that's it!*

'Take off your clothes, get into bed,' he said to Madeline without turning.

'What?' exclaimed Madeline. 'Daniel Lang, how dare –'

'Take off your clothes and get into bed! Do it. If they find us in bed together they will think that's why we have been hiding in here for so long.'

'But – oh. I – I – um, well all right, but keep your back turned while I undress.'

Daniel took the chair away from the door and extinguished the light. Standing in the darkness, he pressed his ear against the door, straining to hear what was going on outside. Seconds passed, then minutes. He removed his shirt, then his shoes and socks.

'What is happening?' asked Madeline.

'People are still shouting.'

'Even I can hear them now. Daniel, I think –'

'They're coming!' hissed Daniel, removing his trousers and flinging them aside as he made for the bed.

'Now what are you doing?' asked Madeline as Daniel climbed in beside her.

'Putting my pistol and radiocomm under your pillow. Where is your gun?'

'In my hand.'

'Well, put it under the pillow.'

'But what if —'

'Trust me, Madeline, no girl takes a boy to bed with a loaded Webley in her hand.'

They settled down under the covers. There were more raised voices outside as the Lionhearts reached another cabin where the inhabitants had expected a little more privacy in first class.

'Do you think this looks suspicious enough?' asked Daniel.

'Daniel Lang, was that meant to be a joke?'

'Of course not! It's just that this is all a bit unfamiliar to me.'

'Same for me.'

'But I've seen pictures. Barry had a book called *A Scientific Guide to Human Reproductive Biology*, and there were some rather lurid pictures on page thirty-seven. It's in my cabin if you want to have a read.'

'If we live through the next five minutes, I'll be sure to. In the meantime we shall have to rely on your memory.'

'Just keep your arms around me, but when they come in remember to scream and look embarrassed.'

'Look embarrassed, he says.'

'Actually, do you speak French?'

'*Mais oui, je parle très bien français, mais —*'

'Good, good. When they break in just cower behind me, speak a few words of French, then let me do all the talking.'

'If only my mother could see me now. Lying in bed with a boy in a first-class cabin, with two pistols under my pillow, pretending to be a French courtesan for the benefit of some armed men from a British secret society who are trying to start a worldwide war.'

'Just send a postcard from Port Said saying, "Wish you were here" and – what are you doing?'

'Making us look more convincing.'

'Oh. But –'

'Come now, Daniel, as lovers we need tousled hair and some of my make-up smeared over your face.'

'But surely not –'

'Daniel, this is for Britain, this is for the king.'

'But what if Muriel found out?'

'Well *I'm* not going to tell her!'

They waited. Beyond the door the Lionhearts entered a third cabin, to be greeted by a shriek of alarm and some angry shouting. The minutes passed. The Lionhearts surprised the inhabitants of a fourth cabin.

'I, ah, do apologise for this,' said Daniel.

'Can't be helped. I never thought I could disguise myself by taking my clothes off.'

'They are taking rather a long time.'

'I suppose the other passengers are being less than cooperative.'

'Perhaps I should have waited at the door a bit longer.'

'No matter,' replied Madeline. 'You were very clever to think of this.'

'I learned it from my sister, Emily.'

'Your sister did *this*?' gasped Madeline.

'Not as far as I know. It's just that she has a way with people. Her attitude is that if you do or say something so incredibly embarrassing that people just don't know where to look, they will probably go away and leave you alone.'

'Clever,' said Madeline. 'Emily must be a formidable girl.'

'Formidable? Try growing up as her younger brother.'

They heard the sound of a key rattling in the lock, then the door was flung open. Several men rushed into the cabin, and one of them flicked the switch to the light. Daniel and Madeline sat up together. Madeline screamed and cowered behind Daniel. Her scream was followed by a long silence.

'You filthy young devils,' hissed the scandalised purser at last.

Two of the Lionhearts smirked, but Harris scowled at the sight of such immoral behaviour.

'Monique Cluny and Lucielle Chasseur are supposed to be here,' said Harris.

'I am Daniel Lang, from another cabin,' said Daniel softly.

'And you, young woman?'

'*Daniel, je ne comprends pas,*' said Madeline.

'She only speaks French,' said Daniel, who then turned to Madeline. '*Comment tu t'appelles?*'

'*Ah, je m'appelle Monique Cluny,*' said Madeline. '*Il y a un problème?*'

'She asks if there is a problem,' said Daniel.

'There will be when your parents are informed, you decadent young wretches. Where is Lucielle Chasseur?' asked Harris.

'Lucielle? We, ah, suggested that she might stay in my cabin because it's, um, nicer there,' said Daniel.

'When did you last see her?'

'Ah, some days ago. Four or five days, I think.'

'Four or five days!' exclaimed Harris.

'We pretended to be seasick. The stewards brought us meals.'

'Young woman, how long have you known your travelling companion, this Lucielle Chasseur?' asked Harris.

'She doesn't speak English,' Daniel reminded him.

'Well, you ask her.'

'I already know her story, sir. They met in Colombo, in a hotel, just before the *Andromeda* sailed. They were both travelling alone, and Lucielle speaks French and English so it seemed like a good idea to share a cabin on the *Andromeda* so that Lucielle could translate –'

'Get on with it!'

'They were walking from the hotel to the docks to board the steam launch for this ship when some ruffians attacked them, but I came along and drove them off.'

'Yes, yes, yes, and you were not slow to take advantage of Mademoiselle Cluny's gratitude,' said the purser.

'Did Mademoiselle Chasseur mention a youth named Barry Porter, or perhaps Barold Chalmer?' asked Harris.

'No, sir.'

The purser turned to Harris, his face grim.

'Do you have any more questions?' he asked.

'Is your cabin number fifteen, Master Lang?'

'Yes.'

'Mademoiselle Chasseur is not there.'

'I can't account for that, sir.'

'She is probably elsewhere on the ship, in similar circumstances to yourselves,' said Harris. 'Purser, I have heard all that I need to.'

'In that case, we had best leave these disgraceful young people to their amusement,' said the purser, turning back to Daniel and Madeline. 'You can both be certain that your families will be informed of what I have just witnessed. Good night to you both.'

The men filed out of the room, and the purser's key rattled in the lock again. Daniel and Madeline sat absolutely still, listening to the footsteps receding along the corridor.

'It worked!' whispered Madeline, putting her arms around Daniel and kissing his cheek. 'What a fantastic warrior you are!'

'Warrior? What do you mean? I just let myself get caught stark naked in bed with a girl and did a lot of fast talking.'

'You drove five armed men out of the cabin by being very brave and clever. You may not be a conventional warrior, but you are a warrior without any doubt.'

Daniel put a finger to his lips, listening for any sign that the Lionhearts were returning, or might have left someone at the door. The moments dragged past like hours.

'Well . . . should we get dressed again?' asked Madeline.

'They may come back.'

'Good point. So when will we know they are not coming back?'

'The radiocomm will make scratchy sounds.'

'Daniel, cheri?'

'Yes?'

'Cela t'as plu?'

'Very funny.'

'Je l'ai trouvé sensationnel. Et tu?'

'Stop it!'

'Just teasing.'

Some seconds of silence passed, with only the distant rumble of the ship's triple expansion engines as a background. Madeline turned and reached under the pillow. Pulling out the radiocomm, she held it at arm's length and pointed it at them.

'Well, I do wish I could take a photo of us just as we are, so that I could send it to my mother. Horrid old bat, taking me away from my father and trying to marry me to that draper's son.'

'Give it here, please,' said Daniel, taking the radiocomm from her and putting it back under the pillow.

'Daniel?'

'*Oui* – oh, for goodness sake, I mean *yes*?'

'What do you think of Liore?'

'She's wonderful, but she's not . . .'

'Not human?'

'Not really.'

'Then what is she to you? Why did you want her to kill you?'

'Because I worship her. She is the Angel of Death, and I am honoured to have been brushed by her wings. Liore is my queen. I am not worthy to touch her.'

'That's ridiculous. What if she were wounded? Would you let her bleed to death rather then touch her?'

'The sight of blood makes me faint.'

'So you *would* let her bleed to death?'

'No! I suppose I would bandage her wounds – but I would apologise for touching her.'

'Daniel, Daniel, you are more twisted than –'

'The radiocomm!'

A soft, scratchy sound was coming from beneath the pillow. Daniel snatched the radiocomm out and looked at the flickers on the screen, then translated the Morse code for Madeline.

'THREE LEFT STOP CREATURE FROM MILLENNIUM ABOARD ANDROMEDA STOP KILLING US STOP SEARCH COMPLETE STOP WEAPON NOT ON ANDROMEDA STOP PORTER MUST HAVE WEAPON ON AJAX STOP INTERCEPT AJAX AT PORT SAID STOP STAY CLEAR OF ANDROMEDA IF YOU VALUE YOUR LIVES STOP OUT STOP.'

Daniel and Madeline looked at each other for a moment, then Daniel got out of bed.

'I think it's safe to get dressed again,' he said. 'I wonder how they know Barry is on the *Ajax*?'

'Barry would have escaped from this ship on one of the tenders,' said Madeline. 'The Lionhearts would have asked all the tender captains if they had taken a short, ratty boy with a large, tatty bag to another ship.'

'Oh. And what was all that about the creature from the *Millennium*?'

'A man on the *Millennium* worked out that I was a girl and tried to – to have his way with me three nights before Colombo. Liore splattered him all over the poop deck.'

Barnes awoke to water being splashed on his face. He was bound hand and foot.

A faintly illuminated face floated in the darkness in front of him.

'By your leave, speaking courtly. Benjamin Barnes, I am Battle Commander Liore of the Imperial War Academy operational crews,' declared the face. 'The rank of Battle Commander allows me to charge, assess and execute any British citizen who endangers the empire of his majesty King Charles the Third by an act of treason.'

Untie me at once, you damn – Barnes realised that he could not hear his own voice.

'Your voice has been silenced, but I can read what you say,' said Liore. 'You are trying to start a war that will lead to the deaths of six billion people over the next hundred years. How do you plead?'

Britons never shall be slaves!

'I do not accept pleas of insanity. Guilty as charged.'

Harris and Edwards stood with their backs to the railing of the aft games deck. There was only one dim light nearby, and they both had their guns drawn. There was a clear field of fire for twenty feet across the deck.

'It has to cross clear space to reach us,' said Harris. 'If it comes, I will be ready. Now get the jolly boat ready to lower.'

'Don't like it,' said Edwards as he began to untie the boat's ropes. 'That thing can see in the dark and we can't.'

'Whatever it is, a gun will stop it,' said Harris.

'But what is it?'

'Some sort of trained ape with claws. Fantastically strong.'

'But how'd it get aboard?'

'Use your brain. It probably swam out and climbed up the anchor chain in Colombo. Now get that boat lowered.'

'Oi! Something over there,' said Edwards, pointing.

'Don't shoot!' called a familiar voice. 'It's me, Greely.'

'Purser! What the hell are you doing here?'

'I'm going with you.'

'Absolutely not, sir!' exclaimed Harris.

'What do you think we're running, a bloody ferry?' added Edwards.

'You can't leave me on the *Andromeda*. Not with that thing on the loose. It knows I helped you. It knows I'm a Lionheart.'

'You're no Lionheart. Five hundred pounds of good British money bought your loyalty.'

'That's no good to me if I'm dead. Besides, I know all about that weapon you're after. Just say that thing corners me. I'll agree to say all I know to the officials at —'

A shot barked out and the purser fell to the deck. Harris walked across to the dark shape and groped for his wrist. After confirming that the purser no longer had a pulse, Harris went through his pockets and retrieved the bribe. His bag appeared to contain nothing more than clothes and papers. Harris flung the bag over the side.

'Edwards, get him into the sea and clean up that mess,' said Harris.

'Edwards has been charged, assessed and executed,' said Liore from behind him.

Harris managed to get the gun out of his belt, but not before Liore's foot connected with his jaw. As she seized his wrist he began firing, but she twisted around under his arm, bending it back and sweeping his right foot from under him with her heel. As Harris fell, Liore smashed the hand holding the gun down onto the deck, so that he dropped it. The gun was in her hand as they stood up.

'I only regret that I have but one life to give for my king,' said Harris as he raised his hands.

Liore flung the gun over the side, then warily closed on Harris.

'Captain Harris, what a hero you were destined to become,' said Liore. 'Terrier Harris, scourge of the huns. If only they knew.'

Harris lashed out with a kick to her head, but Liore did a pivot-dodge and brushed the kick past harmlessly. Harris threw several more kicks, but Liore managed to dodge them all.

'I know all about you, Terrier Harris. I know that you spent time in Paris, and there you learned savate, French foot boxing. You can kick as readily as other men can punch, and your left hand has been hardened like an iron club.'

'What traitor told you all that?' asked Harris.

'I am from a century in the future, Harris. I have read your biography, there is even a Harris Gymnasium at the Imperial War Academy. In that gymnasium I learned UBS, Unified British Style. That makes me a very dangerous girl indeed.'

'Girl?' gasped Harris.

'Girl, Captain Harris. Thanks to the Century War that you started, even girls from good families get to kill people. I have been training since the age of five, and I am not yet sixteen. You created me. Not a pretty sight, am I?'

Liore dropped and swung a leg out to trip Harris, but Harris skipped over her foot and lashed a kick at her head. Liore brushed the kick past and dropped onto her back. Harris closed in for the kill, not knowing that UBS taught people to fight on their backs. Liore's foot caught his next kick, then her other foot slammed into a pressure point just above his knee. Harris dropped, but was back on his feet in an instant, a knife drawn from his boot. He and Liore faced off again.

'Captain Peter Harris, I am Battle Commander Liore of the Imperial War Academy operational crews,' declared Liore. 'The rank of Battle Commander allows me to charge, assess and execute any British citizen who endangers the empire of his majesty King Charles the Third by an act of treason.'

'Just try to execute me, you mad bitch.'

'Actually I could have, several times over, but I am stepping outside the regulations to indulge myself and really hurt you first. I like hurting people that I hate. You have trashed the world, allowed Britain to be occupied, and caused six billion deaths. You could have me on a charge for killing you slowly, but I have a feeling you will not tell anyone.'

Harris feinted a low kick, then lunged at Liore with his left hand. He caught her in the ribs a moment before her fist swept up from a block to backhand him across the temple. On the return swing she closed with him, and her elbow caught him across the mouth, smashing teeth and dislocating his jaw, yet Harris rolled backwards as Liore locked his left arm and tried to snap the elbow.

Harris now swept Liore's foot, and although she rolled as she came down on the deck, breaking her fall, she did not quite avoid Harris's knife. Thinking he had injured her seriously, Harris now stabbed down, but Liore twisted aside and the blade plunged into the well-scrubbed wood of the deck and stuck fast. Harris made the mistake of trying to draw the knife out of the deck, and lingered just long enough for Liore to land a kick on his left elbow, snapping it. The Lionheart seemed immune to pain as he bounced to his feet again, but Liore tangled her legs in his and slammed him back down on the deck. Harris was rolled onto his stomach, and felt his legs locked together as Liore pressed down on him. She had one hand on his jaw and another on the back of his head.

'I believe you know what comes next,' said Liore, who then snapped his neck.

The pain from a broken rib and several cuts and bruises was beginning to make itself felt as Liore heaved Harris and the purser over the side to join Edwards in the Red Sea.

❂

While the fight at the stern of the ship had been taking place, Daniel and Madeline had been crouched behind their beds with their pistols trained on the cabin door. By now they were almost wishing for someone to burst in to relieve the boredom.

'Daniel, can I ask a question?' asked Madeline.

'You just have,' replied Daniel, who was fairly sure that it would be something intensely personal.

'Where does Liore come from, and where did she get those incredible inventions?'

'She comes from Melbourne, and as for the radiocomms and weapon, see here.'

Daniel flipped a coin across to Madeline.

'It's just a shilling,' she said.

'It's the king's shilling. It was given to me when I entered Liore's squad.'

Madeline looked more closely at the coin.

'CHARLES III REX . . . *1997*?' she gasped.

'Yes.'

'But – but that's ninety-six years in the future.'

'Liore is from the future, too. So are her radiocomms and weapon.'

Madeline looked up from the coin to Daniel and frowned sceptically.

'People cannot travel through time,' she said bluntly.

'We are all travelling into the future,' said Daniel, 'but in Liore's future the scientists devised a machine to fling people and weapons backwards through time. She broke into their laboratory with some very brave cadets, intending to travel back to this year to stop something terrible called the Century War. All but Liore and a youth named Fox were killed in the fighting.'

Madeline thought about this, glanced doubtfully at the shilling, then tried to bend it.

'Say, just say, you're speaking the truth: how does, how will this war start?'

'Federal parliament was to be bombed when it opened last May. We stopped that. Liore also saved the crown prince from assassination in Albury.'

'I read in the newspapers about a railway wagon blowing up.'

'That was it. Either event would have triggered the Century War between Britain and Germany.'

'So it won't happen?'

'Liore is from the future, so she gets new memories of the future when history changes. She now remembers her own weapon being used to start the war. The Lionhearts on the *Millennium* use it to attack the entire German fleet.'

Madeline flipped the shilling back to Daniel.

'I don't believe any of that, but nothing else makes sense, so I might have to. I –'

Daniel held up his hand for silence as the radiocomm in his pocket vibrated. He pressed a green stud to accept the connection.

'Liore?' he asked.

'Approaching door, don't shoot,' said Liore from the unit.

Daniel opened the door just as Liore arrived. There was blood down her left side.

'About shirt, sorry,' she said.

'The Lionhearts did this to you?' whispered Madeline as Daniel closed the door and locked it.

'To Lionhearts, did worse.'

'You're bleeding,' said Daniel.

'Do assessment, then repairs,' said Liore, looking straight at Daniel.

'Me?' quavered Daniel.

'Your sewing, high standard, was told, by Emily.'

'I'll need to soak some thread and a needle in iodine solution,' said Madeline.

'The infirmary has iodine,' said Daniel.

'That's where I stole this while visiting you,' said Madeline, holding up a little bottle. 'Soldiers do tend to get injured.'

Daniel was about to insist that Madeline do the sewing when a scene flashed through his mind, a scene from only four months past, although it seemed like a lifetime ago. Liore, lying wounded on a packing case. Barry arriving with a few stolen things that might be useful. Emily boiling water. Fox sewing up the wound in Liore's stomach.

If Fox can sew up a wound, so can I, Daniel decided.

Madeline brought towels and a bowl with needles, thread and scissors soaking in iodine. Liore removed the shirt to reveal a long but shallow gash down the ribs on her left side. Her breasts were smaller and firmer than Madeline's, and were padded out with quite astonishing pectoral muscles. Liore raised her left arm and rested it on Daniel's shoulder. Madeline handed him a facecloth soaked in iodine, and he began trying to clean up the blood around the wound with his eyes closed.

'For goodness sake, Daniel, open your eyes!' snapped Madeline.

'Is problem?' asked Liore.

'Please, this is very hard for me,' pleaded Daniel. 'I don't cope well with the sight of blood.'

'My blood is not real blood,' said Liore.

'What do you mean?'

'It works better than real blood, but – but never mind, it is too hard to explain.'

Daniel teetered on the brink of nausea for the entire half hour that it took to sew up Liore's wound, but he did a very neat job. Finally he was able to turn his patient over to Madeline to do the bandaging. He sat on the edge of a bed, looked at the blood and iodine on his hands, and then made the mistake of thinking about what he had just done. The room began revolving before Daniel's eyes as he fainted.

Chapter 9

HUNTER

The following morning Liore and Madeline attended breakfast together in the saloon. Liore showed no sign of stiffness from her injuries, and her dress covered her cuts and bruises. Daniel arrived ten minutes later, still looking pale. He was beckoned over by the chief engineer and some officers as he tried to decide whether or not to join the girls.

'I've not seen much of you down in the engine hall lately,' said the engineer as Daniel sat down.

'I've not been well, sir,' Daniel replied.

'Ha ha, a touch of *mal de mer*, my lad?' laughed an officer.

'Young Daniel is tougher than he looks,' said the chief engineer. 'Came to the aid of those two young ladies over there in Colombo. Saw off five ruffians, all by himself.'

'Five of them, you say?' asked another officer.

'At least five, the young ladies said,' another officer added.

'There were only three, sir,' said Daniel.

'Ha ha, *only* three, he says.'

'How are your injuries?' asked the engineer.

'My skin is still blue, green and purple in places, but I am well enough,' said Daniel.

'So, a real young warrior, this schoolboy!' exclaimed the second officer.

'Not at all, sir, I only let myself be beaten by the attackers to distract them until the police arrived.'

'Modest, too,' said the engineer. 'Well, you're welcome in the engine hall whenever you like.'

'I shall come down in the afternoon. The young ladies want me to sit with them on the promenade deck this morning.'

'Do they indeed? Mind yourself, lad. The next thing you know they'll be inviting you to walk arm-in-arm to lunch, and in London you will be asked to meet their mothers.'

If only you knew, thought Daniel.

'I say, has anyone seen the purser?' asked the third officer.

'Not seen him since yesterday,' said the engineer.

'I saw him late last night,' said Daniel. 'He was with some men, checking cabins. I am not sure why.'

'Interesting. There have been several complaints this morning. It seems that Mr Greely exceeded his authority last night in his zeal to find some stolen property. The captain wants a word with him, but a steward said that his bed has not been slept in.'

'Strange,' said the third officer. 'Where could he

be? Think I should send the stewards in search of him?'

'Seems a good idea,' said the second officer.

When Daniel walked out onto the promenade deck he found that Liore and Madeline had saved a deckchair between them. He was not sure what to make of this, but had the impression that he was being flanked.

'Ladies, may I join you?' he asked.

'Welcome, Daniel, do sit down,' said Madeline.

'By your leave, speaking courtly,' said Liore.

Slowly and uneasily, Daniel sat down between the two girls.

'Any news of the purser?' asked Madeline softly.

'Nobody has set eyes on him since . . . since we saw him last night,' replied Daniel.

'Perhaps he has had an accident,' suggested Liore. 'Ships can be very dangerous.'

They sat in silence for a while, with the balmy breeze of the ship's passage blowing over them. Liore glanced about, then took out her radiocomm, holding it like a little book.

'Daniel, you have learned a lot about the operation of the radiocomms,' she said. 'For someone born a century before they were invented, you have done well.'

'Thank you, um, Commander.'

'But you still have a lot to learn.'

'Well, I *am* only a schoolboy.'

'What happens when you press this stud?'

'That switches it on.'

'And this one?'

'It lights up the screen.'

'*All* the studs light up the screen, Daniel. This stud also activates transceive.'

'I don't know that word.'

'It means transmit and receive. Only a double click puts it into receive-only.'

'Oh. Thank you, I shall remember that and – Oh, good heavens!'

'What is it?' asked Madeline.

Daniel went totally limp, and had he not been lying down he might have fainted again. He seriously considered jumping over the side.

'It was transceiving last night,' said Liore when Daniel proved incapable of replying. 'My unit was on receive.'

'Daniel, what does she mean?' asked Madeline.

'Battle Commander Liore heard *everything* that went on in your cabin last night.'

'Oh – ah, *merde*!' exclaimed Madeline.

Liore folded her hands over the radiocomm and looked out over the Red Sea.

'Remember, Daniel and I both speak French,' she said to Madeline.

'I can explain,' ventured Daniel.

'Go on,' said Liore.

'Actually, I can't.'

'Neither can I,' said Madeline.

'I think you did very well,' said Liore. 'You drove the Lionhearts out of the cabin without firing a shot. If only all battles could be settled as cleverly. Oh, and the camera was working too, so when Madeline held it up and –'

'Don't show me!' exclaimed Daniel, putting his hands over his face.

'Can I have a look?' asked Madeline. Liore pressed some keys then handed the radiocomm to her. 'Oh. Here we are, sitting up together.'

'Please!' exclaimed Daniel.

'How can I watch more?' said Madeline.

'Press this stud and you go back in five minute jumps, this to go forward, this to play. The sound is off, because we are in a public place.'

'Oh! Here's Daniel, getting into his trousers. Nice legs.'

'Here shark, shark, shark, I feel like jumping over the side,' said Daniel.

Liore stood up slowly, then gestured along the promenade deck. 'Come along Daniel, we have much to discuss, especially regarding the weapon.'

They set off at a casual pace, leaving Madeline to the images of the night before.

'I suppose you think I'm pathetic,' said Daniel.

'Actually no, but more of that in a moment. Daniel, until Colombo I felt so betrayed by you. I considered you my friend, and I was so angry when I thought you had betrayed me. I wanted to kill you slowly and really hurt you because my feelings got the better of me. That is not good discipline. Being alone in your century is eroding my training. I have no CO to give me orders.'

'CO?'

'Commander of Operations. Last night, after the Lionhearts left the cabin, you called me your queen. I am a lot of things, but not that. Do you know who *I* admire most out of our former squad?'

'Fox, probably. He can do everything, and –'

'No.'

'Then it's Muriel. She's the most alluring girl in the whole world.'

'No.'

'Then who? Barry has cartloads of cunning, but nobody in their right mind would admire him. Emily can force people to do things by shouting at them, but so can a drill sergeant. That leaves nobody.'

'That leaves you.'

'What?' exclaimed Daniel, stopping dead and staring in astonishment at Liore.

'That leaves you.'

'I heard you the first time. *You* admire *me*?'

'On target – I mean true.'

'Why? I'm a skinny schoolboy, not a hero like you. I mean – look, a month ago I was bending over and getting caned by old Mr Jackson in front of the whole Applied Maths class for writing poetry about Muriel when I should have been doing equations.'

'You are also witty, innocent, brave, clever, kind, romantic and very resourceful. I want to be all of those things, but I am not, and never can be.'

'You're brave,' said Daniel.

'I have no fear at all, that is not bravery. I am good at killing people, but anyone can do that. It made me so sad to see you pining for Muriel, but I could do nothing. I solve problems by fighting and killing, but that could not help you.'

'This is impossible!' whispered Daniel, looking away from her and out to sea. 'I'm an insect, good for nothing, worthy of nobody. You are so far above me.'

'Silly Daniel. I really am a bit human, and I keep hearing about romance and the allure of the tropics. Last night I did something about it.'

'What? You found time to court a boy while you were killing Lionhearts?'

'Not quite. I let myself get wounded so that you would have to sew me up.'

'Liore! That is the most *twisted* thing I have ever heard.'

'So Death-Wish Daniel dares to call me twisted?'

Daniel thought about this, and decided that she had a very good point. 'I am . . . flattered,' he managed.

'Muriel is a fool for preferring Fox over you. You may not believe me, but it is true.'

They turned and walked back, both with their hands clasped behind them and their heads bowed. Other passengers smiled and nodded to each other, thinking that they were courting, but were a little too shy to hold hands.

'Returning to the fate of the world,' said Liore, 'I estimate that the *Ajax* will reach Port Said this evening. The *Andromeda* is due to dock there tomorrow morning.'

'Barry will have to really use his wits to stay alive with both you and the Lionhearts after him.'

'Barry is proving to be fantastically resilient, considering how far he has come, alone, without getting caught or killed. Like you, he is just a schoolboy, yet he has managed to flee halfway around the world with only quick wits and petty theft to rely upon. I achieved a first-class distinction in Hunter-Killer 507 at the Imperial War Academy, yet he has managed to stay one step ahead of me. That takes talent.'

'Are you going to kill him?'

'Were the fate of the world depending on his death, would you kill him?'

'I . . . I would have to be very sure,' said Daniel unhappily.

'Do you want me to spare him?'

'I . . . well . . . yes. We're mates.'

'What is mates? I hear the word a lot, but nobody defines it.'

'That's when boys are sort of best friends. You do things together, you are totally loyal to each other, and sometimes you even die for your mates.'

'Ah, I see. In my time, there are no more mates. The empire always comes first.'

They stood at the rail for a while, in silence. Daniel could see the distant shoreline of the Arabian Peninsula, which was a low line of lighter colour amid the horizon's shimmers. The Red Sea was definitely narrowing.

'Daniel, I am still trying to understand why Fox ran off with Muriel. He deserted our mission for her.'

'I noticed.'

'And she left you, yet you still love her?'

'Yes.'

'Why?'

'I don't know.'

'This is very confusing. All my life I have had the empire to live and die for. My CO gave the orders, and my squad followed me. Now I need advice and orders, but there is no CO. I have mutinied, and set myself the objective of stopping a war in the future. I shall probably do that, and I may survive.'

'But that's good.'

'Not so. I do not fit into your time, or into peace.'

'People don't always need an objective. Why not just live a normal life?'

'Because I am not normal, Daniel.'

'Of course you are.'

'I am genetically modified.'

'Oh. Did it hurt?'

'I am a monster. I have shot cadets for even kissing during missions, yet last night you and Muriel saved yourselves by a show of – of recreational reproductive activities. The worst possible operational crime actually saved the mission. Worse, I do believe I felt jealous for the first time. Why should Madeline feel your touch but not me? I let myself be wounded, and you know the rest. It was worth it. I cannot say why, and I do not like that. I want control, but all I get is uncertainty.'

'This is very hard to cope with,' said Daniel, who was by now feeling quite drained, and desperately in need of a coffee.

'You have no answers, so there is no more to discuss. Thank you for listening.'

'You're welcome.'

'What about Barry? He is dangerous and

resourceful. In my century he would have got a higher distinction than me in Hunter-Killer 507.'

'Leave Barry to Madeline and me. He is also more stupid and predictable than you could believe.'

'Then you had better do whatever you are going to do to Barry in Port Said. The disruptor that I am building in our cabin is nearly complete. If the worst happens and we cannot get the weapon back, the disruptor can destroy it from a distance.'

'But that's wonderful!' exclaimed Daniel. 'Why didn't you do this earlier?'

'Because a very, very large amount of energy will be released.'

'Oh. So Barry might find himself standing in front of a chap with wings and wearing a white nightshirt?'

'In his case it might be someone with horns and a pitchfork, but yes.'

'What happens if we fail? The *Millennium* will reach Port Said before the *Andromeda*. If the Lionhearts catch Barry there, they shall have the weapon.'

'Then there will be one last chance to stop them. That will be in September, at Wilhelmshaven.'

The *Andromeda* entered the Suez Canal at sunset, so that most of Daniel's view of this engineering marvel were the parts of the banks and the desert beyond that were illuminated by the lights of the ship. After dinner Daniel went to the forward deck, and stared out into the darkness in the hope of seeing something exotic like a camel. He was accosted by a girl named Elizabeth. She was about Muriel's height, and was dressed in a serge skirt and striped tennis shirt with puffed sleeves. She was so concerned about her complexion that she carried a frilly parasol everywhere, even at night. By now she had given up on courting Daniel, and was just looking for someone to complain to.

'Before we sailed everyone was telling me that I would see the world and have lots of adventures,' said Elizabeth peevishly as they waved to some soldiers on the bank. 'Instead, it has been boring, like living in a huge hotel, surrounded by water.'

'True,' replied Daniel. 'I have been surprised by how little one actually sees from a ship on a voyage halfway around the world.'

'So you are going to England to become a lawyer?'

'That is the plan. And what about yourself?'

'I am to go to lots of dinners, parties and balls, become sophisticated, and marry someone with a title.'

'The voyage must have been good practice for that.'

'The voyage has been hopeless. You are the only eligible boy in first class, and you have been, ah, secured by those girls you rescued in Colombo.'

'Not a bit of it,' said Daniel. 'We are indeed friends, but my heart was already lost to a girl named Muriel who jilted me for another.' Daniel decided to make it clear that his heart was still lost. 'She was quite wonderful at kissing, her lips were like warm roses.'

'Ah, now that explains so much about you. Who was your rival in love?'

'A soldier.'

'Only a soldier? You're handsome, your family is rich, your manners are perfect, you're a wonderful musician, yet she left you for a soldier?'

'I'm actually very shy, and he was more skilled at courtship than me,' said Daniel, hoping that this would explain everything. 'That counts for more than anything else.'

'It does indeed. My father has a tannery and is quite rich, but that will not help me charm some earl's son away from some ugly baggage who has a title as well as money. I need to excel at the arts of courtship.'

'We do seem to have some problems in common.'

'We do indeed,' said Elizabeth. 'Actually, would you be so kind as to escort me back to my cabin, Daniel? The air is getting rather chill.'

'Of course, but what about your mother?'

'Mother likes chill air. Come along.'

The moment that the cabin door closed behind

them, Elizabeth flung her arms around Daniel and jammed her lips against his. In spite of his continued yearnings for Muriel, Daniel had by now learned that there was something strangely magnetic about the female body. Once contact was made, it was very hard to pull away.

'What about your mother?' hissed Daniel once he was able to draw breath.

'She's making sure we are not disturbed,' whispered Elizabeth.

'What?'

'How was my kiss compared to Muriel's kisses?'

'Oh, much too hard, it made my lip bleed.'

'Sorry. What about this?'

Their second kiss was indeed an improvement, and Daniel said as much. Several kisses later they moved on to more subtle refinements.

'You need to pout a little as you prepare to kiss me, and to half-close your eyes,' said Daniel. 'And Muriel put a hand behind my head as we kissed, then traced her fingertips down my cheek and ran her tongue across her lips as we drew apart.'

'Oh, wonderful! Stand in front of that mirror so I can see what I'm doing.'

'But if Muriel finds out –'

'Muriel will never find out, and neither will whoever I marry. That is the whole point of shipboard romances. Yield to our circumstances,

Daniel. We shall both step ashore at London as far more accomplished lovers. You may even win Muriel back.'

Three hours later Daniel emerged from the cabin looking rather dishevelled, pulled the door shut, turned, and walked straight into Elizabeth's mother. He gasped with horror, and began casting about for words of explanation that he did not have when she smiled, kissed him lightly on the cheek, then winked and entered the cabin. Daniel returned to the forward deck, which was by now almost deserted. Madeline was waiting there.

'Where in the world have you been?' she demanded as she strode across to him. 'I've been looking for you for hours.'

Daniel was tempted to say that he had indeed been in heaven, but unlike Barry he had the sense not to say whatever popped into his head.

'Oh, here and there,' said Daniel. 'The smoking room, the gymnasium, my cabin, even here.'

'I checked all those places.'

'We must have just kept missing each other.'

'Do I smell perfume?'

'I was chatting with that girl Elizabeth – and her mother.'

'The one with the parasol who wears a tennis

blouse but never plays tennis?'

'Yes. We were practising deportment and manners and –'

'Later, later. Liore has finished the disruptor thing she's been building. We need to see how to use it.'

Daniel and Madeline entered the cabin, where the disruptor stood ready on the writing desk. Curiously, Liore was dressed in her old parade uniform from the future, and was standing to the left of the desk.

'My, my, you do look dashing in uniform!' exclaimed Madeline.

'From now on I can wear nothing else,' said Liore.

'What do you mean?'

'All in good time.'

Daniel had seen the pieces of the device as Liore had been assembling it, but now that it was complete, it still made no sense. There were several heavy batteries from the Lionhearts' spark gap transmitter, some coils and pipes, crystals mounted in ivory with sealing wax, glass tubes containing wires, crystals and mercury, six barrels, and brackets for the radiocomms. On the top was a small telescope. On the bottom was a makeshift switch in the shape of a trigger. Along the side was a row of light switches that had been taken from various parts of the ship, and two small electrical meters.

'By your leave, speaking courtly,' said Liore.

'Of course,' said Daniel.

'Have you ever wondered why Fox and I did not cease to have ever existed after we stopped the bombing of parliament and changed the future?' Liore asked as Daniel peered more closely at the disruptor.

'Yes, but it made my head hurt,' he replied.

'The PR-17 is powered by a thing called a Macro-Quantum Device, and the radiocomms use tiny versions of MQDs as well. You don't need to know what they are, but among their strange properties, they have an interaction with time that is poorly understood. Bringing Macro-Quantum Devices back through time with us was a total unknown, but I discovered a very curious thing. The power lattice of the weapon stored a huge amount of energy from the journey backwards, rather like a spring being stretched out.'

'And the radiocomms, too?'

'Yes, but ten orders of magnitude more energy is now crammed into the weapon's MQD than those of the radiocomms.'

'What does all that mean?' asked Daniel, who was having trouble matching up the numbers with reality.

'The weapon gathered a huge amount of energy by being flung back through time, and it is using it to maintain a time loop that repairs itself and maintains the existence of everything sent back from the future to 1901.'

'I still understand nothing,' Daniel admitted.

'Whenever we try to change the events that cause my future, the loop repairs itself.'

'Um . . . so your *weapon* thing is keeping the future the same?'

'Yes. We made two attempts to change history, and we did change history, yet the Lionhearts still manage to start a war that gets Britain invaded and that lasts for a century. Whatever we do, the Lionhearts survive and they try again. The Century War always starts, but just a little later.'

'So destroy the weapon and you break the time loop?'

'Yes, but that is easier said than done. It must be done at a great distance, for the explosion would kill anyone nearby. I was designing a device to do that when Barry stole the weapon. As you can see, that device is now complete.'

'I'll take your word for it.'

'You will need to do more than that. You and Madeline must use it if we do not recover the weapon at Port Said.'

'I could never use something as complicated as this!' exclaimed Daniel.

'Playing the piano is harder,' said Liore dismissively. 'Madeline will read the meters and operate the power switches. Madeline, when you see that the inductance meter has reached the right level you will wait until Daniel has the target acquired, then throw the main power channel switch. When the feedback meter reaches this little red line, you will tell Daniel to fire. Daniel, you only have a half-second to pull the trigger.'

'You mean the batteries will drain in half a second?'

'No, the device will overload and explode.'

'Oh. Will it be a big explosion?'

'Yes.'

'So . . . we may all be killed?'

'Yes. Thanks to travelling back eleven decades through time, each radiocomm has the explosive power of an artillery shell with two hundred and fifty pounds of explosive.'

Daniel stared at the innocent-looking device.

'So I was carrying something with the power of a two hundred and fifty pound shell in my pocket for most of the voyage?'

'Yes.'

Daniel sat down heavily, closed his eyes, then took out his handkerchief and dabbed at his forehead.

'I wish you had not told me that.'

'Had it exploded, you would never have known what hit you.'

'And that's supposed to make me feel better?' asked Daniel.

'No.'

'One last question.'

'Ask.'

'Why do I have to use it? Surely you are better at, well, everything.'

'Because I can't. Someone from this time must do it.'

'Then you know something I don't,' he replied doubtfully, opening his eyes and staring fearfully at the device.

'Indeed I do. Madeline, light a candle.'

Madeline struck a match and touched the flame to a candle's wick. She held it up, uncertain of what to do next. Liore held her hand in front of the flame. The flame was visible right through her flesh. Madeline cried out and dropped the candle.

'That's like magic!' exclaimed Daniel. 'How did you do that?'

'The time loop that allows me to exist is now destined to break, so I am fading. It started the moment that I completed the disruptor, three hours ago. Someone has fired this disruptor in the future. The Century War will not happen. The future that I was born into is becoming more and more unlikely.'

'So you will not exist at all once we fire it?'

'True. I shall fade into nothingness.'

'But that would be killing you.'

'This is war, Daniel, and I am a warrior. Warriors die. All my life I have existed to destroy targets. Now

I have no CO and no orders, but I have a target. Once the target is destroyed, I shall not matter.'

'But what about eating, and, well, everything else?'

'I can no longer eat, but I can breathe and interact with the ship just enough to get around. My uniform from the future is all that I can wear, for my body cannot support the clothing of 1901. I shall have to stay in this cabin, of course, or people are going to get really alarmed.'

'I for one am already alarmed,' said Daniel.

In his short but harrowing career at sea, Barry had made a great many discoveries. One was that a seminar on picking locks will gain you instant acceptance and a great number of friends in a ship's engine hall. Another was that as long as you kept a low profile outside the engine hall, the rest of the crew left you alone. He also learned that voyages were quite boring, and that the stokers, slaggers and greasers spent most of their spare time playing cards and dice, talking about women, fighting about nothing in particular, and drinking.

Barry had the sense to balance his winnings and losses at gambling, but his most important breakthrough came on the second day when a stoker offered him a tin whistle in return for the lesson on making pickwires. Rumble Bill Markey, the deputy foreman, also had a whistle, and he offered to teach Barry how to play a few tunes. If Barry was playing the whistle he could not talk, and because he definitely did not want to talk about his immediate past, this meant that he practised his whistle whenever he got a chance. He could soon play 'Three blind mice', 'Pop goes the weasel', 'Spirits of whiskey' and some jigs that nobody knew the names for.

Barry's conclusion about shipboard life was that it was like working on a really big railway station that moved. He knew that the ocean contained a very large amount of water, but wondered where all the fish in the South Melbourne market came from, because he saw very few from the ship. On having the Horn of Africa pointed out to him, he was disappointed not to see any lions, giraffes or elephants. His glimpse of the Arabian Peninsula was similarly free of camels, and the Red Sea was not red.

As the *Ajax* reached the Suez Canal, Barry knew that another crisis was looming. He was going to have to cope with another port. He had learned from his fellow crewmen that ports were really bad and dangerous places, where people checked your papers and locked you in jail if they were not in order, where beautiful women lured you into dark alleys where very bad men beat you up and robbed you, and worst of all, where the local people did not speak English. Actually that was not the very worst prospect of all, for he knew that telegrams travelled faster than ships, and that Liore might telegram ahead to Port Said and have him arrested.

When the *Ajax* arrived in Port Said it was 4 am, and Barry was all ready to slip away and board another ship, just as he had in Colombo. The *Ajax* dropped anchor and awaited the coal tender, but what came out first was a steam launch with a dozen sailors carrying bolt action rifles. They came aboard, and Barry watched as an officer showed papers to the captain. The captain nodded, and Barry caught the words, 'Search the entire ship, it's like a gun with three barrels.'

The next half hour saw Barry slipping back and forth through the bowels of the *Ajax* like a grubby shadow, clutching his bag and trying to stay out of sight. The invaders were alarmingly thorough and professional in their search.

The coal tender won't be allowed near this friggin' ship till I'm caught, Barry decided, but it seemed like a good idea to lurk about near the coaling doors anyway. He arrived there to discover the doors open and the ramp attached to the ship already. The only oddity was that nobody was loading coal, but that was probably because they were all away being searched. The sky beyond the doors was clear and moonless, but a light from the coal tender was shining into the ship.

Barry was silently rehearsing a story about being an inspector when someone carrying a sack pack walked through the doors and was illuminated as he stepped onto the ramp. Barry recognised the tall, gangly figure wearing a fez as Big Abdul, one of five Abduls among the stokers. A shot barked out. Big Abdul fell. Some men came running up from the coal tender.

'Not him,' said one quietly. 'Barry Porter's white and about eighteen inches shorter.'

'Nothing in his bag but a fancy knife.'

'Toss him.'

Barry heard a splash. The men returned to the tender to wait for anyone else trying to escape.

So much for callin' meself Inspector of Coal Rodents an' hopin' they don't speak English, thought Barry as he slipped away along the dark but familiar paths of the engine hall. Voices echoed all around him. Angry, harsh voices.

'By all the saints, I'm Paddy O'Rourke!' someone was shouting.

'Then what's this in your sea chest?'

'It's an old flintlock, and it's not mine. I stole it.'

Bad times if Paddy the Pincher is 'fessin to theft, thought Barry as he crawled beneath a huge pipe to circle the group. In the lamplight Barry could see Paddy being held by two of the armed sailors, while the others kept the rest of the crew back. The officer was pointing into Paddy's sea chest. Its lock had been smashed off.

'I say you're Barry Porter,' said the officer. 'You're coming with us.'

'Barry Porter's six inches shorter than him,' called one of the stokers.

'Yeah, leave 'im be!' bawled another.

'Pick up his trunk. We have what we came for,' said the officer.

Paddy the Pincher was a bit like Barry, because he had the look of someone harmless. He was thin, grubby, had a permanent cringe, and a very deferential manner. Unlike Barry, he had fifteen years of being a stoker behind him, as well as the experience of countless brawls in pubs, bars and taverns all around the world. Paddy raised his foot and brought it down hard on the foot of the man holding his left arm, snapping some metatarsal bones. He then wrenched his arm free and delivered a left hook to the face of the man on his right. He had just turned to flee into the crowd of watching stokers when the officer raised his Webley-Fosberry and fired three large calibre bullets into his back.

There was instant bedlam as the armed sailors panicked and opened fire on the stokers. The stokers in turn flung lanterns back, and these smashed and splashed burning paraffin all about. Knives, bullets and lumps of coal flew in the light of the rapidly spreading fire, and Barry cowered as far into the shadows as he could as the sailors picked up Paddy's sea chest and retreated for the coal doors. Barry scuttled in the opposite direction.

Once on deck, Barry made for the side of the ship opposite the coal tender. Gunshots were barking out from that side, and he had the feeling that the sharks were also loitering there in search of easy meals. Looking out over the water to the west, Barry saw that the Suez Canal was not particularly wide. Even better, the canal divided Port Said, and there were plenty of buildings on the west bank, picked out by a scatter of streetlights. For Barry, who had spent his life vanishing down alleys, the poorly lit streets beckoned like the gates to paradise.

Barry glanced about, found a length of rope and tied it to the bottom of the railing where nobody would notice it. Climbing over the railing, he groped about for his rope, grasped it, slung his bag over his shoulder by the strap and let go. Unfortunately, he had grasped the wrong piece of rope, and this one had not been tied to anything. Barry fell straight down the side of the ship to the water.

Fortunately for Barry, the waves in the Suez Canal were little more than ripples. He could not swim, but as he had hoped, his bag kept him afloat. He located the lights of the west side of Port Said, then with his left arm clinging to his bag and his right arm paddling, he set out for the beckoning lights, trying not to think about sharks. The water was placid, the current minimal, and the distance should have taken only minutes to swim, so Barry had everything in his favour.

An hour later, with the sun on the horizon, Barry finally crawled up the steps of a landing on the west side of the canal, still clutching his beloved bag. Fully clothed but dripping wet, he immediately drew a lot of attention from the local Egyptians. He staggered over to a man who was dressed in European clothes. While among the stokers he had learned the words 'Seamen's Mission' and 'Please' in six languages, and he now repeated all six versions before he realised that the man spoke English.

'Oi matey, I'm the victim of a lark by me shipmates, wot flung me in the water off me ship out of high spirits,' Barry now explained.

'Ah, so you wish to be directed to the police?'

'No no no, nuffin' like that, they's good coves, jus' larkin' about with no criminal intent. I just want the Seamen's Mission so's I can get me circumstances sorted out, sorta.'

'Ah, if you mean the house for distressed sailors that the Christian priestly men have established, it is not far. Come along, I shall take you there.'

❂

Unlike most other sailors, Barry did not arrive at the door of the Seamen's Mission with a severe hangover and no money. His very first act upon being admitted was to donate ten shillings that he had won at cards to the mission before pouring out a story of how he was a little boy of fourteen from London who had gone to sea as a slagger to support his poor dear mother in her declining years.

He was given a bath, and supplied with dry clothes from a pool of clothing. The clothes had been left at the mission by sailors who had departed without their bags because the police were watching the mission, because they had become drunk again and forgotten that they had ever been to the mission, or because they had died on the premises.

After a breakfast of some sort of crumbly biscuit washed down by something that looked like milk, but had pieces of cucumber and mint floating in it, Barry attended his first prayer service in several years.

Next he explained to a sympathetic Redemptorist priest that he needed to get aboard the next ship going to London, and that he was willing to work as a slagger. He had by now worked out that the crews of ships were given a lot less scrutiny than the passengers by port officials because they were so transitory. The fact that Barry's papers were supposedly still on his ship was no problem because it could all be sorted out in London.

Port Said had few attractions for tourists, although a few passengers went ashore and bought trinkets just so that they could say that they had been to Egypt.

For Barry, its main virtues were that the city did not move or sway, nobody knew who he was or that he was there at all, there were kindly people who believed his story, and nobody was trying to kill him.

While obviously distressed about being marooned in a foreign city with no friends or papers, it was infinitely preferable to being shot at on the *Ajax* or being strangled by Liore.

At lunchtime Barry was given a list of ships that would be sailing to London that afternoon, and there was a tick next to three ships that needed stokers or slaggers. As he sat eating in the mission's refectory, he noted with great relief that the *Millennium* was marked as having already sailed.

Barry my man, things is goin' your way at last, he thought as he worked his way through a plate of rice and roast lamb shavings. *Before long it's gonna be Sir Barry, wot's good mates with the king. Give yerself a pat on the back.*

He prodded at a pair of meatballs that looked suspiciously like parts of the lamb's anatomy that were not at all to his taste. He decided to finish the rest of the rice instead.

'Barry Porter, time to go sailing.'

Barry gasped, and in the process breathed in a mixture of air and rice. During the choking fit that followed he turned to see a girl with one hand in a large cloth bag that hung from her shoulder.

'I am Madeline Drake, special contract detective,' she said quietly.

'You're a copper?' wheezed the incredulous Barry.

'I'm a detective. A special, secret detective. In my bag is a Webley Bulldog pointed at your heart.'

'Ya can't shoot me with all these sailors an' priests around, like,' said Barry hopefully. 'You'll get arrested. Even coppers can't murder people.'

'In my bag is also a cushion, which will muffle the shot and absorb the smoke. You will just fall down as if you have fainted, and I shall walk away with your bag.'

'Oh. So wot ya gonna do? Hand me to the Gyppy coppers?'

'I could do that.'

'Oh well, jail is jail.'

There was a soft pop. A hole appeared in the bag. Barry looked down at the table and saw another hole. Nobody else in the refectory noticed that a shot had been fired.

'Now then, coming?' asked Madeline.

'Er, yeah, I reckon. Wotcha gonna do to me?'

'That depends entirely upon you,' said Madeline. 'Stand up, pick up your bag, and come with me. We are going to a nice ship called the *Andromeda* that's going to take us to London.'

'But I ain't got no tikky.'

'You left your ticket behind when you abandoned ship in Colombo, Barry, I have it here. Come along.'

Barry was not at all surprised to find Daniel waiting outside the mission.

'It's been a long chase, but the hunters have caught their rat,' Madeline announced.

Daniel took Barry's bag from him at once.

'I can explain,' said Barry as they set off for the steam tenders' landing.

'We can all explain, Barry,' said Daniel with an ominously hard edge to his voice. 'The problem is that some true explanations will get you shot, while all false explanations are not even worth listening to.'

'But I'm a poor little orphan, me old man got shot and I ain't been thinkin' clear.'

'Please accept my condolences about your father, but that does not make you an orphan. Your mother is still alive.'

'Danny boy, I thought we was mates.'

'I'm afraid a lot of young men abandon their mates when they get involved with a girl,' said Madeline.

'Wot? This daft detective baggage is yer sweetheart?'

'No, I am still faithful to Muriel,' said Daniel.

'Here is the tender,' said Madeline, gesturing to a steam launch. 'Are you coming quietly, or do you want another demonstration of my knitting bag?'

'Bleedin' hell, what sorta choice is that?'

'And speaking of having no choices, hand over your pickwires,' said Daniel.

'Where's that Liore baggage?' asked Barry as he fished about in his pockets.

'Liore is no longer able to hurt you, Barry, so come along.'

The deputy purser was at the *Andromeda*'s gangway as they climbed aboard from the steam tender. Daniel announced that he had spotted Barry while he had been seeing the sights in Port Said, so he had taken hold of him and dragged him back to the ship.

'Danny is very brave,' added Madeline.

Barry was presented to the master-at-arms, who added vandalism to the shipping line's property and escaping from legal custody to the charges already against his name. He was put back in the first-class 'brig'.

The following day Barry was let out to take the air, but only on the condition that he be handcuffed to Daniel by the deputy purser.

'Wot ya done with me bag?' asked Barry peevishly

as they walked through the corridors of the first-class cabin area.

'It's in my cabin,' replied Daniel.

'So wot now? Ain't I supposed to be gettin' the air on the prommy deck?'

'We are going to my cabin, Barry. There you are going to open your bag.'

Madeline was waiting in Daniel's cabin. Barry's bag was on the writing desk.

'Open it,' said Daniel.

'Ain't got the key,' mumbled Barry.

Madeline held up his pickwires.

Barry took them and got to work, but pretended to have trouble with the lock. 'There's glue in it,' he said sullenly.

'It's candle wax, Barry, poured there by you,' said Madeline. 'Half an hour over a candle will have it melted and poured out.'

The padlock was still uncomfortably hot as Barry set about opening it, but the mechanism was as familiar as an old friend and it yielded quickly. He removed the padlock and clicked the latch on the bag.

'I still reckon this friggin' weapon orta go to the king,' he began, then froze with his mouth open as he stared into the bag. 'It's gone!' he finally managed to exclaim.

Daniel and Madeline joined him. Within the bag were three lumps of coal, padded with some grimy cloth.

'Good Cornish steaming coal, I'd say,' said Daniel. 'It would probably hurt if thrown hard enough, but it's not in the same class as a PR-17.'

'But – but me padlock were locked. Waxed, too.'

'May I draw your attention to this seam here,' said Madeline. 'Very carefully slit open, then carefully repaired from the outside.'

'That was me, the day after we left Adelaide,' said Daniel.

'Ya can't sew like that from the outside, ya gotta have the bag open for doin' inside seams.'

'It's called gimlet technique,' said Daniel. 'I read about it in a novel. Not hard, once you know how.'

'Now see here,' said Madeline, pointing to a similar repair on another seam. 'Someone aboard the *Ajax* did the same as Daniel, but took the weapon and inserted some coal as ballast.'

'That bleedin' Paddy the Pincher!' exclaimed Barry angrily. 'Serves him right, gettin' shot an' all.'

'Who shot him?' asked Daniel.

'Some sailors come on the *Ajax* when we stopped in Port Said. They searched the ship an' shot anyone tryin' to get off. Shot some coves who weren't tryin' to get off, neither. They were pointin' in Paddy's sea chest, but I didn't see what were there. They shot him when he punched one of 'em. They kept sayin' he was me, so I says Barry me boy, abandon ship.'

'How did you get off?'

'I swum.'

'You can't swim.'

'I sorta swum. Me bag floats, so I hung onta it an' paddled.'

'There's wax in the seams,' said Madeline, holding a magnifying glass to the bag. 'There is also dried salt on the leather. For once he might be telling the truth.'

'So the weapon is on the *Millennium* now?' asked Daniel. 'Not some other ship?'

'Dunno. The sailors wot searched the ship took Paddy's sea chest. If it were in there, then they got it – but they can't use it. Like they have to know that the bit of Liore's hair gotta be pressed on that lock pad thing.'

'Really?' said Daniel, holding up his radiocomm.

'Er, yeah.'

'Are you absolutely sure?' asked Madeline.

'Yeah, course I'm sure.'

'This radiocomm can tell me when that weapon is fired,' said Daniel. 'It was test-fired five times this morning, out at sea, over the horizon.'

'Oh. Yeah, er, well, I might have forgotten to switch it off.'

Madeline took three paces backwards and collapsed across the bed with her hands over her face.

'Incompetent criminals, how I hate them,' she said. 'Nothing they do is logical.'

Daniel held up the wrist to which he was handcuffed to Barry.

'Were it not for this, I could think of no better place for you than over the side,' he said coldly.

Liore chose that very moment to walk in through the wall.

Madeline and Daniel had been aware of Liore's strange new condition since the night before, but Barry came perilously close to losing his bladder control. It was as if she had just lost substance, and was no longer entirely in their world. She looked solid enough, and could breathe air well enough to talk, but she could also pass through solid objects.

'Danny boy, save me, I can explain,' Barry shrieked, pulling Daniel off his chair by the handcuffs as he lurched for the door.

'You stole my weapon, what else is there to explain?' said Liore softly.

'No I didn't! I stole it from Luker the Lurker.'

'Barry, my landlady saw you burgling my place,' said Liore, the light from the porthole dimly visible through her body.

'Oh! Er, yeah, but I were just a little wheel in a great big steam engine.'

'You planned the whole thing.'

'I was all shocked 'cause I was an orphan.'

'Your father was shot *after* you stole the weapon.'

'Oh, yeah. But we was gonna give it to the king, but them Lionhearts come after us. Luker was shot. So was Lurker the Worker. So was me old man. It was them Lionhearts.'

'Out of all those people, only you knew about the weapon,' said Liore, advancing on him.

Barry put his hand out to stop her. It passed right through her arm.

''Ere, you're a ghost!' he cried.

'Why did you steal it?'

'If you're a ghost you can't hurt me,' said Barry, suddenly smiling and looking relieved.

'But *I* can!' said Madeline, getting up and jamming the barrel of her Webley into Barry's ear. 'Now answer Commander Liore's question.'

'Yeah, well, after ya gave them railway coves the big push I thinks, Barry my man, this stuff's too big for even some warrior baggage from the future. Er, no offence, like. A loyal subject of the king orta give it over, 'cause kings know what to do with that sorta stuff.'

'For a modest consideration,' said Daniel.

'Yeah, well, the king's got lotsa money. Danny boy, I deserve it. I saved the world, I stopped parlyment gettin' bombed. Wot reward did I get?'

'Liore set you up with a proper apprenticeship and a bursary for the mechanics college.'

'I had to study, it were too hard. I'm a *doin'* sorta cove.'

'Barry, you had it all, yet you threw it away, and for what?'

'I was bein' loyal.'

'Undoing what you have done will be harder than stopping the bombing of parliament, Barry Porter,' said Liore. 'I am not sure what to do now. The next stop is London, and –'

'Oh yeah, an' London is where the king lives. Now we can get the weapon back from them Lionheart coves an' hand it on to the king –'

Barry hesitated when he noticed the expression on Liore's face.

'She's gonna murder me, Danny boy! Can ghosts murder people?'

'Shut up!' shouted Daniel. 'Why were your father, Lurker the Worker and Luker the Lurker involved?'

By now Barry was so severely frightened that he was telling the truth without thinking.

'Only Luker. I asked him to give me an introductory to some cove wot knows the king.'

'You what?' snapped Liore.

'Well I don't know how to tell the king I've got somethin' for him. I asked Luker to find me someone important.'

Daniel seized Barry by the collar and glared into his eyes.

'So you told the most untrustworthy character in all of Melbourne that you had the most advanced weapon on the face of the Earth and wanted to sell it to the king, so could he please let His Majesty know that Barry the Bag has a deal that he just can't refuse?'

'Well, I had a business arrangement with old Luker. Thought I did, anyway.'

'Barry, now listen to me and listen very carefully,' said Madeline. 'You are so far out of your depth that you could not touch the bottom with a thousand bargepoles tied together. Leave *everything* to us, do *nothing* unless we tell you to, and do not lie to us under *any* circumstances at all. Oh, and keep your hands off other people's property.'

'But I gotta earn a crust –' began Barry.

'Or I will kill you!' continued Madeline.

'Slowly,' added Daniel.

'Yeah, well, suppose bread's free on the ship,' mumbled Barry.

Chapter 10

HERO

In the days that followed, Daniel always spent the mornings with Madeline. The other passengers began spreading rumours about a romance, or even the makings of a love triangle with her and Liore. Daniel and Madeline always had dinner together in the saloon, and then Madeline attended whatever entertainment had been arranged for the passengers. When Liore was not seen out and about for several days, rumours spread that she was in her cabin, heartbroken because Daniel had not chosen her. Daniel vanished from sight in the evenings, but was generally in Elizabeth's cabin. He was discovering that teaching courtship was the best way to learn more about it.

One night Daniel returned to his cabin a little after midnight, and had just turned off the light and got into bed when he discovered that he had company.

'By your leave, speaking courtly,' a voice announced.

'Liore!' exclaimed Daniel. 'How did you get in here?'

'Through the wall.'

'Oh, yes. So why are you in here?'

'There was not much privacy in Elizabeth Bunting's cabin.'

'You were watching?' exclaimed Daniel. 'Don't tell –'

'Muriel. Upon my word of honour as a battle commander, I swear it, but only if you help me destroy the weapon.'

'I've already said I would.'

'Go to your door and let Madeline in. We need to talk.'

Daniel put on a dressing gown, turned on the light and opened the cabin door to admit Madeline.

'According to the radiocomms, the *Millennium* was doing thirty knots after leaving Port Said,' Liore began, floating in the air before Madeline and Daniel, who were sitting on the bed.

'Even if the captain agreed to give chase with the *Andromeda*, we could never catch up,' said Daniel.

'We are not even bothering to track it any more,' added Madeline.

'There is no need,' added Liore. 'My new memories of the future tell me that the *Millennium* will proceed to the Baltic Sea, and in late September it will attack the German fleet at Wilhelmshaven and start the Century War.'

'All this almost convinces me that you really are

from the future,' said Madeline.

'You need more convincing?' asked Daniel.

'Actually, I don't,' said Madeline.

'What happens if we fail?' Daniel asked Liore.

'If you had failed in the future, I would not be fading.'

'So we succeed,' said Daniel hopefully. 'I mean, that's why you are fading.'

'The time loop has healed itself twice, but I have a good feeling about this, our third attempt to change history. All the important Lionhearts are aboard the *Millennium*, so . . .'

'So?' asked Daniel.

'So nobody will be chasing Madeline, you and Barry,' said Liore, avoiding his eyes. 'You must travel to Wilhelmshaven, and be ready when the *Millennium* appears on the horizon on the twenty-ninth day of September.'

'And when it appears, what then?'

'The disruptor's pulse will release the energy crammed into the PR-17 with the force of . . . of the biggest bomb ever built.'

'The biggest bomb is a torpedo!' said Daniel. 'So, it will be like one of the *Millennium*'s own torpedoes exploding. The Germans will think it's just an accident aboard a British ship.'

'Yes.'

'But that would be murder.'

'Younger boys than you help operate the guns and torpedoes aboard British warships. Remember, you two are just soldiers. I am your commander, so the responsibility is mine.'

While Liore's words were convincing, Daniel could not help feeling that something was wrong. She was being evasive, yet Liore had never been evasive before. On the other hand, everything that she said seemed to make sense, so there was no alternative to doing things her way.

After Liore and Madeline had left, Daniel lay back with a great many thoughts cascading through his head. All that had been happening had distracted him from pining for Muriel, but now thoughts of her were creeping back. If Liore was fading, Fox would be fading, too. When the weapon was destroyed, Fox would vanish and Muriel would be on her own again. Daniel was now much more accomplished at courtship than before, and he suspected that Fox's experience of courting girls was still confined to what Muriel had taught him.

If I arrive after Fox is gone, perhaps I can win Muriel back before some French artist comes along, thought Daniel as he drifted away into sleep. *I wonder how long it takes to travel from Wilhelmshaven to Paris?*

On the 28th of August they passed Malta in the early

morning, and all that day steamed parallel with the coast of Sicily. Daniel gave Barry his daily outing on the promenade deck, and pointed out that they could see part of Italy.

'So that's where spaghetti comes from?' asked Barry.

'Yes,' said Daniel. 'And Italians, the renaissance, universities, Galileo, Michelangelo, the Roman Empire, and –'

'Oi, hang on! The Roman Empire comes from Rome.'

'Rome is in Italy, Barry.'

'Oh. But we're not goin' there?'

'No.'

'That's good. I was told they feed people to lions in a great big footy ground while the crowds bet on wot lion can eat the most.'

'Not for the past sixteen hundred years.'

'Oh,' said Barry, who then borrowed Daniel's telescope and peered at the distant coast. 'Don't look like much.'

'Nothing looks like much from fourteen miles away. Barry, I've been meaning to ask you about how you stole the weapon.'

'Oh jeez, mate!' exclaimed Barry. 'I said I done it, can't ya give it a rest?'

'I want to know *how*. Professional techniques, and all that.'

Given the opportunity to boast, Barry's manner changed completely. He handed back the telescope and puffed out his little chest.

'Oh yeah, well I took me time, kept suspicions down. First I did lots of observationals. I worked out that Liore had regular habits, that's very important. I got me opportunity when Muriel dumped ya, 'cause that give me a reason to call in on Liore, and check out where she lived. She even invited me in, and I saw she had a trunk with a padlock. Dead giveaway, stuff wot's got a lock. Just then her landlady called her away, so I was inter that padlock like a rat up a drain. I just had time to check the weapon was in the trunk 'fore she come back.'

'Liore travelled *regularly* on the *train*, and she left *you* alone in her *room*?' asked Daniel, who suddenly had a very bad feeling about what was going on around him.

'Yeah. Don't ya believe me?'

'I believe you, it's just that she told me that a good spy should never be predictable, and that a padlock on a box is like a sign that says, "Something in here is worth stealing".'

'She did?'

'She did.'

'Jeez Danny boy, ya gone more suspicious than a copper wot's had his truncheon pinched.'

'Being lied to continually by everyone is probably

the cause. What about Liore's hair? How did you get your sample?'

'Easy pickin's, Danny boy. I burgled her landlady's garbage. That Liore, she had all her sweepin's for every day bundled up in neat little packets. Plenty of her hair for a little ring, see?'

Barry rummaged in his pockets, then turned them out while Daniel held the contents. There was no ring of hair to be found.

'It's gone!' he exclaimed. 'Jeez, I was guardin' it with me life.'

'Liore is fading away, so her hair must be fading, too. It probably just passed through the cloth of your pocket and drifted away like smoke.'

'Yeah, well, suppose it's no good without the weapon,' he said grudgingly. 'Oi, if Liore is fadin', why ain't the weapon and raddy things fadin' too?'

'Apparently they are part of the time loop, because of the way their batteries store energy.'

'Wot?'

'Different rules apply to them. Go on.'

'Yeah, yeah, well anyway, I waited until ya was goin' away on this ship before I did the big snatch. Would have got clean away, 'cept the bleedin' dog barked and spoiled it all.'

'Does Liore's room have a fireplace?'

'Yeah, a little pot-belly stove.'

'Was she using it?'

'Yeah. It was still hot one time I sneaked in.'

'So why bundle up her sweepings and put them neatly into the bin when she could just burn them?'

'I reckon that's an obviously, she . . . er . . .'

Barry quickly realised that it was not obvious at all. Daniel frowned and shook his head. Liore had not been outsmarted after all.

'You were set up, Barry,' said Daniel, shaking his head. 'Liore let you know where the weapon was kept, how you could activate it without her permission, and when she would be out of her room.'

'Oi, Danny boy, that can't be right. I worked real hard to do that job.'

'The harder you had to work, the more convinced you would be that Liore was not using you.'

Barry turned away, his mouth hanging wide open but his head shaking.

'She *wanted* you to steal the weapon, Barry, and she wanted the Lionhearts to take it away from you, aboard the *Millennium*.'

'Wot? Why would she do that?'

'Because perhaps it is *she* who starts the Century War.'

'You're daft! Why?'

'I don't know, but I'm trying to be a detective like Madeline. I'm following the evidence.'

'Nah, them's goods I can't buy, Danny boy. That Liore's been workin' flat out tryin' to stop the bleedin' war from startin'.'

'True, but nearly all of the important Lionhearts are aboard their disguised warship, along with the weapon. Even if she's not trying to start the war . . . I have a very bad feeling about this. Come on, back to the brig.'

Daniel jerked at the handcuffs, but as they turned away from the rail they came face to face with Liore.

'I can explain,' she said in a whisper that was almost lost on the wind.

'You no longer have to,' replied Daniel.

In the evening Daniel had dinner alone, because Madeline had told the stewards that she and Liore were seasick again, and were not to be disturbed. Daniel no longer considered himself to be in Liore's service, so he went to the Italian Festival Costume Dance. There he practised his new skills at being charming with Elizabeth and the other girls in her circle of shipboard friends, while yet more girls tried to join in.

A distinct change was taking place in Daniel, yet it was a change that he scarcely noticed. He was no longer pining for Muriel, but practising to be better than Fox. On one level, he wanted to get Muriel back, but on another he wanted to be superior to the boy who had run off with her. Losing Muriel had involved humiliation as well as heartbreak, and although he did not realise it, Daniel wanted to wipe that humiliation away.

Securely locked in their own cabin, Liore and Madeline were discussing Daniel as he danced and flirted.

'Breaking the time loop is something that neither Fox nor I could ever have done,' said Liore. 'I understand it now. Daniel worries that he could never be Fox's equal, but here at last is something that is beyond all of Fox's talents. Neither Fox nor I could stop the Century War and save our world.'

'But now Daniel hates you, and will not help fire the disruptor.'

'Yes. The fate of the world depends on you, Madeline, but I can still help by reading the meters and telling you when to fire. You must travel to Wilhelmshaven alone and destroy the *Millennium* there.'

'But that would mean killing you and Fox,' said Madeline.

'Not kill. Our potential to influence the future will cease to exist. It is the time loop that you will destroy. We depend on the time loop to exist, so we shall vanish when it does.'

'But I would still feel like I was shooting you.'

'Do not think of me as a real girl, Madeline, think of me as a thing. As you might have noticed, I am not human. I have been engineered as a leadership machine, designed to inspire people to follow me and be loyal. The physicians of the future consider that a leader loses some loyalty if they fall in love with one particular person, so my brain has been designed with the capacity for affection sliced out.'

'How awful!' exclaimed Madeline.

'After seeing what love has done to Daniel, I am not so sure. Still, I am not able to make judgements on that. Concerning Fox, he is a deserter, and is subject to execution. Just like an artillery shell, I am designed to be destroyed when I hit the target. You must not worry about killing us.'

'And are you sure it is worth it? There will be no war?'

'Oh, there will be war, I already have new memories from the edge of the time loop. It will be terrible, but will last only four years.'

'I'm fascinated by the way your memories keep changing as future history changes.'

'It is very confusing, having so many alternatives in my head. Now I see that on the twenty-eighth of June 1914, in Serbia, at Sarajevo, Archduke Franz Ferdinand will be shot. He is the heir to the Austro-Hungarian Empire's throne. That leads to a war, but as I said, it does not stretch out over a century and ruin the world.'

'But should I try to stop it?' Madeline asked.

'Do you think the Archduke will listen to you, a waitress?'

'I suppose not. Liore, why did you deceive Daniel?'

'Deception needs to be convincing. Daniel was convinced, as was everyone else.'

'Are you deceiving me?'

'With regard to some details, yes.'

'Daniel thinks it is you who will start the Century War. Is that true?'

'No.'

'And you told him that?'

'Yes, but he did not believe me. Too many people have deceived Daniel, so now he trusts nobody. He also hates everyone who has lied to him.'

'I have never lied to him.'

'Daniel would say that you just never had the chance.'

The following morning Daniel ignored Madeline in the breakfast saloon, instead sitting with Elizabeth and several other girls. After that, he took his leave of them and collected Barry from the brig for his morning excursion. Being Barry's guard gave Daniel a type of status with his admirers, but the price of that status was having Barry next to him. Unless Barry were gagged, this could be a dangerous thing. The compromise was to be seen with Barry on the way down to the engines. None of the girls or their mothers would venture down there, so Barry could say what he liked without offending anyone.

'Why do I get some of my best inspirations when I am talking to you?' Daniel asked Barry as they descended the steps to the engine hall.

'I got good ideas?' suggested Barry.

'It's more likely that I have to simplify things so much before you can understand them that it strips away all the confusing and irrelevant details.'

Barry paused to think through the sentence, and concluded that it might be insulting. On the other hand he was not entirely sure why it was insulting, so he decided to say nothing. Because they were handcuffed together, it was not possible for either Daniel or Barry to do any actual work in the engine hall, but by now this was no longer the point for Daniel.

'So, how ya been goin' with Liore and Madeline?' Barry asked presently.

'We have a very good relationship. I avoid them and they avoid me.'

'So that Liore really did set me up to steal her bleedin' weapon?'

'She admitted as much, yes.'

'Bleedin' hell! Now that's a real bad bit of deviantness.'

'The word is deviousness, Barry, but you are right.'

'Enough to put me off wimmen.'

'Since when have you ever shown any interest in women – I mean real ones, not your French postcard pictures?'

'Er, well, if I'd been plannin' to go courtin' I'd never do it now.'

'Oh, it can be enjoyable, as long as you don't give your heart away.'

'So are ya still helpin' to stop that war wot's not started?'

'No, and I think Liore is still lying to us all. The part about the weapon and the time loop may be true, but there is still a flaw in her logic. Destroy the weapon and the time loop breaks. The trouble is that the Lionhearts will still be around, and would be free to come up with some new idea to start a war. Why not get the Lionhearts together on a ship, with the weapon, then blow up the weapon?'

'But that's wot's happened.'

'Yes, so perhaps this is her plan. She's a clever girl. If Madeline stays loyal to her, they might blow up the *Millennium* when it attacks Wilhelmshaven.'

'Gonna have to be a pretty big bang to blow up a bleedin' ship.'

'Oh yes, it would be. Remember those little radiocomms? They each have the explosive power of a shell with two or three times your weight in explosives.'

'Yeah? An' the PR-17 thing has more?'

'Apparently. Liore said it was ten orders of magnitude more.'

'How much is that?'

'Let's work it out. Twice two hundred and fifty pounds of explosive is five hundred pounds. There's four and a half of those in a ton. Make that four times for simplicity, so the two radiocomms are equal to a quarter of a ton of explosive.'

'Er, and that's lots?'

'Lots and lots. Now, ten orders of magnitude times a quarter ton is . . .'

Daniel did the calculation. The figure did not make sense. He thought through it again. He got the same result. He fished a pencil out of one pocket and a notebook page with Elizabeth's address in London out of the other, then wrote out the calculation. The result remained the same.

'No, that can't be right,' said Daniel as the bottom dropped out of his stomach. 'It comes to two and a half thousand *million* tons of explosive! That's ten thousand million shells.'

'Would that sink a ship?' asked Barry.

'Barry, that would sink Tasmania! That's more explosive than has been set off in all of history.'

'Er, so best to stand well clear?'

'Well clear? No wonder she said her disruptor device has to be fired when the *Millennium* is on the horizon. That's why she didn't tell anyone about what her real plan was. Anyone close enough to fire at the *Millennium* would probably be killed by the explosion.'

'Crikey. Lucky we won't be near that Willy's Haven place, then.'

'Wilhelmshaven, and . . . I really ought to warn Madeline. I mean she should be told that Liore's plan means almost certain death –'

Daniel was cut short by a massive explosion not far from the ship. It was as if some giant had struck the ship with a huge sledgehammer. The entire structure reverberated, and every man in the engine hall froze in terror for a moment, although the engines continued to turn steadily.

'Friggin' hell!' exclaimed Barry. 'Are we somewhere near that Willy place?'

'It's the *Millennium*!' Daniel concluded. 'Come on, make for the stairs!'

Daniel had reacted before the engineering crew had thought to send someone up to see what was happening, so they had the iron steps to themselves.

'I thought the *Millennium* only shot at Germans?' said Barry as they climbed.

'I think they've decided to test the weapon on us first,' said Daniel. 'They know that people who don't like the Lionhearts are aboard the *Andromeda*, so why not sink it to get a feel for the weapon and get rid of us, too?'

Another explosion rattled the ship, very nearly pitching Daniel and Barry off the stairs.

'Lucky they're such bleedin' lousy shots,' said Barry as they began climbing again.

'With cannons you have to allow for wind drift and the parabolic path of the shell. As Liore explained it, the PR-17's shots travel in an absolutely straight line. The people on the *Millennium* have not yet worked out that the weapon does not act like a cannon.'

'Jeez, then I hope they're pretty thick and take a long time,' said Barry as they emerged into the sunlight. 'Where's the lifeboats?'

'Forget the lifeboats, follow me.'

'Haven't got much bleedin' choice with these friggin' handcuffs on, have I?'

Daniel made for the cabin that Liore and Madeline shared. As he suspected, they had left, and in such a hurry that the door was unlocked. The disruptor and its batteries were gone. Daniel dragged Barry across to Madeline's bed and felt under the pillow. He drew out her Webley 32.

'Bleedin' hell, how'd ya know that were there?' gasped Barry.

'Because I've been in bed with her!' snapped Daniel, who was by now beyond polite and discreet ways of explaining things.

'Ya wot? Jeez, and ya got the cheek to call me a dirty little man?'

'Come on!' shouted Daniel, dragging Barry back into the corridor.

'Please tell me we're goin' to the lifeboats now.'

'No, we're going to the forward promenade deck and I'm going to put a bullet through Liore's disruptor device before she and Madeline take a shot at the *Millennium*.'

'Wot? The buggers shoot at us but ya don't wanna shoot back?'

'Barry, if they destroy the PR-17, the explosion will be like dropping Mount Everest into the water from a great height. It won't matter whether you're in the ship or a lifeboat when the wave arrives.'

Their progress was slow, because the decks were crowded with people making for the lifeboats, putting on life jackets, trying to take photographs, screaming at the stewards, or running for their cabins. The water on the starboard side of the ship suddenly erupted skywards, showering everyone with hot, salty spray and knocking nearly everyone off their feet. The sound and shockwave was like a physical blow.

'They're gettin' better with that friggin' weapon!' called Barry. 'Next shot's gonna hit us.'

'All they want to do is sink this ship, then vanish before any other ship sees that they were nearby. There may even be time to launch the lifeboats once they blow a hole in us.'

'Well why aren't we goin' for the lifeboats?'

'Shut up and follow me!'

'Slow down, me wrist is bleedin' from the handcuff.'

Not far away, Madeline was setting up the disruptor under Liore's instructions. They were on the part of the promenade deck directly below the bridge, and could just see the smudge of smoke on the horizon that marked the *Millennium*.

'Battery cable one, *there*,' said Liore, pointing. 'Cable two, *there*. Cable three, *there*.'

'The radiocomm screens have both lit up,' said Madeline.

'Madeline, switches,' continued Liore. 'One *up*. Two, three, four, *down*. Five *up*. Six *down*. Inductance meter, monitor.'

'The needle is moving,' said Madeline. 'It's reading five, six, seven, eight, slowing down . . . nine.'

'Lockdown target,' said Liore. 'Dials, myself monitoring. Switch seven, place thumb, at the ready. Feedback meter, redline, I call.'

It was at that moment that Daniel and Barry arrived from the starboard side. Daniel drew his gun and pointed it at the disruptor.

'Daniel, what do you think you are doing?' cried Madeline, crouching over with the disruptor held against her body.

'Get away from that thing, it will destroy us all!' Daniel shouted.

'It's our only chance to stop the *Millennium*!' cried Madeline. 'The disruptor will make Liore's weapon explode like the biggest of bombs.'

'Tell her what sort of bomb, Liore!' shouted Daniel at the translucent figure. 'One from 1901, or one from 2011?'

For the first time since Daniel had met her, Liore looked truly cornered and frightened.

'Liore, what is he talking about?' asked Madeline.

'1901 or 2011?' shouted Daniel. 'Tell her!'

'Large bomb, as from, 2011,' Liore finally conceded.

'That means about two and a half thousand *million* tons of explosive!' explained Daniel. 'You set that off and the *Andromeda* will sink, too, even fifteen miles away.'

'But if the *Andromeda* is sunk today and the *Millennium* takes that weapon to Wilhelmshaven, the Lionhearts will start the Century War,' replied Madeline. 'This is our only chance to stop the war.'

'We've tried twice, this try will fail, too,' said Daniel. 'Put the disruptor on the deck so I can smash it.'

'No!' shouted Madeline.

This was not the only drama being played out on the deck. Baroness Featherington had been seventeen during the Indian Mutiny of 1858. Her father had been in the army, and like Madeline's father, he believed in women being self-reliant when their men folk were not in the area and educated her accordingly. She had organised fifteen girls and women to dress as native women, then led them to safety at a British garrison. On the way she had shot two sepoys who got too inquisitive about the group.

Now the Baroness was again under fire and surrounded by civilians, and she was determined to take over and save the day. When a steward had tried to tell her that everything was under control and that she should go to her cabin, she had demanded to know who was organising a passengers' militia. Upon being told that no such militia was planned, she had taken charge.

'Just what do you young people think you are doing out here!' she shouted as she bore down on Daniel, Madeline and Liore. 'Get back inside at once and wait for orders in the saloon!'

Daniel turned, the gun still in his hand. Baroness Featherington and the steward stopped at the sight of the gun.

'The ship is under attack,' called the steward. 'You can't stay out here.'

'Daniel, please!' pleaded Liore. 'Hate me as much as you like, but please, please help us destroy the Lionhearts.'

'Danny, wot about a nice lifeboat?' suggested Barry.

'I'm willing to die to save the future, Daniel,' said Madeline. 'Are you?'

Daniel was not aware of deciding to change his mind, but at that very moment he decided to save the world from the Century War, even though it meant near-certain death. Thinking back on it several days later, he also realised that he had not liked the idea of being ordered around by Baroness Featherington because she spoke and acted like his sister. One domineering woman too many had tried to order him about, and Baroness Featherington just happened to be the one who pushed him over the edge. On the other hand, Liore was helpless, and had said please rather than trying to order him about.

While not a very logical reason to side with Liore, it was nevertheless Daniel's reason. *I don't hate you, Liore,* he thought. *You're like Barry, you can't help being what you are and you can't change. Unlike Barry, you're trying to do something good, so . . .*

'Stay where you are, don't try to interfere!' he shouted at Baroness Featherington and the steward.

The steward raised his hands and began to back away, but Baroness Featherington now advanced on Daniel.

'Don't you try to intimidate me, you – you middle-class boy!' she said. 'I know you would not shoot a –'

Daniel's shot passed through Baroness Featherington's hat, blowing it from her head, hatpin and all. She stopped, not quite comprehending that the youth had actually shot at her.

'Just you turn around and run, you ugly old bat!' shouted Daniel, who then fired another shot into the deck at her feet.

'Mr Hammond, do something!' shrieked Baroness Featherington as she backed away, but the steward was already out of sight. Finding herself without support, she turned and fled as well.

'Target lockdown!' called Madeline. 'I'm pressing switch seven. Liore, call redline.'

The soft click of the switch was perhaps the most unsettling sound Daniel had ever heard.

'Fire!' called Liore.

Madeline squeezed the trigger stud. There was a loud bang and the disruptor jerked as six gunpowder charges went off, propelling six magnets through tubes wound with coils of wire, and sending a surge of electricity through the circuit.

'Nothing happened,' said Madeline.

'Daniel, Madeline, over side, throw disruptor!' shouted Liore.

A whining sound came from the disruptor, and it rapidly rose in pitch. A corona of electrical discharge danced between the two radiocomms, and smoke curled up from the coils and tubes. Without another word Madeline detached the batteries while Daniel held the disruptor. The moment that the last connection was free, Daniel carried the device to the starboard side, dragging the terrified Barry behind him. With only his right arm, Daniel heaved the disruptor into the water.

'Close eyes, with hands, cover!' shouted Liore.

Abruptly the entire world turned into pure white light for several seconds. Daniel felt as if there should have been some terrible sound, but there was only the distant rumble of the *Andromeda*'s engines, and a few cries of alarm from others who were nearby. The blaze of light passed, and Daniel opened his eyes. On the western horizon, where the *Millennium* had been only moments before, was an enormous, glowing mushroom cloud rapidly reaching skywards.

'Bleedin', friggin' crikey, did I have *that* in me bag?' cried Barry.

'Liore?' called Daniel. 'Madeline, where's Liore?'

In another sea, in another world, the armed merchant sloop *Entropia* reversed its wind tower engines and began to slow. A steam-powered compression boat was lowered, even before the vessel had stopped, and the deck provost pointed.

'It was a floating body, in some sort of uniform,' he called above the engine as they set off. 'It must be a dead officer. I saw a double row of buttons through my peep glass.'

'What's another dead body?' asked the marshal of marines.

'Officers have papers, orders of the day and such. Veldarian papers might be worth a lot in Gallacia – there! I see him.'

Moments later they had secured the body with a boathook, and were hauling it aboard.

'He's alive!' cried the marshal of marines in surprise.

'Out here, in mid-sea?' exclaimed the deck provost.

'He just coughed and shook his head. The dead ones don't do that.'

'Then all the better. The Gallacians will pay even more for a Veldarian officer to torture for a few secrets.'

Target destroyed, but wherever this is, I still exist, thought Liore.

She opened her eyes and slowly sat up. She was not only alive, but was in a steam-powered boat with a dozen armed men. The odds were definitely in her favour, yet the boat was headed for a small ship with six spinning rotor towers instead of masts or funnels. Nothing like that existed in the time streams that she knew.

'I am a battle commander of the British Empire,' said Liore.

'You speak Angelterrian?' said one of the men.

'Angelterrian?'

'Yes, Angelterrian. And what is this British Empire nonsense?'

I am free, Liore realised. *Wherever this is, there is no British Empire. I am free to do whatever I wish. This world is mine.*

In another reality, the *Andromeda*'s problems were worsening exponentially. After travelling for one minute at the speed of sound, the shock wave from the explosion had hit the *Andromeda* so hard that every window pointing west had shattered, and Madeline, Daniel and Barry had been flung against a wall. They had been lucky, for many others were knocked overboard.

'There's something wrong with the horizon!' cried Madeline, pointing west.

'What happened to Liore?' shouted Daniel, his ears still ringing from the blast of the shockwave.

'Danny boy, will ya check that bleedin' horizon?' cried Barry. 'It's not meant to be getting' bigger, is it?'

Daniel looked up at the cloud that marked where the *Millennium* had been.

'Not the cloud, the horizon itself,' said Madeline. 'It's getting higher.'

'A wave,' exclaimed Daniel, finally comprehending what he was seeing. 'An enormous wave from the weapon blowing up. Madeline, strap on a life jacket, then run to the cabin. Barry, kneel on the deck.'

'Wot, ya want me to pray?'

'Kneel!' shouted Daniel, pulling him down. 'Now put your wrist with the handcuff on the deck.'

Daniel pressed the barrel of the Webley against the handcuff chain, pressed down hard, then pulled the trigger. The shot separated him from Barry.

'Wot now?' asked Barry.

'We find a couple of life jackets, then run to the cabin and hang on.'

The *Andromeda* was saved by the fact that it was facing into the wave from the *Millennium*'s annihilation. It began to rise as the wave approached, and far more alarmingly, it started to tilt. Ragged turbulence on the mountain of seawater crashed over the decks, and those on the bridge who had not been blinded by the explosion watched in horror as the bow became submerged. Foaming white water thundered over the decks, then burst through windows and even tore some of the lifeboats away.

The bow of the *Andromeda* crashed down as the ship rode over the crest of the wave, then the vessel began to slide down the other side, into a maelstrom of choppy, turbulent water. Now the deck was tilting in the other direction, and the bow plunged deep into the bottom of the trough. Steel plates and girders shrieked as they were strained and bent, and rivets popped like gunshots.

Daniel and Madeline gazed out through the porthole in terror, for there was only dim, green gloom beyond the thick glass.

'We've sunk!' shrieked Madeline as she and Daniel clung together. 'We're already dead.'

'I can still hear the engines,' said Daniel. 'They don't work under water.'

'Well how do you explain that?' demanded Madeline, pointing at the porthole.

Even as she was speaking the gloom beyond the porthole changed to a scene of seething, turbulent waves as the lower part of the ship rose above the surface again. In every sense of the word, the *Andromeda* had sunk, yet it had not completely filled with water. As a result, the air that was enclosed within its structure slowly bore the ship upwards.

'Maybe we're going to be all right,' said Daniel.

'So now what do we do?' asked Madeline.

'We've finished saving the world, so we'd better help save the ship. Barry, are you coming?'

Barry was crouched on one of the beds with a pillow held firmly over his head, and could not be persuaded to leave. Daniel and Madeline emerged back on deck to find the *Andromeda* wallowing deep in the churning water, but definitely above the surface. The engines were still turning because not all the furnaces had been quenched. Water had poured in through smashed portholes, stairways, air vents, hatches and ruptured plates, but the ship was mostly intact. There was not a single deck-chair, table or person on the promenade deck, which Daniel found very unsettling.

'We're still afloat!' he shouted.

'But we sank,' panted Madeline.

'We weren't under long enough for the ship to fill with water.'

'So do we jump overboard or what?'

'I think we should stay with the ship.'

A bizarre salty rain was falling out of the clear blue sky, while on the horizon the mushroom cloud that marked the *Millennium*'s doom continued to roil upwards and expand.

Suddenly Madeline took Daniel's head between her hands and kissed him on the lips.

'That's for deciding to help me and Liore stop the Century War,' she said.

An officer of the watch now waded through the dispersing water onto the promenade deck.

'Is anyone hurt?' he called. 'Does anyone need help?'

'My friend Liore, she's gone!' cried Madeline.

'We'll look for her,' he said, even though they all knew that anyone who had been swept overboard would never be seen again.

'Can I do anything?' asked Daniel.

'You're the boy who's been helping in the engine hall, aren't you?' said the officer.

'Yes, I am.'

'Then get down there, we have to keep the pumps and generators running.'

The engine hall was lit by only a few lanterns, but in contrast to the promenade deck, it was full of shadowy activity. The furnaces powering the pumps were still burning, even though the stokers feeding them were up to their knees in water. Daniel joined a group of men who were passing coal along a human chain with their bare hands. For what seemed like hours Daniel passed coal along to the furnace. Slowly the water rose to their thighs.

'We're sinkin', we gotta abandon ship!' shouted someone in the line.

'It's only water pouring down from the upper decks!' shouted Daniel. 'The ship's sound.'

'What the frig do you know?'

'I know specific gravity, I know the principles of displacement, and I'm an imperial officer, you bloody peon!' Daniel shouted back. 'Now get back in line and keep working!'

While some of what Daniel had said was vaguely true, the rest of it was absolutely false. Nevertheless, he had shouted with enough authority to reassure the stokers. Suddenly he was a leader, and the men looked to him for reassurance. If Daniel stood firm and stayed in the line, they would stay. Presently the water level ceased to rise, but did not go down.

Unknown to Daniel, two of the ship's ten watertight bulkheads were flooded, and two more contained a near-critical volume of water. The ship was riding so low that the waterline was up to the lowest row of portholes. Now passengers of all classes descended the stairs, and began bailing the water up and out with buckets passed from hand to hand. The water level did not drop appreciably, but the gesture did wonders for the morale of the engineers, stokers, slaggers and greasers.

An hour after the explosion the chief engineer waded through the water in the dark engine hall, congratulated the crewmen for their courage, and told them that the pumps were being used to drain the two most severely flooded bulkheads. They would see no lowering of the water around them for some time to come, but the ship was definitely not lost.

The hours wore on, but there was no measuring them. Every pocket watch on the ship had been saturated. Still, the situation seemed to get no worse. By sunset the pumps were switched to the engine room, and the main engines were engaged. Word was passed down the chain of command that the *Andromeda* was proceeding to Marseilles at seven knots. They were definitely not going to sink. Someone called 'Three cheers for the captain!' but they had reached eleven cheers before Daniel lost count. They wanted everything to be all right, and cheering seemed to somehow chase away any doubts that the good news was indeed true.

There is no place for heroes in peacetime. The following morning Baroness Featherington had Daniel arrested for shooting at her, a fact that was confirmed by the steward. Madeline pretended that she had only been trying to take pictures with a special camera, but she too was arrested for acting suspiciously. Barry was merely rearrested.

The ship resembled a laundry on the last day of August as everyone aboard tried to dry out their clothes and bedding. The meals were primitive, but nobody went hungry or complained. After enduring such an enormous strain, the ship's plates had lost a lot of integrity, and the pumps had to be worked constantly to keep ahead of the water that was leaking in. Finally, on the morning of the first of September, the *Andromeda* tied up at a pier in the Marseilles harbour.

'So, ya reckon yer old man will have a bit of a turn when he gets to hear about all this?' asked Barry as he and Daniel sat facing each other in their makeshift brig.

'I suspect that the groom will be scraping him off the ceiling,' replied Daniel.

'Where the frig are we? England?'

'It's France.'

'Is that bad?'

'No. They'll just put us onto another ship and send us on to London. There we shall be put on trial for all sorts of things and locked away as convicts for a very long time.'

'Do they still send convicts to Australia?'

'Very funny.'

'Ya reckon we should escape?'

'How? There's an armed steward outside the door.'

Presently there was the rattle of a key in the door's lock. The door was pushed open, but instead of the steward, Elizabeth entered. In one hand she was holding her parasol, but upon catching sight of Daniel she flung it aside, wrapped her arms around him and kissed him. Barry stared in disbelief, then looked at the parasol. It had been weighted by a length of iron pipe. He checked the corridor, and saw a body lying on the floor.

'Bleedin' hell, she's clobbered the guard!' he exclaimed.

Daniel checked that the steward had a pulse while Elizabeth retrieved her parasol. She discarded the pipe.

'Daniel, darling, this is as much as I can do for you,' she said, pressing a small roll of banknotes into his hand. 'Now go.'

'But why?' asked Daniel.

'Because you're – I – because I can't stand to think of you in a cage, because you shot the hat off that horrid Baroness Featherington, because you're wicked, and – and because I probably love you!'

'I shall never forget you,' said Daniel sincerely.

'And no other boy will ever measure up to you,' said Elizabeth, who then kissed him again before hurrying away.

'About Elizabeth,' said Daniel as he and Barry dragged the steward into the brig cabin.

'Yeah, yeah, don't tell Muriel.'

After taking the steward's gun, keys and money, they locked the door then released Madeline from the next cabin.

'How did you get out?' she asked as they hurried away.

'Another one of his bleedin' wimmen!' snapped Barry before Daniel could answer.

Two shots through the lock and a well-placed kick by Daniel opened his cabin's door. He retrieved Barry's bag from the cupboard.

'Why do you want that tatty thing?' exclaimed Madeline. 'It's empty.'

'I knew we would be arrested if the ship survived the wave, so I hid our papers and money in the false bottom.'

'What? Why?'

'Because otherwise they would be confiscated and locked up in the purser's office.'

'How did you know we'd escape?'

'I didn't, but just in case we did I thought it best to keep our papers handy.'

'You're starting to think like Barry.'

'I know, and it worries me.'

'Now just a bleedin' minute,' began Barry.

'Shut up and take your stupid bag,' said Madeline, thrusting it into his hands.

They made their way to the seaward side of the ship. Everyone else was to starboard, facing the pier, as Daniel had hoped. He looped a rope around the rail twice.

'Now Barry, over the side and hold on to the rope,' said Daniel.

'But I can't swim.'

'Your bag floated you across the Suez Canal, so it will get you over to the pier.'

'I don't want to!'

'Then stay here. I think you know where the brig is.'

'Yeah, well, I don't wanna, but I'm bleedin' well gonna have to, aren't I?'

Barry climbed over the rail with his bag strapped across his shoulder, and then Daniel lowered him to the water. Drawing the rope back up, he handed the end to Madeline.

'Daniel, I can't swim either,' she said quietly.

'I thought as much, which is why you will strap on one of those life jackets from that rack.'

Wearing a life jacket, Madeline was lowered into the water. Daniel drew the rope back up, coiled it neatly, then climbed over the rail, grasped his nose and jumped. If anyone heard the splash, nobody came to investigate. Slowly and cautiously, Daniel led Madeline and Barry around the stern of the ship and under the shelter of the pier. On the other side of the pier was a landing for small boats, and it was from here that they crept ashore. Amid all the fuss being made over the other bedraggled passengers and crew who had just come off the *Andromeda*, the trio was not paid any particular attention.

The escapees were soon far from the ship, and they stopped to rest in a small park. It was a secluded place, full of statues, bushes and bowers. Although popular with lovers after sunset, by day it was a place for picnickers to relax. Madeline walked ahead of Daniel and Barry, scanning the layout and those disporting themselves on the grass.

'We can hide here for a while, until our clothes dry out,' said Daniel. 'At least we have some money, so we can buy train tickets to Paris.'

'Australian money,' said Madeline. 'That marks us as foreigners. Better to get some French money and look less suspicious.'

'What do you mean?'

'*There's* a family that looks about right.'

Madeline pointed to a couple and their young son having a picnic on a sheltered patch of lawn between the base of a statue and some bushes. Glancing about to make sure that nobody else was watching, she held out her hand to Daniel. Slowly and reluctantly, he drew out the steward's gun and gave it to her. Madeline strode across to the picnickers and pointed the barrel between the eyes of the man.

'*Vos vêtements, donnez-les-nous!*' she said sternly.

By lunchtime, Daniel, Madeline and Barry were on a train going north. Daniel was wearing a tweed cycling jacket and sports trousers, Madeline was in quite a fashionable dress, and Barry was in shorts, a frilly shirt with a bow, a blue sailor's jacket and a straw hat. A stick with a wooden horse's head on one end was propped up beside him.

'I still feel bad about robbing that French family,' said Daniel.

'We left them our wet clothes,' replied Madeline.

'Still don't see why I gotta dress like some bleedin' frog fairy,' Barry muttered sullenly.

'Being a mother at seventeen is bad enough, but being the mother of Barry the Bag is really too much,' said Madeline.

'Well, I'm not exactly thrilled about being his father,' said Daniel.

'We goin' some place where they speak English?' asked Barry.

'Yes. Our papers for Britain will probably be valid until the *Andromeda*'s people arrive on another ship and raise the alarm.'

'We ought to split up after we reach Paris,' said Madeline. 'I'll go straight on to Calais and take the ferry to Dover. You follow a day or two later.'

'Wot about me?' asked Barry. 'I don't speak frog.'

'You can stay with me,' said Daniel reluctantly. 'We'll spend two days in Paris, but you don't speak French so you can't get us into too much trouble.'

'Two days? Why so long?'

'I must go to Muriel's rooming house and explain what happened to Fox. It's my duty to tell her what we did, and why.'

'Ya gonna tell her about Julia an' Lizzy an' this baggage?' asked Barry with a knowing leer.

'Don't be rude to your father,' said Madeline as she smacked him across the ear.

'What are you going to do, Madeline?' asked Daniel.

'Why, open a detective agency in London, of course. What better job for a wanted, hardened criminal like me?'

It was not often that a family conference was called to read a telegram in the Lang household, so Emily feared the worst when the maid summoned her. As they walked down the hallway together, Martha whispered that the telegram was from the captain of the *Andromeda*, and that it contained bad news. They entered the living room. Mr Lang's face was grim, while Mrs Lang was wide-eyed with shock and strangely subdued. Martha turned to go, but Mr Lang told her to stay because she was Emily's chaperone. He unfolded the telegram.

'IT IS MY MELANCHOLY DUTY TO REPORT UPON YOUR SON DANIEL STOP,' he read.

'Did the ship sink?' gasped Emily. 'Is Daniel dead?'

'No,' said her mother listlessly.

'SINCE THE BEGINNING OF THE VOYAGE DANIEL LANG HAS ASSOCIATED WITH MUSICIANS AND THIEVES STOP BEEN INVOLVED IN SEVERAL FIGHTS STOP FALLEN IN WITH LOOSE COMPANY STOP ESCAPED LEGAL CUSTODY WITH TWO MISCREANTS STOP SHOT AT A BARONESS STOP HAD LEWD AND DECADENT LIAISONS WITH WOMEN OF QUESTIONABLE MORAL STANDARDS STOP.'

Mr Lang let the telegram fall to the floor, then sat there for a time with his hand over his eyes.

'There is more. Daniel fled from the ship at Marseilles with a young woman and a notorious thief, and is currently being sought by the French police for armed robbery,' Mr Lang concluded.

'No child of mine will ever again set foot outside this house without a chaperone,' said Mrs Lang firmly.

'Need I remind you whose idea it was to send Daniel to Britain?' asked Mr Lang.

'Well at least he seems to have forgotten about that horrid Muriel Baker,' said Emily.

'Emily, that was insensitive in the extreme!' exclaimed Mr Lang. 'Go up to your room immediately.'

Emily obeyed, but having climbed the stairs she went to Daniel's old room instead and collected a selection of his clothes. Once in her own room with the door safely locked, she began tailoring her brother's clothes to fit her.

Make me a prisoner in this house, Mother dear? she thought as she worked. *Not likely! Anything that Danny can do, I can do better.*

EPILOGUE

Having been released from their cell in a Paris watch-house, Daniel and Barry collected their possessions and prepared to leave. To Daniel's dismay, the gendarme at the desk spoke English. This meant that Barry could talk to him, and Barry talking to anyone could easily be the cause of yet another disaster.

'I must apologise again for your treatment, but we were not to know that Mademoiselle Baker was fabricating stories,' said the gendarme.

Barry was unused to any sort of policeman apologising to him, and was enjoying the experience. Daniel, however, was agitated and anxious to leave.

'No harm done, my man,' said Barry. 'How was you lot to know that baggage Muriel Baker was a looney?'

'Well as soon as she told the magistrate that her lover was from a century in the future, we got a little suspicious. Then, when she said that young Monsieur Lang had murdered him by changing yesterday so that he no longer existed, well, we knew you had to be innocent.'

'Thank you, monsieur,' said Daniel. 'Now come

along Barold, we have to catch the next train to Calais.'

'Oi, wait up, I gotta do an inventory of me bag,' said Barry, opening his bag on the desk.

'I'm sure the nice gendarmes are much too honest to have taken anything from your bag,' said Daniel.

'No they weren't,' said Barry, rummaging in his bag. 'Me picklocks are gone!'

'Monsieur Chalmer, if you can tell me how picklocks can be put to honest use, you may have them back,' said the gendarme sternly.

'I'm a locksmith's apprentice, aren't I?'

'You have papers to prove it?'

'Er, I reckon they was stolen along with me artistic postcards.'

Daniel took Barry firmly by the arm and dragged him in the direction of the door.

'Hurry now, Barold, the train to Calais is leaving soon and we don't want to miss it,' said Daniel.

'But I gotta –'

'Au revoir, Monsieur Constable, and thank you for being so understanding,' Daniel called over his shoulder as they reached the door.

They set off along the busy street at a brisk pace, with Daniel still grasping Barry's arm.

'Now why's ya in such a hurry?' asked Barry as they crossed the street, dodging wagons, carriages and bicycles. 'There's stuff missin' from me bag.'

'Barry, we are wanted in Marseilles for armed robbery and about a dozen other charges.'

'So wot? This is Paris.'

'Have you heard of a thing called the telegraph? It's only a matter of time before –'

Police whistles suddenly shrilled out in the distance behind them. Barry tried to run, but Daniel held his arm even more firmly.

'We gotta run!' cried Barry.

'The gendarmes will be looking for two boys who are running, so we must not run. Over here, stop at this magazine stand and start browsing.'

'Oh jeez!' exclaimed Barry as he caught sight of a rack of postcards featuring women wearing nothing at all. 'Look at all them artistic French postcards.'

Several gendarmes came running past as Daniel and Barry stood with their backs to the street.

'Time to move on, Barry, but walk slowly and don't look nervous.'

'Wait up,' said Barry, turning to the vendor and holding up a selection of postcards. 'Oi, froggo, how muchie for these postie cardies?'

The man stared blankly at Barry.

'*C'est combien, monsieur?*' asked Daniel, adding two newspapers to Barry's cards.

The vendor held up seven fingers. Daniel paid. They set off again.

'Why'd ya buy two papers?' asked Barry. 'I can't

read frog an' I don't like newspapers anyway.'

'They are for hiding behind.'

'Oh. Well, it's not gonna do us much good. The cops are gonna be watchin' the trains to that Callay place after ya blabbed about it in the copper shop.'

'That was deliberate. While the police watch the trains to Calais, we shall go to Cherbourg instead. The Channel Islands are close to Cherbourg. They are British territory, and we can bribe some fisherman to take us there.'

'So wot? The British coppers want us, too.'

'I doubt that the officials on the Channel Islands will be on the lookout for us yet. From there we can take another boat to Portsmouth.'

'So wot's to do in England, then?' asked Barry.

'Avoid the police, and anyone by the name of Lang or Ashdayle-Potter,' said Daniel.

'Ashdayle-Potter?'

'Mother's family. The Potters made a fortune from ceramics in Coalbrookdale about a hundred years ago, then married into an aristocratic family, the Ashdayles.'

'So why aren't your folks rich?'

'They *are* rich, Barry. How else could I be sent to Britain first class? My father married one of the daughters in 1880 while working in Coalbrookdale as an accountant.'

'So we give this Coalbrook place the swerve?'

'We give it a very wide swerve. My grandmother lives there.'

'So wot we gonna do?'

'Some of Mother's more distant relatives have a very isolated estate in the Lake District. They're the original Ashdayles, and Mother only writes to them every Christmas.'

'If we go there we'll be in trouble at Christmas.'

'Christmas is months away.'

'Oh. So they won't know the coppers are after us?'

'No. We can hide there until things quieten down.'

'And then?'

'I might go on to Glasgow and learn to be a ship's engineer.'

'Thought you'd had enough of ships. I never wanna see another bleedin' ship as long as I live.'

'I quite like ships,' said Daniel. 'Besides, I think I'd better get used to a life at sea, never settling down in case someone checks my past.'

'So ya been cured of wantin' that daft Muriel Baker?' asked Barry.

'I certainly have.'

'But wot if –'

'I never want to see her again, Barry, leave it at that.'

'But –'

'She's a monster. All I did was explain to her what happened to Fox when we saved the world, yet she screamed at me, called me a murderer, threw all those plates and bottles at me, hit me with a chair, then ran out into the street and dragged a gendarme in to arrest me.'

'And me.'

'Would *you* still be in love with a girl like that?'

'I'd never be in love with the baggage in the first place. So ya don't wanna die heroical neither?'

'Absolutely not.'

Daniel had learned his lesson, although it had been at a rather high cost. He had not even wanted to get Muriel back by the time he had visited her earlier that day, but he *had* wanted to show her that he was no longer the awkward boy who she had abandoned for Fox three months earlier. That was a matter of pride, and the plan had seemed harmless enough. He had forgotten that she might be a little distraught, and even irrational, after watching Fox gradually fading for a week, then vanishing completely. Still, he had seen her again, and amid all the hysterics Daniel had been convinced that he no longer had any feelings for her.

Daniel and Barry paused here and there to buy different-looking clothes as they made their way across Paris. Soon Barry was again dressed as a little boy, and Daniel was wearing a herringbone coat and hat, and pretending to be his father.

Although Daniel did not know it, something else was now different within him. Neither Barry nor Liore were still the pivots upon which the direction of history had changed. Because he had chosen to confront Baroness Featherington instead of smashing the disruptor, Daniel was now that pivot, and his life would never be the same again. Wherever he went, weirdness and change would follow him. Although he would one day be a ship's engineer, it would be on a ship with engines such as this world had never seen.

More great reading from Ford Street Publishing

BEFORE THE STORM

'... clever plot, feisty characters ... this is a great story'
Kerry White

Fox and BC travel through time from the distant future to 1901. Elite cadets in the Imperial Army, they are young, handsome, well-mannered ... and now, mutineers.

They have journeyed into the past to save the opening ceremony of Australia's first parliament from being bombed. If the cadets fail, thousands will die, sparking a century of total war.

However, to change the destiny of the world, the young warriors will need the help of three ordinary teenagers ...

About the author

Sean McMullen is one of Australia's leading SF and fantasy authors, with fourteen books and sixty stories published, for which he has won over a dozen awards.

His most recent novels are *The Ancient Hero* (2004) and *Voidfarer* (2006). When not writing he is a computer training manager, and when not at a keyboard he is a karate instructor.

www.fordstreetpublishing.com

FORD ST